"I Don't Want To Be Hurt Again."

"Oliver." She said his name, but her voice made no sound. His going had left her frozen, but now the weight and the warmth of his body warmed her own, melting resolution, and stirring to life long-forgotten instincts. She thought, *oh, no* and laid her hands against his shoulders and tried to push him away, but he was a thousand times stronger than she and her resistance was pathetic, pointless as trying to topple some immense tree.

"Oliver. No."

She might not have spoken aloud. He simply continued his gentle lovemaking, and after a little, her hands, as though of their own volition, slid away from his shoulders, under his jacket, around his back. She heard him say, "You've stopped pretending. . . ."

Wild Mountain Thyme

ROSAMUNDE PILCHER

A DELL BOOK

Published by
Dell Publishing Co., Inc.
1 Dag Hammarskjold Plaza
New York, New York 10017

Dell ® TM 681510, Dell Publishing Co., Inc.

ISBN: 0-440-19352-4

Reprinted by arrangement with St. Martin's Press, Inc.

Printed in the United States of America

First Dell printing—May 1980

For Robin and Kirsty and Oliver

Contents

CHAPTER 1
Friday

Once, before the bypass had been built, the main road ran through the heart of the village, a constant stream of heavy traffic that threatened to rattle the heart out of the gracious Queen Anne houses and the small shops with their bulging windows. Woodbridge had been, not such a long time ago, simply a place you drove through in order to reach some other place.

But since the opening of the bypass, things had changed. For the better, said the residents. For the worse, said the shopkeepers and the garage proprietors and the man who had run the lorry-drivers' restaurant.

Now, the people of Woodbridge could go shopping and cross the road without taking their lives into their hands or having their pet dogs securely leashed. At weekends, children with brown velvet caps jammed down over their eyebrows, and mounted on a variety of shaggy steeds, trotted off to their local pony club meets, and already there had been a positive flowering of open-air events, garden parties and charity fetes. The lorry-drivers' cafe became an expensive delicatessen, a ramshackle tobacconist sold out to a precious young man who dabbled in antiques, and the vicar had begun to plan a festival for next summer, in order to celebrate the tricentenary of his small, perpendicular church.

Woodbridge had come into its own again.

The clock on the church tower was pointing to ten minutes to twelve on a chill February morning when a big shabby Volvo turned the corner by the saddlers, and came slowly down the main street between the wide cobbled pavements. The young man at the wheel saw the whole long empty curve of it, his eye unde-flected by thundering streams of traffic. He saw the charming irregularity of houses and bow-fronted shops, the beckoning perspective, and a distant glimpse of willow-fringed meadows. Far above, in a wintry sky full of sailing clouds, a plane droned in to-wards Heathrow. Otherwise it was very quiet, and there seemed to be scarcely anybody about.

He passed a pub, newly painted and with tubs of bay trees at either side of the door; a hairdresser, Car-ole Coiffures. The wine merchant with his bow-fronted bottle-glass window, and an antique shop stuffed with overpriced relics of better days.

He came to the house. He drew the car into the pavement's edge and switched off the engine. The sound of the plane died, thrumming, into the morning quiet. A dog barked, a bird sang hopefully from a tree, as though deluded that the thin sunshine meant that spring had come. He got out of the car, slammed the door shut, and stood looking up at the flat, sym-metric face of the house, with its fanlighted door and pleasing proportions. Flush on the pavement it stood, a flight of stone steps leading up to the front door and tall sash windows discreetly veiled in filmy curtains.

It was, he thought, a house that had never given any-thing away.

He went up the steps and rang the doorbell. The surround of the bell was brass and brightly polished, as was the lion's head knocker. The door was painted yellow, new and bright looking, without a sunblister or a scratch upon it. In the lea of the house, out of the sun, it was cold. He shivered inside his thick donkey jacket and rang the bell again. Almost at once there

were footsteps, and the next instant the yellow front
door opened for him.

A girl stood there, looking rather cross, as though
she had been interrupted, disturbed by the bell, and
wanted to put off for as little time as possible. She had
long, milk-fair hair, and she wore a tee shirt bulging
with puppy fat, an apron, knee stockings and a pair of
scarlet leather clogs.

"Yes?"

He smiled and said, "Good morning," and her impatience instantly melted into quite a different expression. She had realized that it wasn't the man about the
coal, or someone collecting for the Red Cross, but a
tall and personable young man, long-legged in his
well-scrubbed jeans, and bearded like a Viking. "I
wondered if Mrs. Archer was in?"

"I'm so sorry." She looked quite sorry, too. "But I'm
afraid not. She is gone to London today. To shop."

She was, he reckoned, about eighteen, and from her
accent, some sort of Scandinavian. Swedish, probably.

He said, with what he hoped was engaging rueful-
ness, "Isn't that just my luck? I should have phoned or
something, but I thought I'd take the chance of catching her at home."

"Are you a friend of Mrs. Archer's?"

"Well, I used to know the family, some years ago.
But we've been . . . well, sort of out of touch. I was
passing, on my way up to London from the West
Country. I thought it would be nice to come and say
hello. Just an idea I had. It doesn't matter."

He began, diffidently, to back away. As he had
hoped, the girl delayed him.

"When she comes back, I could tell her that you
have been here. She will be back in time for tea."

At that moment, with splendid timing, the church
clock began to chime for midday.

He said, "It's only twelve o'clock now. I can scarcely
hang around till then. Never mind, I'll maybe be

down this way again some time." He looked up and down the street. "There used to be a little café here . . ."

"Not any more. It is a delicatessen now."

"Well, perhaps I can get a sandwich in the pub. It seems a long time since breakfast." He smiled down at her from his great height. "Goodbye, then. It's been nice meeting you." He turned as though to leave. He could feel her hesitation, her decision, as though he had directed them himself. She said, "I could . . ."

With one foot already on the upper step, he turned back.

"What could you do?"

"Are you really an old friend of the family?" She longed to be put out of her doubt.

"Yes, I really am. But I have no way of proving it to you."

"I mean, I was just going to get the lunch for myself and the baby. I could get it for you, too."

He looked reproachful, and she began to blush. "Now, that's very foolhardy of you. I'm sure you've been warned, time and time again, about strange men coming to the door."

She looked distressed. She obviously had. "It is just that, if you are a friend of Mrs. Archer's, Mrs. Archer would want me to ask you in." She was lonely and probably bored. All au pair girls seemed to be lonely and bored. It was an occupational hazard.

He said, "You mustn't get yourself into trouble."

Despite herself, she began to smile. "I don't think I will."

"Supposing I steal the silver? Or start trying to make violent love to you?"

For some strange reason this possibility did not alarm her in the least. Rather, she seemed to regard it as a joke, and so to be reassured. She even gave a small, conspiratorial giggle. "If you do, I shall scream and the whole village will come to my rescue. Everybody knows what everybody does in Woodbridge. Everybody talks all the time. Chat, chat. Nobody has a secret." She stepped back, opening the yellow door wide. The long, pretty hallway was invitingly revealed.

He hesitated for just long enough to make it seem genuine and then shrugged, said, "All right," and followed her over the threshold, wearing the expression of a man who has been finally, reluctantly, persuaded. She closed the door. He looked down into her face. "But you may have to take the consequences."

She laughed again, excited by the little adventure. She said, in hostess-like tones, "Would you like to take off your coat?"

He did so, and she hung it up for him.

"If you would like to come to the kitchen, perhaps you would like a glass of beer?"

"Well, thank you."

She led the way, down the passage that led to the back of the house, to the modern kitchen, built out into the south-facing garden and flooded now with pale sunlight. Everything shone with cleanliness and order; bright surfaces, a gleaming cooker, stainless steel and polished teak. The floor was blue and white tiles, which looked Portuguese. There were plants along the windowsill, and a table at the window was laid for lunch. He saw the high chair, the bright plastic table mat, the small spoons, the Beatrix Potter mug.

He said, "You've got a baby to look after."

She was at the fridge, getting him a can of beer. "Yes." She closed the fridge door and went to take a pewter mug from a hook on the scrubbed pine dresser. "He's Mrs. Archer's grandchild."

"What's he called?"

"Thomas. He's called Tom."

"Where's he now?"

"In his cot, having his morning rest. In a moment, I'll go up and get him, because he'll be ready for his lunch."

"How old is he?"

"Two." She handed him the can and the mug, and he opened the can and poured it carefully, without a head.

"I suppose he's staying here, is he? I mean, his parents are away, or something."

"No, he lives here. Her smiling, dimpled face took on an expression of woe. "It's very sad. His mother is dead." She frowned. "It is funny that you do not know that."

"I told you. I've been out of touch since I last saw the Archers. I had no idea. I *am* sorry."

"She was killed in a plane crash. She was coming home from a holiday in Yugoslavia. She was their only child."

"So they look after the grandchild?"

"Yes."

He took a mouthful of beer, cool and delicious. "What about the father?"

The girl had turned her rounded back on him, was stooping to investigate something in an oven. A fragrant smell filled the kitchen, and his mouth watered. He had not realized how hungry he was.

She said, "They were separated. I don't know anything about him." She closed the oven and straightened up. She gave him another searching look. "I thought you would have known about that, too."

"No. I don't know about anything. I was out of this country for a bit. I was in Spain and I was in America."

"Yes. I see." She looked at the clock. "If I leave you, will you be all right? I have to go up and get Thomas."

"If you're sure you can trust me not to help myself

to the spoons." He was teasing her, and she cheered up and smiled again. "I don't think you'll do that." She was wholesome, creamy as a tumbler of milk.

He said, "What's your name?"

"Helga."

"Are you Swedish?"

"Yes."

"They're lucky, the Archers. I mean, having someone like you."

"I'm lucky, too. It is a good job, and they are very kind. Some girls get terrible places. I could tell you some stories."

"Do you go to classes in the afternoons?"

"Yes. English and history."

"Your English sounds perfect to me."

"I am doing literature. Jane Austen."

She looked so pleased with herself that he laughed. He said, "Run along, Helga, and get that baby. I'm starving, even if he isn't." For some reason she blushed again, and then went away and left him alone in the shining, sunny kitchen.

He waited. Heard her go upstairs, her footsteps cross the floor of the room above. He heard her voice, speaking quietly; curtains being drawn back. He laid down his beer and went, soft-footed, rubber-soled, back down the hall and opened the door at the bottom of the staircase. He went in. There were the chintzes, the grand piano, the orderly bookshelves, the unassuming water colors. A fire had been laid in the Adam grate, but was, as yet, unlit. Even so, the room was warm with central heating and heavy with the scent of hyacinths.

Its neatness, its order, its air of well-bred, well-moneyed smugness, enraged him, as it always had. He longed for muddled knitting, strewn newspapers, a dog or a cat on some familiar cushion. But there was nothing. Only the slow ticking of the clock on the mantelpiece bore witness to any sort of activity.

He began to prowl around. The grand piano was a repository of photographs. Mr. Archer in a top hat, proudly displaying some minor order bestowed upon him by the queen at Buckingham Palace; his moustache like a toothbrush, his morning coat strained across his spreading stomach. Mrs. Archer as a misty girl, dressed for her wedding. The baby, propped up on a fur rug. And Jeannette.

He picked up the stylized portrait and stood, looking down at it. Pretty, as she had always been pretty. Sexy even, in her extraordinary, fastidious way. He remembered her legs, which were sensational, and the shape of her well-manicured hands. But nothing much else. Not her voice, not her smile.

He had married her because the Archers hadn't wanted their daughter to be the mother of an illegitimate baby. When the disastrous news had been broken to them that their precious only child had been having an affair with, actually living with, that dreadful Oliver Dobbs, their tidy little world had fallen apart. Mrs. Archer had taken to her bed with a *crise de nerfs*, but Mr. Archer, harking back to his brief years as a soldier, had straightened his tie and his back and taken Oliver out to lunch at his London club.

Oliver, unimpressed and not a little amused, had recorded the subsequent discussion with the detachment of a totally impartial observer. Even at the time it had seemed as unreal as a scene from an old-fashioned play.

Only daughter, Mr. Archer had said, plunging in at the deep end. Always had great plans for her. No question of recriminations, hindsight never did a man any good, but the question was, what was Oliver going to do about this baby?

Oliver said that he didn't think he could do anything. He was working in a fish-and-chips shop, and he couldn't afford to marry anyone, let alone Jeannette.

Mr. Archer cleared his throat, and said that he didn't want to tread on toes, or to appear curious, but it was obvious to him that Oliver came from a good family, and he knew for a fact that Oliver had been to a well-known school, so was there any reason that he had to work in a fish-and-chips shop?

Oliver said that yes, there was a reason. The reason was that he was a writer, and the fish-and-chips shop job was the sort of undemanding occupation he needed to keep himself alive in order to be able to write.

Mr. Archer cleared his throat again and began to talk about Oliver's parents, and Oliver told Mr. Archer that his parents, who lived in Dorset, were not only penniless, but unforgiving. Living on an army pension, they had denied themselves everything in order to be able to scrape up enough money to send Oliver to that exclusive school. When he had finally walked out of it at the age of seventeen, they had tried, in a broken-hearted sort of way, to persuade him to follow some sensible, conventional course. To join the army, the navy, perhaps. To become a chartered accountant, a banker, a lawyer. But he could only be a writer, because by then he already was a writer. Defeated at last, they washed their hands of their son, cutting him without the proverbial shilling, and remaining sulkily and stubbornly incommunicado.

This obviously disposed of Oliver's parents. Mr. Archer tried another tack. Did Oliver love Jeannette? Would he make her a good husband?

Oliver said that he didn't think he would make her a good husband, because he was so terribly poor.

Mr. Archer then cleared his throat for the third and last time and came to the point. If Oliver agreed to marry Jeannette and provide the baby with a legitimate father, then he, Mr. Archer, would see to it that . . . er . . . financially, the young couple would be all right.

Oliver asked, how all right? And Mr. Archer elucidated, his eyes steadily holding Oliver's across the table, but his anxious hands shifting his wineglass, straightening a fork, crumbling a roll. By the time he was done, his place setting was in chaos, but Oliver realized that he was onto a good thing.

Living in Jeannette's flat in London, with a steady income coming in each month to his bank account, he could give up the job in the fish-and-chips shop and get down to finishing his play. He already had a book under his belt, but that was still with an agent, and the play was something else, something that he had to get down, before it ate his soul out like some ghastly cancer. That was how it was with writing. He was never happy unless he was living two lives. A real life with women and food and drinking in pubs with friends; and the other life, teeming with his own people, who were more vital and sympathetic than anyone he ever met in the normal course of events. And certainly, he thought, more interesting than the Archers.

Over the lunch table, the two men had come to an agreement. Later, it was consolidated by lawyers' letters and drafts and signatures. Oliver and Jeannette were duly married in a registry office, and this seemed to be all that mattered to the Archers. The alliance lasted no more than a few months. Even before the child was born, Jeannette had gone back to her parents. Boredom she could stand, she said, and loneliness too, but abuse and physical violence were more than she was prepared to endure.

Oliver scarcely noticed her going. He stayed in her flat and peacefully, without any sort of interruption, finished the play. When it was done, he left the flat, locked the door and posted Jeannette the key. He took himself off to Spain. He was in Spain when the baby was born, and still there when he read, in some week-old paper, of his wife's death in the Yugoslavian air disaster. By then Jeannette had become a person who had happened to Oliver a long time ago, and he discovered that the tragedy aroused little emotion in him. She belonged to the past.

Besides, by then he was well into his second novel. So he thought about Jeannette for perhaps five minutes and then plunged thankfully back into the company of the infinitely more compelling characters who were now going about their business within the confines of his own head.

When Helga came downstairs again, he was back in the kitchen sitting on the window seat, with his back to the sun, and enjoying his beer. The door opened, and she appeared, carrying the child in her arms. He was larger than Oliver had imagined, dressed in red overalls with a bib and a white sweater. His hair was a sort of reddish gold, like new pennies, but Oliver couldn't see his face, which was buried in Helga's delectable neck.

Helga smiled at Oliver over Thomas's shoulder.

"He's shy. I have told him that there is a visitor, and he doesn't want to look at you." She bent her head to say to the little boy, "Look, you silly. He is a nice man. He has come to have lunch with us."

The child made a mooing, negative sound and buried his face still deeper. Helga laughed and brought him over to his high chair and inserted him into it, so that at last he had to let go of her. He and Oliver looked at each other. The child had blue eyes and seemed sturdy. Oliver didn't know much about children. Nothing, in fact. He said, "Hi."

"Say hello, Thomas," Helga prompted. She added, "He does not like to talk."

Thomas stared at the stranger. One-half of his face was red from being pressed into a pillow. He smelled of soap. Helga clipped a plastic bib around his neck, but he didn't take his eyes off Oliver.

Helga went to the stove to collect their meal. From

the oven she took a shepherd's pie, a dish of brussels sprouts. She put a little into a round dish, mashed it up with a fork and set it down on the tray of Thomas's high chair. "Now, eat it up," and she put his spoon into his hand.

"Does he feed himself?" asked Oliver.

"Of course. He's two now, not a baby anymore. Are you, Thomas? Show the man how you can eat up your dinner." Thomas responded by laying down his spoon. His blue eyes fixed, unwinking, on Oliver, and Oliver began to feel self-conscious.

"Here," he said. He set down his glass of beer, and reaching over, took up the spoon, filled it with squashed meat and potato, and steered it towards Thomas's mouth. Thomas's mouth opened, and it all disappeared. Thomas, munching, continued to stare. Oliver gave him back the spoon. Thomas finished his mouthful and then smiled. A good deal of the smile was shepherd's pie, but there was, as well, the glimpse of an engaging double row of small pearly teeth.

Helga, putting down Oliver's plate in front of him, caught sight of the smile.

"There now, he has made a friend." She brought another plate and sat herself at the head of the table, so that she could help Thomas. "He's a very friendly little boy."

"What does he do all day?"

"He plays, and he sleeps, and in the afternoons he goes for a walk in his push chair. Usually Mrs. Archer takes him, but today I will take him."

"Does he look at books and things?"

"Yes, he likes picture books, but sometimes he tears them."

"Does he have toys?"

"He likes little cars and blocks. He doesn't like teddies or rabbits or things like that. I don't think he likes the feel of fur. You know what I mean?"

Oliver began to eat the shepherd's pie, which was

very hot and delicious. He said, "Do you know a lot about babies?"

"At home in Sweden I have younger brothers and sisters."

"Are you fond of Thomas?"

"Yes, he is nice," She made a face at the child. "You are nice, aren't you Thomas? And he doesn't cry all the time like some children do."

"It must be rather . . . dull for him, being brought up by his grandparents."

"He is too little to know whether it is dull or not."

"But it'll be dull when he's older."

"A child on his own is always sad. But there are other children in the village. He will make friends."

"And you? Have you made friends?"

"There is another au pair girl. We go to classes together."

"Haven't you got a boyfriend?"

She dimpled. "My boyfriend is at home in Sweden."

"He must miss you."

"We write to each other. And it is only for six months. At the end of six months, I shall go back to Sweden."

"What will happen to Thomas then?"

"I expect Mrs. Archer will get another au pair girl. Would you like some more shepherd's pie?"

The meal progressed. For dessert there was fruit or yoghurt or cheese. Thomas ate yoghurt. Oliver peeled an orange. Helga, at the stove, made coffee.

She said to Oliver, "Do you live in London?"

"Yes, I've got a basement flat just off the Fulham Road."

"Is that where you are going now?"

"Yes. I've been in Bristol for a week."

"On holiday?"

"Who'd go to Bristol for a holiday in February? No, I have a play being put on at the Fortune Theatre there. I went down to do a small rewrite. The actors complained they couldn't get their tongues round some of my lines."

"A writer?" She turned wide-eyed. "You write *plays*? And get them *performed*? You must be very good."

"I like to think so." He filled his mouth with sections of orange. Their taste, and the bitter tang of the peel, reminded him of Spain. "But it's what other people think that really matters. The critics, and the people who pay to come to the theatre."

"What is the play called?"

"*Bent Penny*. And don't ask me what it's about, because I haven't got time to tell you."

"My boyfriend writes. He writes articles on psychology for the university journal."

"I'm sure they're fascinating."

"But it isn't the same as writing plays."

"No. Not quite the same."

Thomas had finished his yoghurt. Helga wiped his face and took off his bib and lifted him out of his high chair. He came to stand by Oliver, balancing himself by placing his hands on Oliver's knee. Through the worn denim, Oliver could feel their warmth, the grip of the little fingers. Thomas gazed up at Oliver and smiled again, a grin with dimples and that row of little teeth. He put up a hand to touch Oliver's beard, and Oliver stooped so that he could reach it. Thomas laughed. Oliver picked him up and held him on his knee. He felt solid and warm.

Helga seemed gratified by all these friendly advances. "Now he has made friends. If I got a book, you could show him the pictures while I put the plates in the dishwasher. Then I have to take him for a walk."

Oliver had already decided that it was time to leave, but he said, "All right" so Helga went to find a book, and he and Thomas were left alone.

Thomas was fascinated by his beard. Oliver hoisted him up so that he stood on Oliver's knee and their eyes were on a level. Thomas tugged his beard. Oliver

yelped. Thomas laughed. He tried to tug it again, but
Oliver caught his hand and held it in his own. "That
hurts, you brute." Thomas stared into his eyes. Oliver
said softly, "Do you know who I am?" and Thomas
laughed again, as though the question were a great
joke.

Helga came back with the book and laid it on the
table, a large and brightly colored book with farm animals on the shiny cover. Oliver opened it at random
and Thomas sat down again on his knee, leaning forward on the table, to peer at the pictures. As Helga
went about her work putting plates away and scrubbing out the dish that had contained the shepherd's
pie, Oliver turned the pages, and said the names of the
animals, and pointed to the farmhouse and the gate
and the tree and the haystack. And they came to a
picture of a dog, and Thomas barked. And then to a
picture of a cow, and he made mooing sounds. It was
all very companionable.

Then Helga said it was time for Thomas to come
upstairs and be dressed in his outdoor clothes, so she
gathered him up and bore him away. Oliver sat and
waited for them to come down again. He looked at the
immaculate kitchen, and out into the immaculate garden, and he thought of Helga leaving and the next au
pair girl coming, and the pattern repeating itself until
Thomas was eight years old, and of an age to be sent
to some well-established and probably useless prep
school. He thought of his son, slotted, labeled, trapped
on the conveyor belt of a conventional education, expected to make the right friends, play the accepted
games, and never question the tyranny of meaningless
tradition.

Oliver had escaped. At seventeen he had cut and
run, but only because he had had the twin weapons of
his writing and his own single-minded, rebellious determination to go his own way.

But how would Thomas fare?

The question made him feel uncomfortable, and he rejected it as being hypothetical. It was none of Oliver's business what school Thomas went to, and it didn't matter anyway. He lit another cigarette, and idly opened Thomas's picture book again, lifting the front cover. He saw on the white fly sheet, written in Mrs. Archer's neat black-inked script,

> Thomas Archer
> For his Second Birthday
> From Granny.

And all at once it did matter. A sort of rage rose within Oliver, so that if Jeannette's mother had been standing nearby, he would have attacked her; with words that only he knew how to use; with his fists if necessary.

He is not Thomas Archer, you sanctimonious bitch. He is Thomas Dodds. He is my son.

When Helga came downstairs, carrying Thomas dressed in a sort of ski suit and a woolen hat with a bobble on it, Oliver was already waiting for her in the hall. He had put on his coat, and he said, "I have to go now. I have to get back to London."

"Yes, of course."

"It was very kind of you to give me lunch."

"I will tell Mrs. Archer that you were here."

He began to grin. "Yes. Do that."

"But . . . I don't know your name. To tell her, I mean."

"Just say Oliver Dobbs."

"All right, Mr. Dobbs." She hesitated, standing at the bottom of the stairs, and then said, "I have to get the pram and my coat from the cloakroom. Will you hold Thomas for a moment?"

"Of course."

He lifted the child out of her arms, hoisting him up against one shoulder.

"I won't be long, Thomas," Helga assured him, and she turned and went down the passage beneath the staircase, and disappeared through a half-glassed door.

A pretty, trusting, stupid little girl. He hoped they would not be too hard on her. *You can be as long as you like, my darling.* Carrying his son he went down the hall, let himself out through the yellow front foor, went down the steps and got into his waiting car.

Helga heard the car go down the street, but she did not realize it was Oliver's. When she returned with the push chair, there was no sign of either the man or the child.

"Mr. Dobbs?"

He had left the front door open, and the house was invaded by the bitter cold of the afternoon.

"Thomas?"

But outside was only the empty pavement, the silent street.

CHAPTER 2
Friday

The most exhausting thing in the world, Victoria Bradshaw decided, was not having enough to do. It was infinitely more exhausting than having far too much to do, and today was a classic example.

February was a bad time for selling clothes. She supposed it was a bad time, really, for selling anything. Christmas was forgotten, and the January sales just a gruesome memory. The morning had started hopefully, with thin sunshine and a light icing of frost, but by early afternoon it had clouded over, and now it was so cold and wet that people with any sense at all were staying at home by fires or in centrally heated flats, doing crosswords or baking cakes or watching television. The weather gave them no encouragement to plan wardrobes for the spring.

The clock edged around to five o'clock. Outside, the bleak afternoon was darkening swiftly into night. The curved shop window had SALLY SHARMAN written across it. From the inside of the shop this presented itself backwards, like writing seen in a mirror, and beyond these hieroglyphics Beauchamp Place was curtained in rain. Passersby, umbrellaed and gusted by wind, struggled with parcels. A stream of traffic waited for the Brompton Road lights to change. A figure, camouflaged by rainproof clothing, ran up the steps from the street and burst through the glass-paneled door like a person escaping, letting in a gust of cold air before the door was hastily slammed shut again.

It was Sally, in her black raincoat and her huge red fox hat. She said, "God, what a day," furled her umbrella, took off her gloves and began to unbutton her coat.

"How did it go?" Victoria asked.

Sally had spent the afternoon in the company of a young designer who had decided to go into the wholesale trade.

"Not bad," she said, draping her coat over the umbrella stand to drip. "Not bad at all. Lots of new ideas, good colors. Rather mature clothes. I was surprised. I thought his being so young, it would have been all jeans and workmen's shirts, but not at all."

She pulled off her hat, shook it free of raindrops, and finally emerged as her usual, lanky, elegant self. Narrow trousers tucked into tall boots, and a stringlike sweater that on anyone else would have looked like an old floor-cloth, but on Sally was sensational.

She had started life as a model and had never lost her beanpole shape or the ugly, jutting, photogenic bones of her face. From being a model, she had gravitated to the editorial pages of a fashion magazine, and from there, using her accumulated know-how, her many connections, and a natural flair for business, had opened her own shop. She was nearly forty, divorced, hard-headed, but far more tenderhearted than she liked anybody to suspect. Victoria had worked for her for nearly two years and was very fond of her.

Now, she yawned. "I really hate business lunches. I always feel hung over by the middle of the afternoon, and somehow that throws me for the rest of the day."

She reached into her immense handbag and took out cigarettes and an evening paper, which she tossed down onto the glass counter. "What's been happening here?"

"Practically nothing. I sold the beige overdress, and

some female came in and dithered for half an hour over the paisley coat, and then she went out again and said she'd think about it. She was put off by the mink collar. She says she's a wildlife supporter."

"Tell her we'll take it off and put on plastic fur instead." Sally went through the curtained doorway into the small office at the back of the shop, sat at her desk and began to open the mail.

She said, "You know, Victoria, I've been thinking, this would be a terribly good time for you to take a couple of weeks off. Things'll start livening up soon, and then I shan't be able to let you go. Besides, you haven't had a holiday since goodness knows when. The only thing is, February isn't very exciting anywhere. Perhaps you could go and ski, or stay with your mother in Sotogrande. What's Sotogrande like in February?"

"Windy and wet, I should think."

Sally looked up. "You don't want to take two weeks off in February," she announced resignedly. "I can tell by your voice." Victoria did not contradict her. Sally sighed. "If I had a mother who had a gorgeous house in Sotogrande, I'd stay with her every month of the year if I could. Besides, you look as though you need a holiday. All skinny and pale. It makes me feel guilty having you around, as though I worked you too hard." She opened another envelope. "I thought we'd paid that electricity bill. I'm sure we paid it. It must be the computer's fault. It must have gone mad. Computers do, you know."

To Victoria's relief the question of her suddenly taking a holiday at the end of February was, for the moment, forgotten. She picked up the newspaper that Sally had tossed down, and for lack of anything better to do, leafed idly through it, her eye skimming the usual disasters, both great and small. There were floods in Essex, a new conflagration threatened in Africa. A middle-aged earl was marrying his third wife, and in Bristol rehearsals were under way at the Fortune Theatre for Oliver Dobbs' new play, *Bent Penny*.

There was no reason why she should have noticed this little scrap of news. It was tucked in at the end of the last column on the entertainments page. There was no headline. No photograph. Just Oliver's name, which leapt out at her, like shout of recognition, from the small print.

". . . . it's a final demand. What a nerve, sending a final demand. I know I wrote a cheque last month." Victoria said nothing, and Sally looked at her. "Victoria . . . ? What are you staring at?"

"Nothing. Just this bit in the paper about a man I used to know."

"I hope he's not being sent to jail."

"No, he writes plays. Have you ever heard of Oliver Dobbs?"

"Yes, of course. He writes for television. I saw one of his short plays the other night. And he did the script for that marvelous documentary on Seville. What's he been doing to get himself in the news?"

"He's got a new production coming off in Bristol."

"What's he like?" Sally asked idly, half her mind still on the iniquities of the London Electricity Board.

"Attractive."

This caught Sally's attention. She was all in favor of attractive men. "Did he attract you?"

"I was eighteen and impressionable."

"Weren't we all, darling, in the dim days of our youth. Not that that applies to you. You're still a blooming child, you fortunate creature." Suddenly she lost interest in Oliver Dobbs, in the final demand, in the day, which had already gone on far too long. She leaned back and yawned. "To hell with it. Let's shut up shop and go home. Thank the Lord for weekends. All at once the prospect of nothing to do for two days is total paradise. I shall spend this evening sitting in a hot bath and watching television."

"I thought you'd be going out."

Sally's private life was both complicated and lively. She had a string of men friends, none of whom seemed to be aware of the others' existence. Like an adroit juggler, Sally kept them all on the go, and avoided the embarrassment of inadvertently muddling their names by calling them all "darling."

"No, thank God. How about you?"

"I'm meant to be going out to have a drink with some friends of my mother's. I don't suppose it will be very thrilling."

"Oh, well," said Sally, "You never know. Life is full of surprises."

One of the good things about working in Beauchamp Place was that it was within walking distance of Pendleton Mews. The flat in Pendleton Mews belonged to Victoria's mother, but it was Victoria who lived there. Most of the time she enjoyed the walk. Down shortcuts and narrow back roads, it only took half an hour and provided a little pleasant exercise and fresh air at the beginning and the end of the day.

But this evening it was so cold and wet that the prospect of a trudge through icy wind and rain was almost more than she could bear; so, breaking her own rule about never taking taxis, she succumbed, without much resistance, to temptation, walked up to the Bromptom Road and finally flagged down a cab.

Because of one-way streets and snarled-up traffic, it took perhaps ten minutes longer to reach the Mews than if she had made the journey on foot, and cost so much that she simply handed the driver a pound note and let him count out the meagre change. He had set her down at the arch that divided the Mews from the road, so there was still a little way to go, across the puddles and the shining wet cobbles before she reached at last the haven of her own blue front door. She opened the door with her latch key, reached inside and switched on the light; climbed the steep, narrow stairs, carpeted in worn beige Wilton, and emerged at the top directly into the small sitting room.

She shed umbrella and basket and went to draw the chintz curtains against the night. The room at once became enclosed and safe. She lit the gas fire and went through to the tiny kitchen to put on a kettle for a cup of coffee; switched on the television and then switched it off again, put a Rossini overture on the record player, went into her bedroom to take off raincoat and boots.

The kettle, competing with Rossini, whistled for attention. She made a mug of instant coffee, went back to the fireside, pulled her basket towards her and took out Sally's evening paper. She turned to the item about Oliver Dobbs and the new play in Bristol.

I was eighteen and impressionable, she had said to Sally, but she knew now that she had also been lonely and vulnerable, a ripe fruit, trembling on its stalk, waiting to fall.

And Oliver, of all men, had been standing at the foot of the tree, waiting to catch her.

Eighteen, and in her first year at art school. Knowing nobody, intensely shy and unsure of herself, she had been both flattered and apprehensive when an older girl, perhaps taking pity on Victoria, had flung a vague invitation to a party in her direction.

"Goodness knows what it'll be like, but I was told I could ask anybody I wanted. You're meant to bring a bottle of something, but I don't suppose it matters if you come empty handed. Anyway, its a good way to meet people. Look, I'll write down the address. The man's called Sebastian, but that doesn't matter. Just turn up if you feel like it. Any time; that doesn't matter either."

Victoria had never had such an invitation in her life. She decided that she wouldn't go. And then decided that she would. And then got cold feet. And finally put on a pair of clean jeans, stole a bottle of her mother's best claret, and went.

She ended up in a top floor flat in West Kensington, clutching her bottle of claret and knowing nobody. Before she had been there two minutes somebody said "How immensely kind," and removed the bottle of claret, but nobody else said a single word to her. The room was filled with smoke, intense men in beads, and girls with grey faces and long seaweed-like hair. There was even a grubby baby or two. There was nothing to eat and—once she had parted with the claret—nothing recognizable to drink. She could not find the girl who suggested that she come and was too shy to join any of the tight, conversational groups gathered on floor, cushions or the single sagging sofa that had curly wire springs protruding from between arm and seat. She was, as well, too diffident to go and get her coat and leave. The air was filled with the sweet and insidious smell of marijuana, and she was standing in the bay window, lost in nerve-wracking fantasies of a possible police raid, when suddenly somebody said, "I don't know you, do I?"

Startled, Victoria swung round, so clumsily that she almost knocked the drink out of his hand.

"Oh, I am sorry . . ."

"It doesn't matter. It hasn't spilled. At least," he added, generously, "not very much."

He smiled as though this were a joke, and she smiled back, grateful for any friendly overture. Grateful too that out of such woebegone company the only man who had spoken to her was neither dirty, sweaty, nor drunk. On the contrary, he was perfectly presentable. Even attractive. Very tall, very slender with reddish hair that reached to the collar of his sweater, and an immensely distinguished beard.

He said, "You haven't got a drink."

"No."

"Don't you want one?"

She said no again, because she didn't and also because if she said that she did, he might go away to get her one and never come back again.

He seemed amused. "Don't you like it?"

Victoria looked at his glass. "I don't exactly know what it is."

"I don't suppose anybody does. But this tastes like . . ." He took a mouthful, thoughtfully, like a professional taster, rolling it round his mouth, finally swallowing it. ". . . red ink and aniseed balls."

"What's it going to do to the inside of your stomach?"

"We'll worry about that in the morning." He looked down at her, a frown of concentration furrowing his brow. "I *don't* know you, do I?"

"No. I don't suppose you do. I'm Victoria Bradshaw." Even saying her own name made her feel embarrassed, but he did not seem to think that there was anything embarrassing about it.

"And what do you do with yourself?"

"I've just started at art college."

"That explains how you got to this little do. Are you enjoying it?"

She looked around. "Not very much."

"I actually meant art college, but if you're not enjoying this very much, why don't you go home?"

"I thought it wouldn't be very polite."

He laughed at that. "You know, in this sort of company, politeness doesn't count all that much."

"I've only been here for ten minutes."

"And I've only been here for five." He finished his drink, tipping back his remarkable head and pouring the remains of the noxious tumbler down the back of his throat as easily as if it had been a cold and tasty beer. Then he set the glass down on the window ledge and said, "Come on. We're leaving." And he put a hand under her elbow and steered her expertly towards the door, and without making the vaguest of excuses or even saying good-bye, they left.

At the top of the dingy staircase, she turned to face him.

"I didn't mean that."

"What didn't you mean?"

"I mean that I didn't want *you* to leave. I wanted *me* to leave."

"How do you know I didn't want to leave?"

"But it was a party!"

"I left those sort of parties behind light years ago. Come on, hurry up, let's get out into the fresh air."

On the pavement, in the soft dusk of a late summer's night, she stopped again. She said, "I'm all right now."

"And what is that supposed to mean?"

"I can get a taxi, and go home."

He began to smile. "Are you frightened?"

Victoria became embarrassed all over again. "No, of course not."

"Then what you running away from?"

"I'm not running away from anything. I simply . . ."

"Want to go home?"

"Yes."

"Well you can't."

"Why not?"

"Because we're going to go and find a spaghetti house or something, and we're going to buy a proper bottle of wine, and you are going to tell me the story of your life."

An empty taxi hove into view, and he hailed it. It stopped, and he bundled her in. After he gave the taxi driver directions, they drove in silence for about five minutes, and then the taxi stopped and he bundled her out again. He paid off the taxi and led her across the pavement into a small and unpretentious restaurant, with a few tables crowded around the walls and the air thick with cigarette smoke and the good smells of cooking food. They were given a table in the corner without enough room for his long legs, but somehow he arranged them so that his feet didn't trip the passing waiters, and he ordered a bottle of wine and asked for a menu, and then he lit a cigarette and turned to her and said, "Now."

"Now what?"

"Now tell me. The story of your life."

She found herself smiling. "I don't even know who you are. I don't know what your name is."

"It's Oliver Dobbs." He went on, quite kindly, "You have to tell me everything, because I'm a writer. A real honest-to-God published writer, with an agent and an enormous overdraft, and a compulsion for listening. Do you know, nobody listens enough. People fall over themselves trying to tell other people things, and nobody ever listens. Did you know that?"

Victoria thought of her parents. "Yes, I suppose I do."

"You see? You suppose. You're not sure. Nobody's ever sure of anything. They should listen more. How old are you?"

"Eighteen."

"I thought you were less when I saw you. You looked about fifteen standing there in the window of that crumby joint. I was about to ring the welfare and tell them that a tiny junior minor was out on the streets at night."

The wine came, uncorked, a liter bottle dumped onto the table. He picked it up and filled their glasses. He said, "Where do you live?"

"Pendleton Mews."

"Where's that?"

She told him and he whistled. "How very smart. A real Knightsbridge girl. I didn't realize they went to art college. You must be immensely rich."

"Of course I'm not rich."

"Then why do you live in Pendleton Mews?"

"Because it's my mother's house, only she's living in Spain just now, so I use it."

"Curiouser and curiouser. Why is Mrs. Bradshaw living in Spain?"

"She's not Mrs. Bradshaw, she's Mrs. Paley. My parents divorced six months ago. My mother married again, to this man called Henry Paley, and he has a house in Sotogrande because he likes playing golf all the time." She decided to get it all over in a single burst. "And my father has gone to live with some cousin who owns a moldering estate in Southern Ireland. He's threatening to breed polo ponies, but he's always been a man of great ideas but little action, so I don't suppose he will."

"And little Victoria is left to live in London."

"Victoria is eighteen."

"Yes, I know, old and experienced. Do you live alone?"

"Yes."

"Aren't you lonely?"

"I'd rather be alone than live with people who dislike each other."

He made a face. "Parents are hell, aren't they? My parents are hell, too, but they've never done anything so definite as divorcing each other. They just molder on in darkest Dorset, and everything—their reduced circumstances, the cost of a bottle of gin, the fact that the hens aren't laying—is blamed on either me or the government."

Victoria said, "I like my parents. It was just that they'd stopped liking each other."

"Have you got brothers or sisters?"

"No. Just me."

"No one to take care of you?"

"I take very good care of myself."

He looked disbelieving. "*I* shall take care of you," he announced, magnificently.

After that evening Victoria did not see Oliver Dobbs

again for two weeks, and by that time she knew that
she was never going to see him again. And then it was
a Friday evening, and she was so miserable that she
compulsively spring-cleaned the flat, which did not
need it, and then decided to wash her hair.

It was while she was kneeling by the bath with her
head under the shower that she heard the bell ring.
She wrapped herself up in a towel and went to open
the door, and it was Oliver. Victoria was so pleased to
see him that she burst into tears, and he came in and
shut the door and took her in his arms, then and
there, at the foot of the stairs, and dried her face with
the end of the towel. After this they went upstairs, and
he produced a bottle of wine out of his jacket pocket,
and she found some glasses, and they sat by the gas
fire and drank wine together. And when they had finished the wine, she went into her bedroom to get
dressed, and to comb out her long, fair, damp tresses,
and Oliver sat on the end of the bed and watched her.
And then he took her out for dinner. There were no
apologies, no excuses for his two weeks silence. He had
been in Birmingham, he told her, and that was all. It
never occurred to Victoria to ask him what he had
been doing there.

And this proved to be the pattern of their relationship. He came and went, in and out of her life, unpredictable, and yet strangely constant. Each time he
came back, she never knew where he had been. Perhaps Ibiza, or perhaps he had met some man who
owned a cottage in Wales. He was not only unpredictable, he was strangely secretive. He never spoke about
his work, and she did not even know where he lived,
except that it was a basement flat in some street off
the Fulham Road. He was moody, too, and once or
twice she had seen a terrifying flash of uncontrollable
temper, but this all seemed to be an acceptable part of
the fact that he was a writer and a true artist. And
there was another side to the coin. He was funny and

loving and immensely good company. It was like having the kindest sort of older brother who was, at the same time, irresistibly attractive.

When they were not together, she told herself that he was working. She imagined him at his typewriter, writing and rewriting, destroying, starting again, never achieving his own goals of perfection. Sometimes, he had a little money to spend on her. At others, none at all, and then Victoria would provide the food and cook it for him in the Mews flat, and she would buy him a bottle of wine and the small cigars that she knew he loved.

There came a bad period when he went through a slough of despondency. Nothing would go right and nothing seemed to be selling, and it was then that he took the night job in a little café, piling dirty dishes into the automatic washer. After that things began to get better again, and he sold a play to Independent Television, but he still went on washing dishes in order to be able to earn enough money to pay his rent.

Victoria had no other men friends, and did not want them. For some reason, she never imagined Oliver with other women. There was no occasion for jealousy. What she had of Oliver was not much, but it was enough.

The first she heard of Jeannette Archer was when Oliver told her that he was going to be married.

It was early summer, and the windows of Victoria's flat were open to the Mews. Below, Mrs. Tingley from number fourteen was bedding out geraniums in her decorative tubs, and the man who lived two doors down was cleaning his car. Pigeons cooed from rooftops, and the distant hum of traffic was deadened by trees in full leaf. They sat on the window seat, and Victoria was sewing a button onto Oliver's jacket. It hadn't fallen off, but it was going to, and she had offered to sew it on before it did. She found a needle and thread and put a knot in the thread and pushed the needle into the worn corduroy when Oliver said, "What would you say if I told you I was going to be married?"

Victoria pushed the needle right into her thumb. The pain was minute but excruciating. She pulled the needle carefully out and watched the red bead of blood swell and grow. Oliver said, "Suck it, quickly, or it'll drip all over my coat," and when she didn't, he took her wrist and thrust her thumb into his mouth. Their eyes met. He said, "Don't look at me like that."

Victoria looked at her thumb. It throbbed as though some person had hit it with a hammer. She said, "I don't know any other way to look."

"Well say something then. Don't just stare at me like a lunatic."

"I don't know what I'm meant to say."

"You could wish me luck."

"I didn't know . . . that you . . . I mean, I didn't know that you were . . ." She was trying, even at this ghastly juncture, to be rational, polite, tactful. But Oliver scorned such euphemisms and interrupted brutally.

"You mean, you never realized that there was anybody else? And that, if you like it, is a line, straight from an out-of-date novel. The kind my mother reads."

"Who is she?"

"She's called Jeannette Archer. She's twenty-four, a nicely brought-up girl with a nice flat and a nice little car, and a good job, and we've been living together for the past four months."

"I thought you lived in Fulham."

"I do sometimes, but I haven't just lately."

She said, "Do you love her?" because she simply had to know.

"Victoria, she's going to have a child. Her parents want me to marry her so that the baby will have a father. It seems to matter to them very much."

"I thought you didn't pay regard to parents."

"I don't if they're like mine, complaining and unsuccessful. But these particular parents happen to have a lot of money. I need money. I need money to buy the time to write."

She knew that she wouldn't. Her thumb still ached. Her eyes were filling with tears, and so that he shouldn't see them, she dropped her head and started to try to sew on the button, but the tears brimmed over and rolled down her cheeks and fell, great drops on the corduroy of his coat. He saw them and said, "Don't cry." And he put a hand under her chin and lifted her streaming face.

Victoria said, "I love you."

He leaned forward and kissed her cheek. "But you," he told her, "don't happen to be having a baby."

The clock on the mantelpiece astonished her by chiming, with silvery notes, seven o'clock. Victoria looked at it, disbelieving, and then at her wrist watch. Seven o'clock. The Rossini had finished long ago, the dregs in her coffee mug were stone cold, outside it was still raining, and in half an hour she was due at a party in Campden Hill.

She was assailed by the usual small panic of one who has lost all trace of time, and all thoughts of Oliver Dobbs were, for the moment, forgotten. Victoria sprang to her feet and did a number of things in quick succession. Took the coffee mug back into the kitchen, turned on a bath, went into her room to open her wardrobe and take out various garments, none of which seemed suitable. She took off some clothes and searched for stockings. She thought about ringing up for a taxi. She thought about calling Mrs. Fairburn and pleading a headache, and then thought better of it, because the Fairburns were friends of her mother's, the invitation was a long-standing one, and Victoria had a horror of causing offense. She went into the steaming bathroom and turned off the taps and splashed in some bath oil. The steam became scented. She disposed of her long hair in a bathcap, slathered cold cream on her face and wiped it all off again with a tissue. She climbed into the scalding water.

Fifteen minutes later she was out once more and dressed. A black silk turtleneck with a peasant-embroidered smock on top of it. Black stockings, black shoes with very high heels. She blackened her thick lashes with mascara, clipped on earrings, sprayed on some scent.

Now, a coat. She drew back the curtains and opened the window and leaned out to gauge the weather. It was very dark and still windy, but the rain, for the moment, seemed to have ceased. Below, the Mews was quiet. Cobbles shone like fish scales, black puddles reflected the light from the old-fashioned street lamps. A car was turning in from the street, under the archway. It nosed down the Mews like a prowling cat. Victoria withdrew her head, closed the windows and the curtains. She took an old fur coat from the back of the door, bundled herself into its familiar comfort, checked for her keys and wallet, turned off the gas fire and all the upstairs lights, and started downstairs.

She had taken one step when the doorbell rang.

She said, "Damn." It was probably Mrs. Tingley come to borrow milk. She was always running out of milk. And she would want to stand and talk. Victoria ran to the foot of the stairs and flung open the door.

On the far side of the Mews, beneath a lamp, the prowling car was parked. A big old Volvo estate car. But of its driver there was no sign. Puzzled, she hesitated, and was about to go and investigate, when, from the dark shadows at the side of the door, a figure moved soundlessly forward, causing Victoria nearly to jump out of her skin. He said her name, and it was as though she had been taken, very swiftly, down twenty-three stories in a very fast lift. The wind blew a scrap of newspapers the length of the Mews. She could hear the beating of her own heart.

"I didn't know if you'd still be living here."

She thought, these things don't happen. Not to ordinary people. They only happen in books.

"I thought you might have moved. I was sure you'd have moved."

She shook her head.

He said, "It's been a long time."

Victoria's mouth was dry. She said, "Yes."

Oliver Dobbs. She searched for some change in him but could find none. His hair was the same, his beard, his light eyes, his deep and gentle voice. He even wore the same sort of clothes, shabby and casual garments that on his tall, lean frame did not look shabby at all but somehow contrived and distinctive.

He said, "You look as though you're just going out."

"Yes, I am. I'm late as it is. But . . ." She stepped back ". . . you'd better come in, out of the cold."

"Is that all right?"

"Yes." But she said again, "I have to go out," as if her going out were some sort of an escape hatch from a possibly impossible situation. She turned to lead the way back upstairs. He began to follow her and then hesitated. He said, "I've left my cigarettes in the car."

He plunged back into the outdoors. Halfway up the stairs Victoria waited. He returned in a moment, closed the door behind him. She went up, turning on the light at the head of the stairs, and going to stand with her back to the unlit gas fire.

Oliver followed her, his eyes alert, instantly scanning the pretty room, the pale walls, the chintzes, patterned with spring flowers. The pine corner-cupboard that Victoria had found in a junk shop and stripped herself, her pictures, her books.

He smiled, satisfied. "You haven't changed anything. It's exactly the way I remembered. How marvelous to find something that hasn't changed." His eyes came back to her face. "I thought you'd have gone. I thought you'd have married some guy and moved. I was so certain that the door would be opened by a complete stranger. And there you were. Like a miracle."

Victoria found that she could think of absolutely nothing to say. She thought, I have been struck speechless. Searching for words, she found herself looking around the room. Beneath the bookcase was the cupboard where she kept a meagre collection of bottles. She said, "Would you like a drink?"

"Yes, I'd like one very much."

She laid down her bag and went to crouch by the cupboard. There was sherry, half a bottle of wine, a nearly empty bottle of whisky. She took out the whisky bottle. "There isn't much, I'm afraid."

"That's marvelous," He came to take the bottle from her. "I'll do it." He disappeared into the kitchen, at home in her flat as if he had walked out only yesterday. She heard the chink of glass, the running of the tap.

"Do you want one?" he called.

"No thank you."

He emerged from the kitchen with the drink in his hand. "Where's this party you're going to?"

"Campden Hill. Some friends of my mother's."

"Is it going on for long?"

"I don't suppose so."

"Will you come back for dinner?"

Victoria almost laughed at this, because this was Oliver Dobbs, apparently inviting her to have dinner with him in her own flat.

"I imagine I will."

"Then you go to your party, and I'll wait here." He saw the expression on her face and added quickly, "It's important. I want to talk to you. And I want to have time to talk to you."

It sounded sinister, as though someone was after

him, like the police, or some Soho heavy with a switch knife.

"There's nothing wrong, is there?"

"How anxious you look! No, there's nothing wrong." He added, in a practical fashion, "Have you got any food in the house?"

"There's some soup. Some bacon and eggs. I could make a salad. Or, if you wanted, we could go out. There's a Greek restaurant around the corner, it's just started up . . ."

"No, we can't go out." He sounded so definite that Victoria began to be apprehensive all over again. He went on, "I didn't want to tell you right away until I knew what the form was with you. The thing is, there's someone else in the car. There are two of us."

"Two of you?" She imagined a girlfriend, a drunken crony, even a dog.

In answer Oliver laid down his glass and disappeared once more down the stairs. She heard the door open and his footsteps crossing the Mews. She went to the head of the stairs and waited for him to return. He had left the door open, and when he reappeared he closed this behind him, carefully with his foot. The reason that he did this was that his arms were otherwise occupied with the weight of a large, mercifully sleeping, baby boy.

CHAPTER 3
Friday

It was a quarter past seven, at the end of a grueling day, before John Dunbeath finally turned his car into the relative quiet of Cadogan Place, down the narrow lane between tightly parked cars, and edged it into a meagre gap not too far from his own front door. He killed the engine, turned off the lights, and reached into the back seat for his bulging briefcase and his raincoat. He got out of the car and locked up.

He had left his office, and commenced the daily ordeal of the journey home, in lashing rain, but now, half an hour or so later, it seemed to be easing up a little. Dark and still windy, the sky, bronzed with the reflected glow of the city lights, seemed to be full of ominous, racing clouds. After ten hours spent in an overheated atmosphere, the night air smelled fresh and invigorating. Walking slowly down the pavement, his briefcase slapping against his leg, he took one or two deep and conscious lungfuls, and was refreshed by the cold wind.

With his key ring in his hand, he went up the steps to the front door. It was black, with a brass handle and a letter box that the porter polished every morning. The tall old London house had been turned, some time ago, into flats, and the lobby and staircase, although carpeted and neatly kept, always smelled stale and stuffy, unaired and claustrophobic with central heating. This odor greeted him now, as it greeted him every evening. He shut the door with the seat of his pants, collected his mail from its pigeon hole and began to climb the stairs.

He lived on the second floor, in an apartment that had been cunningly contrived from the main bedrooms of the original house. It was a furnished flat, found for him by a colleague when John had left New York and come to work in London at the European headquarters of the Warburg Investment Corporation, and he had arrived at Heathrow off the plane from Kennedy and taken instant possession. Now, six months later, it had become familiar. Not a home, but familiar. A place for a man alone to live.

He let himself in, turned on the lights and saw on the hall table his message from Mrs. Robbins, the daily lady whom the porter had recommended should come in each morning and clean the flat. John had only seen her once, at the very beginning, when he had given her a key and told her more or less what he wanted her to do. Mrs. Robbins had made it clear that this was quite unnecessary. She was a stately person, portentously hatted and wearing her respectability like armor. At the end of the encounter he was fully aware that he had not been interviewing her, but that Mrs. Robbins had been judging him. However, it seemed that he had passed muster, and she duly took him on, along with one or two other privileged persons who also lived in the house. Since then, he had never set eyes on her, but they corresponded by means of notes that they left for each other, and he paid her, weekly, in the same fashion.

He dropped his briefcase, slung his raincoat onto a chair, picked up Mrs. Robbins' letter, and along with the rest of his mail took it into the sitting room. Here all was beige and brown and totally impersonal. Another person's pictures hung upon the wall, another person's books filled the shelves which flanked the fireplace, and he had no wish for it to be any different.

Sometimes, for no particular reason, the emptiness of his personal life, the need for welcome, for love, would overwhelm him, breaking down the careful barriers which he had painfully built. On these occasions, he could not stop the memories flooding back. Like coming home to the shining brilliance of the New York apartment, with its white floors and its white rugs, and a sort of perfection which Lisa had achieved with her eye for color, her passion for detail and her total disregard for her husband's bank balance. And, inevitably, Lisa would be there, waiting for him,—for these memories belonged to the beginning of their marriage—so beautiful that she took your breath away, wearing something gauzy by de la Renta, and smelling unbearably exotic. And she would kiss him, and put a martini into his hand, and be glad to see him.

But most times, like this evening, he was grateful for quiet, for peace; for time to read his mail, to have a drink, to reassemble himself after the day's work. He went around the room turning on lights; he switched on the electric fire which instantly became a pile of rustic logs, flickering in the pseudo firebasket. He drew the brown velvet curtains and poured himself a Scotch, and then read the message from Mrs. Robbins.

Her notes were always brief and abbreviated, rendering them as important sounding as cables.

Laundry missing pair sox and 2 hankchfs.
Miss Mansell called says will you ring her this evng.

He leafed through the rest of his mail. A bank statement, a company report, a couple of invitations, an airmail letter from his mother. Putting these aside for later perusal, he sat on the arm of the sofa, reached for the telephone and dialed a number.

She came on almost at once, sounding breathless as

she always did, as though perpetually in a tearing hurry.

"Hello?"

"Tania."

"Darling. I thought you'd never call."

"Sorry, I'm only just back. Just picked up your message now."

"Oh, poor sweet, you must be exhausted. Listen, something maddening's cropped up, but I can't make this evening. The thing is, I'm going down to the country *now*. Mary Colville rang up this morning, and there's some dance going on, and some girls got flu, and she's desperate about her numbers, and I simply had to say I'd go. I tried to say no, and explain about this evening, but then she said would *you* come down tomorrow, for the weekend."

She stopped, not because she hadn't got plenty more to say, but because she had run out of breath. John found himself smiling. Her spates of words, her breathlessness, her confused social arrangements were all part of the charm that she held for him, mostly because she was so diametrically different from his ex-wife. Tania had, perpetually, to be organized, and was so scatty that the thought of organizing John never entered her pretty feather-head.

He looked at his watch. He said, "If you're going to be at some dinner party in the country this evening, aren't you running things a little fine?"

"Oh, darling, yes, I'm going to be desperately late, but that's not what you're meant to say at all. You're meant to be desperately disappointed."

"Of course I'm disappointed."

"And you will come down to the country tomorrow?"

"Tania, I can't. I just heard today. I have to go to the Middle East. I'm flying out tomorrow morning."

"Oh, I can't bear it. How long are you going for?"

"Just a few days. A week at the outside. It depends on how things go."

"Will you call me when you get back?"

"Yes, sure."

"I rang Imogen Fairburn and told her I couldn't make it this evening, so she understands, and she says she's looking forward to seeing you even if I can't be there too. Oh, darling, isn't everything grim? Are you furious?"

"Furious," he assured her, mildly.

"But you do understand, don't you?"

"I understand completely, and you thank Mary for her invitation and explain why I can't make it."

"Yes, I will, of course I will, and . . ."

Another of her characteristics was that she could never finish a phone call. He interrupted firmly.

"Look, Tania, you have an appointment this evening. Get off the line and finish your packing and get moving. With luck, you'll arrive at the Colvilles no more than two hours late."

"Oh, darling I do adore you."

"I'll call you."

"You do that." She made kissing sounds. "Bye." She hung up. He put the receiver back on the hook and sat looking at it, wondering why he couldn't feel disappointed when a charming and engaging female stood him up for a more exciting invitation. He mulled over this problem for a moment or two, and finally decided that it didn't matter anyway. So he dialed Annabel's and cancelled the table he had ordered for this evening and then he finished his drink and went to have a shower.

Just as he was on the point of leaving for the Fairburns' a call came through from his vice president, who had had, on his journey home in the company Cadillac, one or two important thoughts about John's projected trip to Bahrain. Discussing these, getting them collated and noted, had taken a good fifteen minutes, so that by the time John finally arrived at the house in Campden Hill, he was nearly three quarters of an hour late.

The party was obviously in full swing. The street outside was jammed with cars—it took him another frustrating five minutes to find a scrap of space in which to park his own—and light and a steady hum of conversation emanated from beyond the tall, curtained first-floor windows. When he rang the bell the door was opened almost immediately by a man (hired for the occasion?) in a white coat, who said, "Good evening," and directed John up the stairs.

It was a pleasant and familiar house, expensively decorated, thickly carpeted, smelling like an extravagant hothouse. As John ascended, the sound of voices swelled to a massive volume. Through the open door that led into Imogen's drawing room, he could discern an anonymous crush of people, some drinking, some smoking, some munching canapés, and all intent on talking their heads off. A couple was sitting at the head of the stairs. John smiled and excused himself as he stepped around them, and the girl said, "We're just having a tiny breath of air," as though she felt she must apologize for being there.

By the open door was a table set up as a bar, with another hired waiter in attendance.

"Good evening, sir. What'll it be?"

"Scotch and soda, please."

"With ice, sir, naturally."

John grinned. The "naturally" meant that the barman had recognized him for the American that he was. He said, "Naturally," and took the drink. "How am I going to find Mrs. Fairburn?"

"I'm afraid you'll just have to go and look for her, sir. Like a needle in a ruddy haystack, I'd say."

John agreed with him, took a spine-stiffening slug of whiskey and plunged.

It wasn't as bad as it night have been. He was recognized, greeted, almost at once, drawn into a group, offered a smoked salmon roll, a cigar, a racing tip. "Absolute certainty, old boy, three-thirty at Doncaster tomorrow." A girl he knew slightly came and kissed him and he suspected, left lipstick on his cheek. A tall young man with an old man's balding head swam forward and said, "You're John Dunbeath, aren't you? Name's Crumleigh. Used to know your predecessor. And how are things in the banking world?"

He was nursing his drink, but a waiter nipped up and refilled his glass when he wasn't looking. Somebody trod on his shoe. A very young man wearing a brigade tie materialized at his elbow, trailing a protesting female by the arm. She was perhaps seventeen years old, and her hair looked like dandelion floss. ". . . . this girl wants to meet you. Been eyeing you across the room."

"Oh, Nigel, you are *awful*."

Mercifully, he spied his hostess. He excused himself, and edged, with some difficulty, across the room to her side. "Imogen."

"John! Darling!"

She was immensely pretty. Grey-haired, blue-eyed, her skin smooth as a young girl's, her manner unashamedly provocative.

He kissed her politely, because she was obviously expecting to be kissed, with that flower-face turned up to his.

"This certainly is a party."

"So gorgeous to see you. But Tania couldn't come. She telephoned, something about having to go down to the country. So terribly disappointing. I was so looking forward to seeing you *both*. Never mind, you came and that's all that matters. Have you had a word with Reggie? He's longing to have a long, boring chat with you about the stock market or something." A couple hovered, waiting to say good-bye. "Don't go away," Imogen told John out of the corner of her mouth, and then turned from him, all smiles. "Darling. Do you really have to go? Such a sadness. Heavenly to see you. So glad you enjoyed it . . ." She came back to John. "Look, as Tania hasn't come, and you're on your own, there's a girl that perhaps you could go and chat up. She's pretty as paint, so I'm not letting you in for anything gruesome, but I don't think she knows many people. I mean, I asked her, because her mother's one of our greatest friends, but somehow she seems a little out of her depth. Be an angel, and be sweet to her."

John, whose party manners had been rigorously drilled into him by his American mother (Imogen knew this, otherwise she would never have appealed to him for help) said that he would be delighted. But where was the girl?

Imogen, who was not tall, stood tiptoes, and searched with her eyes. "There. Over in the corner." Her little feminine hand closed over his wrist like a vice. "I'll take you over and introduce you."

Which she proceeded to do, shouldering her way across the stifling room without once releasing her grip of him. John tagged along, willy-nilly, feeling like a bulky liner in the tow of a tug. They emerged at last, and it seemed to be a quiet corner of the room, perhaps because it was furthest from the door and the bar, but all at once there was room to stand, or move your elbows or even sit.

"Victoria."

She was perched on the arm of a chair, talking to an elderly man who was obviously going on to some other party, for he was wearing a dinner suit and a black tie. When Imogen said her name, she stood up, but whether this was out of politeness to Imogen, or to escape from her companion, it was impossible to say.

"Victoria, I do hope I'm not interrupting something absolutely riveting, but I do want you to meet John,

because his girlfriend hasn't been able to come to-night, and I want you to be terribly kind to him."
John, embarrassed both for himself and the girl, con-tinued to smile politely. "He's an American, and he's one of my most favorite people . . ."

With a clearing of the throat, and a small, imper-ceptible gesture of farewell, the elderly man in the dinner suit also stood up and eased himself away.

". . . and John"—the grip on his wrist had not less-ened. Perhaps the blood stream to his hand had al-ready seized up and in a moment his fingers would start falling off—"this is Victoria, And her mother is one of my best friends, and when Reggie and I were in Spain last year, we went and stayed with her. At Soto-grande. In the most heavenly house you've ever seen. So now you've got *lots* to talk about."

She let go of his wrist at last. It was like being freed from handcuffs.

He said, "Hello, Victoria."

She said, "Hello."

Imogen had chosen the wrong words. She was not pretty as paint. But she had a scrubbed, immaculate look to her that reminded him, with some nostalgia, of the American girls he had known in his youth. Her hair was pale and silky, straight and long, cut cun-ningly to frame her face. Her eyes were blue, her face neatly boned, her head supported by a long neck and narrow shoulders. She had an unremarkable nose, dis-armingly freckled, and a remarkable mouth. A sweet and expressive mouth with a dimple at one corner.

It was an out-of-doors sort of face. The sort of face one expected to encounter at the tiller of a sailboat or at the top of some hair-raising ski-slope; not at a Lon-don cocktail party.

"Did Imogen say Sotogrande?"

"Yes."

"How long has your mother lived out there?"

"About three years. Have you ever been to Soto-grande?"

"No, but I have friends who golf, and they get out there whenever they can."

"My stepfather plays golf every day. That's why he chose to go and live there. Their house is right on the fairway. He steps out of the garden gate and he's playing the tenth hole. It's as easy as that."

"Do you play golf?"

"No. But there are other things to do. You can swim. Play tennis. Ride, if you want to."

"What do you do?"

"Well, I don't very often go out, but when I do I play tennis mostly."

"Does your mother come back to this country?"

"Yes. Two or three times a year. She dashes round from one art gallery to another, sees about six plays, buys some clothes, and then goes back again."

He smiled at this, and she smiled back. There came a small pause. The subject of Sotogrande seemed to have exhausted itself. Her eyes moved over his shoulder, and then quickly, as though she did not wish to appear ill-mannered, back to his face again. He wondered if she was expecting somebody.

He said, "Do you know many people here?"

"No, not really. Not anybody really." She added. "I'm sorry your girlfriend couldn't come."

"Like Imogen said, she had to go down to the country."

"Yes." She stooped to take a handful of nuts out of a dish that had been placed on a low coffee-table. She began to eat them, putting them into her mouth one at a time. "Did Imogen say you were an American?"

"Yes, I think she did."

"You don't sound like an American."

"How do I sound?"

"Sort of halfway between. Mid-Atlantic. Alistair Cooke type American."

He was impressed. "You have a sharp ear. I have an American mother and British father. I'm sorry . . . a Scottish father."

"So you're really British?"

"I have a dual passport. I was born in the States."

"Whereabouts?"

"Colorado."

"Was your mother skiing at the time, or do your parents live there?"

"No, they live there. They have a ranch in Southwest Colorado."

"I can't imagine where that is."

"North of New Mexico. West of the Rockies. East of the San Juans."

"I'd have to have an atlas. But it sounds very spectacular."

"It is spectacular."

"Were you riding a horse before you could walk?"

"Just about."

She said, "I can imagine it," and he had a strange feeling that she probably could. "When did you leave Colorado?"

He told her. "At eleven years old I was sent East to school. And then I came over to this country and I went to Wellington, because that's where my father had been. And after that I went to Cambridge."

"You really do have a dual nationality, don't you? What happened after Cambridge?"

"I went back to New York for a spell, and now I'm back in London. I've been here since the summer.

"Do you work for an American firm?"

"An investment bank."

"Do you get back to Colorado?"

"Sure, whenever I can. Only I haven't been for some time, because things have been pretty busy over here."

"Do you like being in London?"

"Yes, I like it very much." Her expression was very thoughtful. He smiled. "Why, don't you?"

"Yes. But just because I know it so well. I mean I can't imagine, really, living anywhere else."

There came, for some reason, another lull. Once more her eyes strayed, only this time it was to the gold watch strapped to her slender wrist. Having a pretty girl look at her watch while he was chatting her up was an unfamiliar experience for John Dunbeath. He expected to be irritated, but instead found himself mildly amused, although the joke was against himself.

"Are you expecting someone?" he asked her.

"No."

He thought that her face had a private look about it; composed, polite, but private. He wondered if she was always like this, or if their lines of communication were being cut by the murderous impossibility of cocktail party conversation. In order to keep this going, she had asked him a number of friendly questions, but there was no knowing whether she had listened to half of his polite replies. They had talked banalities and found out nothing about each other. Perhaps she wanted it this way. He could not decide whether she was totally disinterested or simply shy. Now, she had started glancing around the crowded room once more as though desperate for a means of escape, and he began to wonder why she had come in the first place. Suddenly exasperated, and ready to cast formalities aside, he was about to ask her this, but she forestalled him by announcing, without preamble, that she ought to be going. ". . . its getting late, and I seem to have been here for ages." At once she seemed to realize that this remark was, perhaps not much of a compliment to him. "I am sorry, I didn't mean it that way. I didn't mean that I seem to have been *here* for ages, I meant that I seem to have been at the party for ages. I . . . I've very much enjoyed meeting you, but I shouldn't be too late." John said nothing. She smiled brightly, hopefully. "I ought to get home."

"Where's home?"

"Pendleton Mews."

"That's very close to where I live. I'm Cadogan Place."

"Oh, how nice." Now, she was beginning to sound desperate. "It's so quiet, isn't it?"

"Yes, it's very quiet."

Stealthily, she set down her glass, and hitched the strap of her bag up onto her shoulder. "Well, then, I'll say good-bye . . ."

But all at once he was consumed with an unfamiliar and healthy annoyance, and told himself that he was damned if he was going to be palmed off like this. Anyway, with his Scotch finished and no Tania to attend to, the party had gone sour for him. Tomorrow, and the long flight to Bahrain loomed on the edge of his mind. He still had to pack, check his papers, leave messages for Mrs. Robbins.

He said, "I'm going too."

"But you've only just arrived."

He finished his drink and laid down the empty tumbler. "I'll take you home."

"You don't need to take me home."

"I know I don't need to, but I may as well."

"I can get a taxi,"

"Why get a taxi, when we're going in the same direction?"

"There's really no need . . ."

He was becoming bored by the tedious argument. "No problem. I don't want to be late either. I have a plane to catch in the early morning."

"To America?"

"No, to the Middle East."

"What are you going to do there?"

He put a hand under her elbow in order to propel her in the direction of the door. "Talk," he told her.

Imogen was torn between astonishment that he had hit it off so swiftly with her dearest friend's daughter, and a certain peevishness that he had stayed at her party for such a short time.

"But, John darling, you've only just come."

"It's a great party, but I'm headed for the Middle East tomorrow; an early flight, and . . ."

"But tomorrow's *Saturday*. It's too cruel having to fly off on a Saturday. I suppose that's what happens if you're a budding tycoon. But I wish you could stay a little longer."

"I wish I could too, but I really must go."

"Well, it's been divine, and sweet of you to come. Have you talked to Reggie? No, I don't suppose you have, but I'll tell him what's happening, and you must come for dinner when you get home again. Good-bye, Victoria. Heaven to see you. I'll write and tell your mother you're looking fabulously well."

On the landing he said, "Have you got a coat?"

"Yes. It's downstairs."

They went down. On a chair in the hall was a mound of coats. She dug from this an unfashionable fur, probably inherited and much worn. John helped her into it. The man in the starched white coat opened the door for them, and they emerged into the windy darkness and walked together up the pavement to where he had parked his car.

Waiting at the end of Church Street for the lights to change, John became aware of pangs of hunger. He had eaten a sandwich for lunch and nothing since. The clock on his dashboard told him that it was nearly nine o'clock. The lights changed, and they moved out and into the stream of traffic that poured east towards Kensington Gore.

He thought about eating dinner. He glanced at the girl beside him. Her closeness, her reserve, was a challenge. It intrigued him, and against all reason he found himself wanting to break it down, to find out what went on behind that private face. It was like being confronted by a high wall, a notice saying No

Trespassers, and imagining that beyond lay the promise of enchanting gardens and inviting tree-shaded walks. He saw her profile, outlined against the lights, her chin deep in the fur collar of the coat. He thought, well, why not?

He said, "Do you want to come and have dinner with me someplace?"

"Oh . . ." She turned towards him. "How kind."

"I have to eat, and if you'd like to join me . . ."

"I do appreciate it, but if you don't mind, I really should get back. I mean, I'm having dinner at home. I arranged to have dinner at home."

It was the second time she had used the word "home," and it disconcerted him, with its implication of close relatives. He wondered who waited for her. A sister, a lover, or even a husband. Anything was possible.

"That's all right. I just thought if you weren't doing anything."

"Really so kind of you, but I can't . . ."

A long silence fell between them, broken only by her giving him directions as to how to get most easily to Pendeleton Mews. When they reached the archway that separated the Mews from the street, she said, "You can put me down here. I can walk the rest."

But by now he was feeling stubborn. If she would not have dinner with him, at least he would drive her to her door. He turned the car into the narrow angle beneath the arch and let it idle its way down between the garages and the painted front doors and the tubs that would soon be bright with spring flowers. The rain had stopped, but the cobbles were still damp and shone, like some country street, in the lamplight.

"Which number?" he asked.

"It's right at the very end. I'm afraid there's scarcely room to turn. You'll have to back out."

"That's all right."

"It's this one."

The lights were on. They shone from upstairs windows and through the small pane of glass at the top of the blue front door. She peered anxiously upwards as though expecting a window to be flung open and a face to appear, announcing bad news.

But nothing happened. She got out of the car, and John got out too, not because he wanted to be invited in, but because he had been meticulously brought up, and good manners insisted that a girl should not be simply dumped on her doorstep, but that her latchkey should be located, her door politely opened, her safety and well-being assured.

She had found her key. She had opened her door. She was, obviously, anxious to get away and up the stairs.

"Thank you so much for bringing me back. Really kind of you, and you didn't need to bother . . ."

She stopped. From upstairs there came the unmistakable wail of a furious child. The sound rooted them to where they stood. They stared at each other, the girl looking as astonished as John felt. The wails continued, rising in volume and fury. He expected some sort of an explanation, but none came. In the hard light from the staircase, her face was, all at once, very pale. She said in a strained sort of way, "Good night."

It was a dismissal. He thought, damn you. He said, "Good night, Victoria."

"Have a good time in Bahrain."

To hell with Bahrain. "I will."

"And thank you for bringing me home."

The blue front door was closed in his face. The light beyond was turned off. He looked up at the windows, secret behind the drawn curtains. He thought, and to hell with you too.

Getting back into his car he reversed at top speed down the length of the Mews and out into the street, missing the side of the archway by inches. There he sat for a moment or two endeavouring to recover his natural good humor.

A baby. Whose baby? Probably her baby. There was no reason why she shouldn't have a baby. Just because she looked such a child herself, there was no reason why she shouldn't have a husband or a lover. A girl with a baby.

He thought, *I must tell Tania that. It'll make her laugh. You couldn't come to Imogen's party, so I went by myself and got hooked up with a girl who had to go home to her baby.*

As his annoyance abated, so did his hunger, and their going left him feeling flat. He decided to skip dinner and instead go back to his flat and make a sandwich. His car moved forward, and deliberately, his thoughts moved with it, ahead to the following day, to the early start, the drive to Heathrow, the long flight to Bahrain.

CHAPTER 4
Friday

Oliver was on the sofa, holding the child standing up on his knees. As Victoria came up the stairs the first thing she saw was the back of Oliver's head and the round, red, tear-drenched face of his son. He, surprised by her sudden appearance, stopped crying for an instant, and then, realizing that it was no person he knew, at once started up again.

Oliver jigged him hopefully up and down, but it did no good. Victoria dropped her bag and came around to stand in front of them, unbuttoning her coat.

"How long has he been awake?"

"About ten minutes." The child roared furiously, and Oliver had to raise his voice in order to make his voice heard.

"What's wrong with him?"

"I imagine he's hungry." He got to his feet, heaving his burden with him. The little boy wore dungarees and a wrinkled white sweater. His hair was copper-gold, the curls at the nape of his neck tangled and damp. The only information Victoria had managed to elicit from Oliver before she had left for the Fairburns' was that the child was his son, and with that she had had to be content. She had left them together, the baby sound asleep on the sofa and Oliver peacefully downing his whisky and water.

But now . . . She gazed with sinking apprehension. She knew nothing about babies. She had scarcely held a baby in her life. What did they eat? What did they want when they wept so heartbreakingly?

She said, "What's he called?"

"Tom." Oliver jigged him again, tried to turn him around in his arms. "Hey, Tom. Say hello to Victoria."

Tom took another look at Victoria and then let them know, lustily, what he thought of her. She took off her coat and dropped it onto a chair. "How old is he?"

"Two."

"If he's hungry, we should give him something to eat."

"That makes sense."

He was being no use at all. Victoria left him and went into the kitchen to search for suitable food for a baby. She stared into the cupboard at racks of spices, Marmite, flour, mustard, lentils, stock cubes.

What was he doing, back in her flat, back in her life, after three years of silence? What was he doing with the child? Where was its mother?

Jam, sugar, porridge oats. A packet brought, the last time she had been in London, by Victoria's mother, for the purpose of making some special sort of biscuit.

"Will he eat porridge?" she called.

Oliver did not reply, because over the yells of his son he did not hear the question; so Victoria went to the open door and repeated it.

"Yes, I suppose so. I suppose he'll eat anything, really."

Feeling near exasperation, she went back to the kitchen, put on a pan of water, poured in some oats, found a bowl, a spoon, a jug of milk. When it had started to cook, she turned down the heat and went back into the sitting room and saw that already it had been taken over by Oliver, it was no longer hers. It was filled with Oliver, with his possessions, his empty glass, his cigarette stubs, his child. The child's coat lay on the floor, the sofa cushions were crushed and flattened, the air rang with the little boy's misery and frustration.

She could bear it no longer. "Here," she said and took Thomas firmly in her arms. Tears poured down his cheeks. She said to Oliver, "You make sure the porridge doesn't burn," and she bore Tom into the bathroom and set him down on the floor.

Steeling herself to cope with steaming nappies, she unbuttoned his dungarees and found that he wasn't wearing nappies at all, and was, miraculously, dry. There was, obviously, no pot in this childless establishment, but with a certain amount of contriving she persuaded him to use the grown-up lavatory. For some reason this mild acomplishment stopped his tears. She said, "What a good boy," and he looked up at her, still tear-drenched, and disarmed her with a sudden grin. Then he found her sponge and began to chew it, and she was so thankful that he had stopped crying that she let him. She buttoned up his clothes and washed his face and hands. Then she led him back into the kitchen.

"He's been to the loo," she told Oliver.

Oliver had poured himself another whisky, thus finishing Victoria's bottle. He had his glass in one hand and a wooden spoon in the other, with which he stirred the porridge. He said, "I think this sort of looks ready."

It was. Victoria put some into a bowl, poured milk over it, sat at the kitchen table with Tom on her knee, and let him get on with it, which he did. After the first mouthful, she hastily reached for a tea towel and wrapped it around his neck. In a moment the bowl was empty and Thomas apparently ready for more.

Oliver eased himself away from the cooker. "I'm going out for a moment."

Victoria was filled with alarm, and suspicions that if

he went he would never come back and she would be left with the child. She said, "You can't."

"Why not?"

You can't leave me alone with him. He doesn't know who I am."

"He doesn't know who I am either, but he seems quite happy. Eating himself to a standstill." He laid the palms of his hands flat on the table and stooped to kiss her. It was three years since this had happened, but the aftereffects were alarmingly familiar. A melting sensation, a sudden sinking of the stomach. Sitting there with his child heavy on her knee, she thought, oh, no. "I shall be gone about five minutes I want to buy cigarettes and a bottle of wine."

"You'll come back?"

"How suspicious you are. Yes, I'll come back. You're not going to get rid of me as easily as that."

He was, in fact, away for fifteen minutes. By the time he returned, the sitting room was once more neat, cushions plumped up, coats put away, the ashtrays emptied. He found Victoria at the kitchen sink, wearing an apron and washing a lettuce. "Where's Thomas?"

She did not turn round. "I put him into my bed. He isn't crying. I think he'll go to sleep again."

Oliver decided that the back of her head looked implacable. He put down the brown grocery bag containing the bottles and went to turn her to face him.

"Are you angry?" he asked.

"No. Just wary."

"I can explain."

"You'll have to." She turned back to the sink and the lettuce.

He said, "I'm not explaining if you won't listen properly. Leave that and come and sit down."

"I thought you wanted to eat. It's getting terribly late."

"It doesn't matter what time it is. We've all the time in the world. Come on. Come and sit down."

He had brought wine and another bottle of whisky. While Victoria untied her apron and hung it up, he found ice cubes and poured two drinks. She had gone back to the sitting room, and he joined her there and found her settled on a low stool with her back to the fire. She did not smile at him. He handed her the glass and raised his own.

"Reunions?" he suggested as a toast.

"All right." Reunions sounded harmless enough. The glass was cold to her fingers. She took a mouthful and felt better. More able to deal with what he was about to tell her.

Oliver sat on the edge of the sofa and faced her. There were artistic patches in the knees of his jeans, and his suede boots were worn and stained. Victoria found herself wondering on what he chose to spend the fruits of his considerable success. Whisky, perhaps. Or a house in a more salubrious part of London than the Fulham back street where he had lived before. She thought of the big Volvo parked in the Mews outside. She saw the gold watch on his long, narrow wrist.

He said again, "We have to talk."

"You talk."

"I thought you'd be married."

"You said that before. When I opened the door."

"But you're not."

"No."

"Why not?"

"I never met anybody I wanted to marry. Or perhaps I never met anybody who wanted to marry me."

"Did you go on with your painting?"

"No, I threw that up after a year. I wasn't good enough. I had a little talent, but not enough. There's nothing more discouraging than having just a little talent."

"So what do you do now?"

"I have a job. In a dress shop in Beauchamp Place."

"That doesn't sound very demanding."

She shrugged, "It's all right." They were not meant to be talking about Victoria, they were meant to be talking about Oliver. "Oliver . . ."

But he did not want her questions, perhaps because he had not yet made up his mind what the answers would be. He quickly interrupted her. "How was the party?"

She knew that this was a red herring. She looked at him, and he met her gaze with watchful innocence. She thought, what does it matter? Like he says, we have all the time in the world. Sooner or later he's going to have to tell me. She said, "The usual. Lots of people. Lots of drink. Everybody talking and nobody saying anything."

"Who brought you home?"

She was surprised that he was sufficiently interested to want to know this, and then remembered that Oliver had always been interested in people, whether he knew them or not; whether he even liked them. He would sit in buses and listen to other people's conversations. He would talk to strangers in bars, to waiters in restaurants. Everything that happened to him was filed away in the retentive storehouse of his memory, mulled over and digested, only to reappear at some later date in something he was writing, a scrap of dialogue or a situation.

She said, "An American."

He was instantly intrigued. "What sort of an American?"

"Just an American."

"I mean bald-headed, middle-aged, hung about with cameras? Earnest? Sincere? Come along now, you must have noticed."

Of course Victoria had noticed. He had been tall, not as tall as Oliver, but more heavily built, with wide shoulders and a flat stomach. He looked as though he played furious squash in his spare time, or jogged round the park in the early mornings, wearing sneakers and a track suit. She remembered dark eyes, and hair almost black. Crisp, wiry hair, the sort that has to be closely cut or it gets out of hand. His had been expertly barbered, probably by Mr. Trumper or one of the more exclusive London establishments, so that it lay on his well-shaped head like a smooth pelt.

She remembered the strong features, the tan, and the marvelous white American teeth. Why did Americans all seem to have such beautiful teeth?

She said, "No, he wasn't any of those things."

"What was his name?"

"John. John something. I don't think Mrs. Fairburn's very good at introductions."

"You mean he didn't tell you himself? He can't have been a true-blooded American. Americans always tell you who they are and what they do, before you've even decided whether you want to meet them or not. 'Hi!' He put on a perfect New York accent. 'John Hackenbacker, Consolidated Aloominum. Glad to have you know me.'"

Victoria found herself smiling, and this made her feel ashamed, and as though she must stand up for the young man who had brought her home in his sleek Alfa-Romeo. "He wasn't a bit like that. And he's flying to Bahrain tomorrow," she added as though this were a point in the American's favor.

"Ah! An oil man."

She was becoming tired of his teasing. "Oliver, I have no idea."

"You seem to have made remarkably little contact. What the hell did you talk about?" An idea occurred to him, and he grinned. "I know, you talked about me."

"I most certainly didn't talk about you. But I think it's about time you started talking about you. And about Thomas."

"What about Tom?"

"Oh, Oliver, don't fence."

He laughed at her exasperation. "I'm not being kind, am I? And you're simply bursting to know. All right, here it is. I've stolen him."

It was so much worse than she had imagined that Victoria had to take a long, deep breath. When that was safely over, she was calm enough to ask, "Who did you steal him from?"

"Mrs. Archer. Jeannette's mother. My erstwhile mother-in-law. You probably didn't know, but Jeannette was killed in an air crash in Yugoslavia, just a little while after Tom was born. Her parents have looked after him ever since."

"Did you go and see him?"

"No. Never went near him. Never set eyes on him. Today was the first time I ever saw him."

"And what happened today?"

He had finished his drink. He got up and went into the kitchen to pour himself another. She heard the clink of the bottle, the ice going into the glass, the tap being turned on and off. Then he returned and resumed his seat, leaning back on the deep cushions of the sofa, with his long legs stretched out in front of him.

"I've been in Bristol all week. I've got a play coming off at the Fortune Theatre, it's in rehearsal now, but I had to do some work with the producer, rewrite some of the third act. Driving back to London this morning, I was thinking about the play. I wasn't really paying attention to the road, and suddenly I realized I was on the A.30, and there was a signpost to Woodbridge, and that's where the Archers live. And I thought, why not? And I turned the car and went to call. As simple as that. A whim, you might say. The hand of fate stretching out its grubby paw."

"Did you see Mrs. Archer?"

"No. Mrs. Archer was in London, buying sheets at

Harrods or something. But there was a choice au pair
girl called Helga who needed little encouragement to
invite me in for lunch."

"Did she know you were Tom's father?"

"No."

"So what happened?"

"She sat me down at the kitchen table and went upstairs to fetch Tom. And then we had lunch. Good
healthy fare. Everything was good and healthy, and so
clean it looked as though it had been through a sterilizer. The whole house is one enormous sterilizer.
There isn't a dog or a cat or a readable book in the
place. The chairs look as though no one ever sat in
them. The garden's full of horrible flower beds, like a
cemetery, and the paths look as if they've been drawn
with a ruler. I'd forgotten its utter soullessness."

"But it's Tom's home."

"It stifled me. It's going to stifle him. He had a picture book with his name written in the front. 'Thomas
Archer. From Granny.' And somehow that finished
me, because he's not Thomas Archer, he's Thomas
Dodds. So then the girl went to get his beastly peram-
bulator, to take him out for a walk, and I picked him
up and carried him out of the house and put him in
the car and drove him away."

"But didn't Thomas *mind*?"

"He didn't seem to. Seemed quite pleased, in fact.
We stopped off somewhere and spent the afternoon in
a little park. He played on the swings and in the sand-
pit, and a dog came up and talked to him. And then it
began to rain, so I bought him some biscuits and we
got back into the car again and came back to London.
I toook him to my flat."

"I don't know where your flat is."

"Still in Fulham. Same place. You've never been
there I know, but you see, it isn't really a living place,
it's a working place. It's a basement and grotty as hell,
and I have an arrangement with a large West Indian

lady who lives on the first floor, and she's meant to come and clean it up once a week, but it never seems to look any better. Anyway, I took Tom there, and he obligingly fell asleep on my bed, and then I rang the Archers."

He came out quite casually with this. Moral coward-ice was something from which Oliver had never suf-fered, but Victoria felt quite weak at the thought.

"Oh, *Oliver*."

"No reason why I shouldn't. After all, he's my child."

"But she must have been out of her mind with worry."

"I told the au pair girl my name. Mrs. Archer knew he was with me."

"But . . ."

"You know something? You sound the way Jean-nette's mother sounded. As though I had nothing but evil intentions. As though I were going to harm the child, bash his brains out on a brick wall, or some-thing."

"I don't think that at all. Its just that I can't help but be sorry for her."

"Well don't be."

"She'll want him back."

"Yes, of course she wants him back, but I've told her that for the time being I'm keeping him myself."

"Can you do that? Legally, I mean? Won't she get the police, or lawyers, or even high court judges?"

"She's threatened all those things. Litigation, ward of court, in the space of ten minutes she threw every-thing at my head. But you see, she can't do anything. Nobody can do anything. He's my child. I'm his fa-ther. I'm neither a criminal nor otherwise unfit to take care of him."

"But that's just the point. You can't take care of him."

"All that's required of me is to provide a home for

Tom with resources and facilities for taking care of him."

"In a basement in Fulham?"

There was a long silence while Oliver, with slow deliberation, stubbed out his cigarette. "That," he told her at last, "is why I am here."

So, it was out. The cards were on the table. This was why he had come to her.

She said, "At least you're being honest."

Oliver looked indignant. "I'm always honest."

"You want me to look after Tom?"

"We can look after him together. You wouldn't want me to take him back to that moldy flat, would you?"

"I can't look after him."

"Why not?"

"I'm working. I have a job. There isn't any room for a child here."

He said, in a false voice, "And what would the neighbors say?"

"It's nothing to do with the neighbors."

"You can tell them I'm your cousin from Australia. You can say that Tom is my aborigine offspring."

"Oh, Oliver, stop joking. This is nothing to joke about. You've stolen that child of yours. Why he isn't howling his head off with misery and fright is beyond my comprehension. Mrs. Archer is obviously distraught, we're going to have the police on the doorstep at any moment, and all you do is make what you think are funny remarks."

His face closed up. "If you feel like that about it, I'll take the child and go."

"Oh, Oliver, it's not that. It's just that you have to be sensible."

"All right, I'll be sensible. Look, I've got on my most sensible expression." Victoria refused even to smile at him. "Oh, come along. Don't be angry. I wouldn't have come if I'd thought it would make you angry."

"I don't know why you did come."

"Because I thought of you as being exactly the right sort of person who'd help me. I thought of you, and I thought of telephoning first, but then I imagined some stranger—or worse, some stiff-necked husband— answering the call. And then what was I going to say? This is Oliver Dobbs, the well-known author and playwright, speaking. I have a baby I'd like your wife to look after. Wouldn't that have gone down a treat?"

"What would you have done if I hadn't been here?"

"I don't know. I'd have thought of something. But I wouldn't have taken Tom back to the Archers."

"You may have to. You can't take care of him . . ."

Oliver interrupted her, as though she had never started to speak. "Look, I have a plan. Like I said, the Archers haven't got a leg to stand on, but still there's the chance that they'll try to make trouble. I think we should get out of London. Go away for a little. There's this play of mine coming off in Bristol, but as far as that's concerned I've done all I can do. The first night's on Monday, and after that it's at the mercy of the critics and the general public. So let's go away. You and me and Tom. Let's just take off. We'll go to Wales or the north of Scotland, or down to Cornwall and watch the spring coming. We'll. . . ."

Victoria gazed at him in total disbelief. She was shocked, outraged, indignant. Did he imagine—did he really imagine—that she had so little pride? Had he never truly known how much he had hurt her? Three years ago Oliver Dobbs had walked out of her life, shattering everything, and leaving her alone to put the pieces together as best she might. But now he decided that he needed her once more, simply to look after his child. And so here he sat, already making plans, trying to seduce her with words, believing that it was only a matter of time before he wore down her resistance.

". . . no tourists, empty roads. We won't even have to book in at hotels, they'll all be longing for business, desperate to have us . . ." He went on, hatching plans, leading Victoria on to images of blue seas and fields of yellow daffodils; of carefree escape, and winding country lanes. And she listened, marveling at his selfishness. He had helped himself to his son. He wanted, for the time being, to keep his son. He needed someone to take care of his son. And so, Victoria. It was as simple as an elementary mathematical formula.

He stopped at last. His face was alight with enthusiasm, as though he could not envisage any objection to this delightful project. After a little, Victoria said, because she really wanted to know, "Out of interest, what made you think of me?"

"I suppose because you're the sort of person that you are."

"You mean, stupid?"

"No, not stupid."

"Forgiving, then?"

"You could never be unforgiving. You wouldn't know how. Besides, it was a good time we had together. It wasn't a bad time. And you're pleased to see me again. You have to be otherwise you'd never have let me into your house."

"Oliver, some bruises don't necessarily show."

"What's that supposed to mean?"

"For my sins, I loved you. You knew that."

"But you see," he reminded her carefully, "I didn't love anybody. And you knew that."

"Except yourself."

"Perhaps. And what I was trying to do."

"I don't want to be hurt again. I'm not going to be hurt again."

A smile touched his mouth. "You sound very determined."

"I'm not coming with you."

He did not reply, but his eyes, pale and unblinking,

never left her face. Outside, the wind rattled a window pane. A car started up. A girl's voice called some person's name. Perhaps she was going to a party. From far off came the distant hum of London traffic.

He said, "You can't spend the rest of your life avoiding being hurt. If you do that, then you turn your back on any sort of relationship."

"Just say that I don't want to be hurt by you. You're too good at it."

"Is that the only reason that you won't come with us?"

"I think it's enough of a reason, but there are other things as well. Practical considerations. For one thing, I have a job . . ."

"Selling clothes to idiotic females. Ring up and make some excuse. Say your grandmother's died. Say you've suddenly had a baby . . . now that would be nearly true! Send in your resignation. I'm a rich man now. I'll take care of you."

"You've said that before. A long time ago. But you didn't."

"What a prodigious memory you have."

"Some things really can't be forgotten." From the mantelpiece her little clock chimed. It was eleven o'clock. Victoria stood up and put her empty glass beside the clock, and as she did so, she saw his reflection, watching her through the looking glass which hung on the wall behind it.

He said, "Are you afraid? Is that what it is?"

"Yes."

"Of me, or of yourself."

"Both of us." She turned from the mirror. "Let's go and have some supper."

It was nearly midnight by the time they finished the makeshift meal, and Victoria was suddenly so tired that she had not even the energy to collect the plates and the empty glasses and wash them up. Oliver was pouring the last of the wine into his glass and reaching for another cigarette, apparently settled for the night, but Victoria stood up, pushing back her chair, and said "I'm going to bed."

He looked mildly surprised. "That's very unsocial of you."

"I can't help it if it's unsocial. If I don't go to bed I'll fall asleep on my feet."

"What do you want me to do?"

"I don't want you to do anything."

"I mean," he spoke patiently, as though she were being immensely unreasonable, "Do you want me to go back to Fulham? Do you want me to spend the night in my car? Do you want me to wake Thomas up and bear him off into the night, never to darken your door again? You only have to say."

"You can't take Thomas. He's sleeping."

"Then I'll go back to Fulham and leave him here with you."

"You can't do that either. He might wake up in the middle of the night and be frightened."

"In that case I'll stay here." He assumed the expression of a man prepared to be accommodating, at whatever cost to himself. "Where would you like me to sleep? On the sofa? On top of some chest of drawers? On the floor outside your bedroom door, like an old dog, or a faithful slave?"

She refused to rise to his teasing. "There's a divan in the dressing room," she told him. "The room's full of suitcases and my mother's London clothes, but the bed's longer than the sofa. I'll go and make it up . . ."

She left him, with his cigarette and his glass of wine and the chaos of unwashed dishes. In the tiny slip of a dressing room, she found blankets and a pillow. She removed dress boxes and a pile of clothes from the divan and made it up with clean sheets. The room smelled stuffy and rather mothbally (her mother's fur coat?) so she opened the wide, and the curtains stirred in the cold damp air which blew in from the darkness beyond.

From the kitchen now came sounds as if Oliver had decided to stack the supper plates, or possibly wash them. Victoria was surprised, because domesticity had never been his strong suite, but she was touched as well, and tired as she was, knew an impulse to go and help him. But if she went to help him, they would only start talking again. And if they started talking, then Oliver would start, all over again, trying to persuade her to go away with him and Thomas. So she left him to it, and went into her bedroom. Here, only a small lamp burned on the dressing table. On one side of the double bed, Thomas slumbered, one arm outflung, his mouth plugged by his thumb. She had taken off everything except his vest and pants, and folded clothes lay on a chair, his small shoes and socks on the floor beneath it. She stooped to lift him out of the bed. His weight was warm and soft in her arms. She carried him to the bathroom and somehow persuaded him to use the lavatory again. He scarcely woke: his head lolled, his thumb stayed determinedly in his mouth. She put him back into the bed, and he sighed contentedly and slept once more. She prayed that he would sleep until morning.

She straightened up, and listened. It seemed that Oliver had decided that he had had enough of the supper dishes, and he had returned to the living room, where he had started telephoning. Only Oliver would start telephoning at midnight. Victoria undressed, brushed her hair, put on her nightdress and cautiously slipped into the other side of the bed. Tom never stirred. She lay on her back and stared at the ceiling, and then closed her eyes, waiting for sleep. But sleep would not come. Her brain whirled with images of Oliver, with memories, with a sort of throbbing excitement which maddened her because it was the last thing in the world that she wanted to feel. Finally, in desperation, she opened her eyes again, and reached for a book, intending to read herself to calmness and so to unconsciousness.

From the next room, the telephoning stopped, and the television was switched on. But most of the programs had finished by now anyway, and eventually Oliver apparently decided to call it a day. She heard him moving about, switching off lights. She heard him go to the bathroom. She lay down her book. His footsteps crossed the little landing, and stopped outside her door. The handle turned. The door opened. His tall figure appeared, silhouetted against the bright light beyond.

He said, "Not asleep?"

"Not yet," said Victoria.

They spoke softly, so as not to disturb the sleeping child. Oliver, leaving the door open, crossed the floor and came to sit on the edge of the bed.

"Just a guy. Nothing important."

"I made up the bed for you."

"I know. I saw."

But he made no move to go. "What will you do tomorrow?" she asked him. "With Thomas?"

He smiled. He said "I'll decide tomorrow." He touched her book. "What are you reading?"

It was a paperback. Victoria held it up for him to see the front cover. She said, "It's one of those books that you read over and over again. About once a year, I take it out, and it's like being with an old friend."

Oliver read the title aloud. *"The Eagle Years."*

"Have you read it?"

"Perhaps."

"It's by this man called Roddy Dunbeath and it's all about being a little boy in Scotland between the wars. I mean, it's a sort of autobiography. And he and his brothers were brought up in this beautiful house called Benchoile."

Oliver had laid his hand over her wrist. His palm was warm, his fingers strong, but the caress very gentle.

"It was in Sutherland, somewhere. With mountains all around and their own private loch. And he had a falcon that used to come and take food out of his mouth . . ."

His hand began to move up her bare arm, pressing the flesh beneath his touch, as though he were massaging life back into some limb which had been paralyzed for years.

". . . and a pet duck and a dog called Bertie that liked eating apples."

"I like eating apples," said Oliver. He lifted a long strand of hair away from her neck and laid it on the pillow. She could feel the solid, throbbing beat of her own heart. Her skin, where he had touched her, felt as though it were standing on tip toe. She went on talking, desperately, trying to control these alarming physical manifestations with the sound of her own voice.

". . . and there was a place with a waterfall, where they used to go for picnics. And there was a stream running across the beach, and the hills were filled with deer. He says that the waterfall was the heart of Benchoile . . ."

Oliver leaned down and kissed her mouth and the flow of words was mercifully stopped. She knew that he hadn't been listening anyway. Now, he drew aside the blankets which covered her, and slid his arms beneath her back, and his lips moved away from her mouth and across her cheek and into the warm hollow of her neck.

"Oliver," She said his name, but her voice made no sound. His going had left her frozen, but now the weight and the warmth of his body warmed her own, melting resolution, and stirring to life long-forgotten instincts. She thought, *oh, no,* and laid her hands against his shoulders and tried to push him away, but he was a thousand times stronger than Victoria and the puny resistence was pathetic, pointless as trying to topple some immense tree.

"Oliver, No."

She might not have spoken aloud. He simply continued his gentle love-making, and after a little, her hands, as though of their own volition, slid away from his shoulders, under his jacket, around his back. He smelled clean, of clothes dried in the open air. She felt the thin cotton of his shirt, the rib cage, the hard muscles beneath his skin. She heard him say, "You've stopped pretending."

The last shred of common sense made her say, "But Oliver, Thomas . . ."

She sensed his amusement, his silent laughter. He drew away from her and stood up, towering over her. "That can easily be arranged," he told her, and he stooped and lifted her up into his arms as easily and lightly as he had carried his son. She felt weightless, dizzy, as the walls of her bedroom spun and slid away and he bore her through the open door, across the bright landing, and into the airy darkness of the little dressing room. It still smelled of camphor, and the bed on which he placed her was hard and narrow, but the curtains stirred in the soft wind, and the starched linen of the pillow lay cool beneath her neck.

She said, looking up into the shadowed blur that was his face, "I never meant this to happen,"

"I did," said Oliver, and she knew that she should be angry, but by then it was too late. Because by then she wanted it to happen anyway.

Much later—she knew it was much later, because she had heard the clock in the sitting room strike two with its silvery chimes—Oliver hoisted himself up onto one elbow and leaned over Victoria in order to grope for his jacket and take his cigarettes and lighter from the pocket. The flame illuminated the tiny room for a second, and there came the gentle darkness again and the glow of the cigarette tip.

She lay in the curve of his arm, her head pillowed on his naked shoulder.

He said, "Do you want to make plans?"

"What sort of plans?"

"Plans for what we're going to do. You and me and Thomas."

"Am I coming with you?"

"Yes."

"Have I said I'm coming with you?"

He laughed. He kissed her. "Yes." he said.

"I don't want to be hurt again."

"You mustn't be so afraid. There's nothing to be afraid of. Just the prospect of a holiday, an escape. Lots of laughter. Lots of love."

Victoria did not reply. There was nothing to say, and her thoughts were so confused that there was nothing much to think, either. She only knew that for the first time since he had left her, she felt safe again, and at peace. And she only knew that tomorrow, or perhaps the next day, she was going away with Oliver. Once more, she was committed. For better or for worse, but maybe it would work this time. Maybe he had changed. Things would be different. And perhaps, if he felt so strongly about Thomas, he would feel strongly about other things. Permanent things. Like loving one person and staying with her forever. But whatever happened, the die had been cast. Victoria had passed the point of no return.

She sighed deeply, but the sigh was prompted by confusion rather than unhappiness. "Where shall we go?" she asked Oliver.

"Anywhere you like. Is there an ashtray in this benighted cupboard of a room?"

Victoria reached out and groped for the one she knew lay on the bedside table, and handed it to him.

He went on, "What was the name of that place you

were babbling about, when you were so patently anxious not to be made love to? The place in the book, *The Eagle Years?*"

"Benchoile."

"Would you like to go there?"

"We can't."

"Why not?"

"It's not a hotel. We don't know the people who live there."

"I do, my darling innocent."

"What do you mean?"

"I know Roddy Dunbeath. I met him about two years ago. Sat next to him at one of those dismal television award dinners. He was there on account of his last book, and I was there because I was given some piddling little statue for a television script I wrote about Seville. Anyway, there we were, surrounded by moronic starlets and shark-like agents, and thankful for each other's company. By the end of the evening we were friends for life, and he gave me a standing invitation to visit him at Benchoile whenever the spirit moved me. So far I haven't taken it up, but if you want to go there, there's no reason on earth why we shouldn't."

"Do you really mean that?"

"Of course I do."

"Are you certain it wasn't just one of those things people say at the end of a good evening and then forget about, or even regret for the rest of their lives?"

"Not at all. He meant it. Even gave me his card in a rather old-fashioned way. I can find out the telephone number and ring him up."

"Will he remember you?"

"Of course he'll remember me. And I shall tell him that I and my wife and my child want to come and spend a few days with him."

"It sounds like an awful lot of people. And I'm *not* your wife."

"Then I shall say my mistress and my child. He'll jump at that. He's rather Rabelasian. You'll love him. He's very fat, and extremely, politely drunk. At least, he was by the end of that dinner. But Roddy Dunbeath, drunk, is ten times more charming than most men are stone cold sober."

"It'll take us a long time to drive to Sutherland."

"We'll take it in stages. Anyway, we have a long time."

He stubbed out his cigarette, and leaned over Victoria once more, in order to put the ashtray on the floor. She found that she was smiling into the darkness. She said, "You know, I think I'd rather go to Benchoile than anywhere else in the world."

"It's better than that. You're going to Benchoile with me."

"And Thomas."

"You're going to Benchoile with me and Thomas."

"I can't think of anything more perfect."

Oliver gently placed his hand on her stomach; slowly, he slid it up her body, over her rib cage, to cup one small, naked breast. "I can," he told her.

CHAPTER 5

Sunday

In the middle of February, the cold weather arrived. Christmas had been sunny and the New Year mild and still, and the weeks of winter crept past, with some rain and a little frost and nothing much else. "We're going to be lucky," said people who knew no better, but the shepherds and the hill-farmers were wiser. They eyed the skies and smelled the wind and knew that the worst was still to come. The winter was simply waiting. Biding its time.

The real frosts started at the beginning of the month. Then came the sleet, swiftly turning to snow, and then the storms. "Straight from the Urals," said Roddy Dunbeath, as the bitter wind whined in over the sea. The sea turned grey and angry, sullen as the color of wet slate, and creaming breakers flooded in over the Creagan sands, depositing a long tidemark of undigested rubbish. Old fish boxes, ragged nets, knotted twine, plastic detergent bottles, rubber tires, even a disfigured shoe or two.

Inland, the hills were cloaked in white, their summits lost in the dark, racing sky. Snow blew from the open fields and piled in steep drifts, choking the narrow roads. Sheep, heavy in their winter wool, could survive, but the cattle searched for shelter in the angles of the drystone dikes, and the farmers tractored fodder to them twice a day.

Accustomed to, and expecting, cruel winters, the local people accepted all this hardship with stoic calm.

The smaller hill crofts and isolated cottages were cut off entirely, but walls were thick and peat stacks high, and there was always plenty oatmeal, and feedstuff for the stock. Life continued. The scarlet post-van made its daily round of the glens, and sturdy housewives, wearing rubber boots and three cardigans, emerged from doorways to feed hens and hang out lines of washing in the freezing wind.

Now, it was Sunday.

> The Lord's my Shepherd, I'll not want
> He makes me down to lie
> In pastures green . . .

The pipes in the church were faintly warm, but the draughts excruciating. The congregation, thinned to a mere handful by the weather, bravely raised their voices in the last hymn of the morning service, but their efforts were almost drowned by the fury of the wind outside.

Jock Dunbeath, standing alone in the Benchoile pew, held his hymnbook in mittened hands but did not look at it, partly because he had sung this hymn all his life and knew the words by heart and partly because, by some oversight, he had left his reading spectacles at home.

Ellen had fussed over him. "You must indeed be mad thinking you'll get to the kirk today. The roads are blocked. Would you not stop off at Davey's and get him to drive you?"

"Davey has enough to do."

"Then why not sit by the fire and listen to the nice man on the wireless? Would that not do as well for once?"

But he was stubborn, immovable, and she finally sighed and tossed her eyes to heaven and gave in. "But don't be blaming me if you die in a drift on your way."

She sounded quite excited at the thought of such a happening. Disaster was the spice of life to Ellen, and she was always the first to say "I told you so." Irritated by her, in a hurry to get away, he forgot his spectacles, and was then too pigheaded to go back for them. However, his determination was vindicated, and, in the old Landrover, grinding in bottom gear down the four miles of the glen, he had managed to make it safely and had come to church. Chilled as he was, and blind as a bat without his glasses, he was glad that he had made the effort.

All his life, unless prevented by illness, war, or some other act of God, he had come to church on Sunday mornings. As a child because he had had to; as a soldier because he needed to; as a grown man because he was the Laird of Benchoile and it was important to be involved, to uphold the established traditions, to set a good example. And now, in his age, he came for comfort and reassurance. The old church, the words of the service, the tunes of the hymns, were some of the very few things in his life that hadn't changed. Perhaps, at the end of the day, the only thing.

> Goodness and mercy all my days,
> Shall surely follow me,
> And in God's house for ever more
> My dwelling place shall be.

He closed his hymnbook, bowed his head for the blessing, collected his driving gloves and his old tweed cap from the seat beside him, buttoned up his overcoat, wound himself up in his scarf, started up the aisle.

"Morning, sir." It was a friendly sort of church. People came out with conversation in their ordinary voices—none of those pious whispers as though there were a body dying in the next room. "Terrible weather. Good morning, Colonel Dunbeath, and how are the roads up with you . . . ? Well, Jock, and you're a fine one, making the trip to the kirk on a day like this."

That was the minister himself, coming up at Jock from behind. Jock turned. The minister, the Reverend Christie, was a well-set-up man with a pair of shoulders like a rugby player, but still Jock topped him by half a head.

He said, "I thought you'd be a bit thin on the ground this morning. Glad I made the effort."

"I imagined you all cut off up at Benchoile."

"The telephone's dead. There must be a line down somewhere. But I managed the road in the Landrover."

"It's a bitter day. Why don't you come into the Manse for a glass of sherry before you start back?"

His eyes were kind. He was a good man, with a homely and hospitable wife. For a moment Jock let himself imagine the living room at the Manse. The chair, which would be drawn up for him by an enormous fire, the air fragrant with the smell of roasting Sunday mutton. The Christies had always done themselves very well. He thought of the dark, sweet, warming sherry, the comfortable presence of Mrs. Christie, and for a small instant was tempted.

But, "No," he said. "I think I'd better get back before the weather worsens. Ellen will be expecting me. And I would not want the constable to find me frozen in a snowdrift with the smell of alcohol on my breath."

"Ah, well, that's understandable," The minister's kindly countenance and robust manner masked his concern. He had been shocked this morning to see Jock sitting solitary in his pew. Most of the congregation, for some reason, gathered themselves at the back of his church, and the laird, isolated like some outcast, had stuck out like a sore thumb.

He looked old. It was the first time that Mr. Christie had seen him looking really old. Too thin, too tall, his tweed hanging loose on the lanky frame, the fingers of his hands swollen and red with the cold. The collar of his shirt was loose on his neck, and there had been a hesitancy in his actions, fumbling for his hymnbook, for the pound note that was his weekly contribution to the offertory plate.

Jock Dunbeath of Benchoile. How old was he? Sixty-eight, sixty-nine? Not old for nowadays. Not old for hereabouts, where the menfolk seemed to go on well into their eighties, sprightly and active, digging their gardens and keeping a few hens, and making small tottery excursions to the village inn for their evening dram. But last September Jock had suffered a slight heart-attack, and since then, thought Mr. Christie, he seemed to have gone visibly downhill. And yet, what could one do to help? If he had been one of the country folk, Mr. Christie would have gone visiting, taken a batch of his wife's scones, perhaps offered to cut a stack of kindling; but Jock was not country folk. He was Lieutenant Colonel John Rathbone Dunbeath, late the Cameron Highlanders, the Laird of Benchoile and a Justice of the Peace. He was proud, but he was not poor. He was old and lonely, but he was not poor. On the contrary, he was a well-respected landowner with a large house and a farm in hand, twelve thousand or so acres of hill, a thousand or more sheep, some arable land, some stalking, some fishing. In all respects, an enviable property. If the big house was rambling and shabby, and the laird's shirt had a frayed collar, it was not because he was poor. It was because his wife was dead, he was childless, and old Ellen Tarbat, housekeeper to Jock and his brother Roddy, was getting beyond it.

And somewhere, sometime, before the eyes of them all, the old man seemed to have given up.

Mr. Christie searched for some remark that would keep their conversation going. "And how is the family" was a useful starter on most occasions, but not this one, because Jock didn't have a family. Only Roddy. Oh well, thought the minister, any port in a storm.

"And how is your brother keeping."

Jock responded with a gleam of humor. "You make him sound like a box of herring. I think he's all right. We don't see that much of each other. Keep to ourselves, you know, Roddy in his house and me in mine." He cleared his throat. "Sunday lunch. We have Sunday lunch together. It's companionable."

Mr. Christie wondered what they talked about. He had never known two brothers so different, one so reserved and the other so outgoing. Roddy was a writer, an artist, a raconteur. The books that he had written, some almost twenty years or so ago, were all still in print, and the paperback editions could always be found on station bookstalls and in the racks of the most unlikely country shops. *A classic* said the blurb on the back covers, under the photograph of Roddy that had been taken thirty years ago. *A breath of the outdoors. Roddy Dunbeath knows his Scotland and presents it, with native perception, within the pages of this book.*

Roddy did not come to church unless it was Christmas or Easter or somebody's funeral, but whether this was due to his inner convictions or his inherent idleness, the minister did not know. Roddy did not even appear very often in the village. Jess Guthrie, the shepherd's wife, did his shopping for him. "And how is Mr. Roddy, Jess?" the grocer would inquire, fitting the two bottles of Dewars down the side of the carton of groceries, and Jess would avert her eyes from the bottles and reply, "Oh, he's no so bad," which could have meant anything.

"Is he working on anything just now?"

"He mentioned something about an article for the *Scottish Field*. I . . . I never really know." Jock ran a diffident hand down the back of his head, smoothing down the thinning grey hair. "He never talks much about his work."

A lesser man might have been discouraged, but Mr. Christie pressed on, and asked after the third Dunbeath brother.

"And what news of Charlie?"

"I had a letter at Christmas. He and Susan were skiing. At Aspen. That's in Colorado, you know," he added in his mannerly way, as though Mr. Christie mightn't.

"Was John with them?"

There was a small pause. Jock put back his head. His eyes, pale and watering a little in the cold, fixed on some distant, unfocused spot beyond the minister's head.

"John doesn't work in New York any longer. Got sent to the London branch of his bank. Works there now. Been working there for six months or more."

"But that's splendid."

The church was nearly empty now. They began to tread, side by side, up the aisle towards the main door.

"Yes. Good thing for John. Step up the ladder. Clever boy. Suppose he'll be president before we know where we are. I mean president of the bank, not president of the United States of America . . ."

But Mr. Christie was not to be diverted by this mild joke. "I didn't mean that, Jock. I meant that if he's living in London, it shouldn't be too hard for him to get up to Sutherland and spend a few days with you and Roddy."

Jock stopped dead and turned. His eyes narrowed. He was suddenly alert, fierce as an old eagle.

Mr. Christie was a little taken aback by that piercing glance. "Just an idea. It seems to me that you need a bit of young company." And someone to keep an eye on you, as well, he thought, but he did not say this aloud. "It must be ten years since John was last here."

"Yes. Ten years." They moved on, slow-paced. "He was eighteen." The old man appeared to be debating with himself. The minister waited tactfully, and was rewarded. "Wrote to him the other day. Suggested he come up in the summer. He was never interested in the grouse, but I could give him a bit of fishing."

"I'm sure he needs no such bait to lure him north."

"Haven't had an answer yet."

"Give him time. He'll be a busy man."

"Yes. The only thing is, these days I'm not quite sure how much time I have to give." Jock smiled, that rare wry smile that warmed the chill from his features and never failed to disarm. "But then, it comes to all of us. You of all men know that."

They let themselves out of the church, and the wind caught the minister's robes and sent the black skirts ballooning. From the porch, he watched Jock Dunbeath clamber painfully up into the old Landrover and set off on his uncertain journey home. Despite himself he sighed, heavy-hearted. He had tried. But, at the end of the day, what could anybody do?

No more snow had fallen and Jock was glad of this. He trundled through the quiet, shuttered village and over the bridge and turned inland where the road sign pointed to Benchoile and Loch Muie. The road was narrow and single-tracked, with passing places marked by black and white painted posts, but there was no other traffic of any sort. The Sabbath, even in weather like this, cast its gloom over the countryside. Beset by icy draughts, hunched over the wheel, with his scarf up to his ears and his tweed cap pulled down over his beak of a nose, Jock Dunbeath let the Landrover take its own way home, like a reliable horse, up the tracks in the snow that they had made themselves that morning.

He thought about what the minister had said. He was right, of course. A good man. Concerned and trying not to show it. But he was right.

You need a bit of young company.

He remembered Benchoile in the old days when he, and his friends, and his brothers' friends, had all filled the house. He remembered the hall overflowing with fishing boots and creels, tea on the lawn beneath the silver birches, and in August the sunlit purple hills echoing to the crack of guns. He remembered house parties for the Northern Meetings Hunt Ball in Inverness, and girls coming downstairs in long, pretty dresses, and the old station wagon driving off to collect guests off the train at Creagan Halt.

But those days, like everything else, were gone. For the brothers, youth had gone. Roddy had never married; Charlie had found himself a wife, and a sweet one too, but she was an American girl, and he had gone back with her to the States, and made a life for himself as a cattleman, ranching his father-in-law's spread in Southwest Colorado. And although Jock had married, he and Lucy had never had the children they so ardently wanted. They had been so happy together that even this cruel trick of fate could not mar their content. But when she had died, five years ago, he had realized that he had never before known the true meaning of loneliness.

You need a bit of young company.

Funny, the minister bringing John's name up like that, just days after Jock had written him the letter. Almost as though he had known about it. As a child, John had visited Benchoile regularly, in the company of his parents, and then, as he grew older, alone with his father. He had been a quiet, serious little boy, intelligent beyond his years, and with a searching curiosity that manifested itself in a long stream of endless questions. But even in those days, Roddy had been his favorite uncle, and the two of them would go off for hours on end, to search for shells, or watch the birds, or stand, on still summer evenings, casting their trout rods over the deep brown pools of the river. In all respects, a likeable and satisfactory boy, but still, Jock had never been able to get close to him. The main reason for this was that John did not share with Jock his abiding passion for shooting. John would blissfully lure and catch and slay a fish, and very soon became accomplished at the sport, but he refused to go up the hill with a gun, and if he stalked a deer, would carry nothing more deadly than his camera.

And so the letter had not been an easy one to write. For John had not been to Benchoile for ten years, and this gap of time had left a yawning void that Jock had found almost impossible to bridge with words. Not, he assured himself quickly, that he didn't like the boy. He remembered John Dunbeath at eighteen as a composed, reserved young man with disturbingly mature attitudes and opinions. Jock respected these, but he found his coolness and his polite self-confidence a little disconcerting. And since then they had somehow lost touch. So much had happened. Lucy had died and the empty years had slipped away. Charlie had written, of course, giving news. John had gone to Cambridge, played squash and rackets for the University, and left with an honors degree in economics. He had then returned to New York and there joined the Warburg Investment Corporation, a position that he achieved entirely on his own merits and without any assistance from his influential American connections. For some time he had been at the Harvard Business School, and after some time, inevitably, he had married. Charlie was too loyal a father to spell out the details of this misalliance to Jock, but gradually, reading between the lines of his brother's letters, Jock realized that all was not well with the young couple. So he was distressed, but not surprised, when the news came through that the marriage had broken up, divorce proceedings were being taken, and legal settlements made. The only good thing about it was that there were no children.

The divorce, painfully, was finally accomplished, and John's career, apparently untouched by the traumas of his personal life, continued to go from strength to strength. The appointment in London was the latest in a succession of steady promotions. Banking was a world about which Jock Dunbeath knew nothing, and this was another reason why he felt so totally out of touch with his American nephew.

> *Dear John,*
>
> *You father tells me that you are now back in this country and working in London.*

It wouldn't have been so hard if he had felt that he had anything in common with the young man. Some shared interest that would have provided him with a starting point.

> *If you are able to get a little time off, perhaps you would think about making the journey north and spending a few days at Benchoile.*

He had never been much of a letter writer and it had taken him nearly half a day to finally compose this one, and even then the finished result did not satisfy him. But he signed it, and wrote the address on the envelope and stuck down the flap. It would have been so much easier, he thought wistfully, if only John had shown some interest in the grouse.

These reflections had brought him halfway home. The narrow, rutted, snow-filled road took a turn and the length of Loch Muie slid into view, grey as iron beneath the lowering sky. There was a light on in Davey Guthrie's farmhouse, and away at the end of the loch stood Benchoile itself, sheltered by the stand of pines which stood silhouetted, black as ink, against the snow-covered slopes of the hill.

Built of grey stone, long and low, turreted and gabled, it faced south, across a wide sloping lawn, to the loch. Too big, draughty and unheatable, shabby and constantly in need of repair, it was, nevertheless, his home, and the only place, in all his life, that he had ever really wanted to be.

Ten minutes later, he was there. Up the slope and through the gates, over the rattle of the cattle grid, and down the short tunnel of wild rhododendrons. In front of the house the drive opened up into a wide gravel sweep. At the far end of this was an ornate stone arch which attached the house, by one corner, to the old stable block where Jock's brother Roddy lived. Beyond the arch was a spacious cobbled yard, and at the far end of this were the garages, which were originally built to house carriages and shooting brakes but now contained Jock's old Daimler and the aged green MG into which Roddy squeezed his bulk when the spirit moved him to make some excursion into the outside world.

Alongside these two ill-assorted vehicles, in a thick gloom occasioned by the dreariness of the day, Jock Dunbeath finally homed the Landrover, pulled on the brake, and killed the engine. He took the folded wad of Sunday newspapers off the seat beside him, got out of the car, slammed the door shut, and went out into the yard. Snow lay thick on the cobbles. The light was on in Roddy's sitting room. Cautiously, anxious not to slip or fall, he made his way across the yard to Roddy's front door, and let himself in.

Although it was often referred to as a flat, Roddy's house was, in fact, a two-story dwelling, converted out

of the old stables at the end of the war, when Roddy
had come back to Benchoile to live. Roddy, fired by
enthusiasm, had architected the conversion himself.
The bedrooms and bathrooms were downstairs, the
kitchen and the living room upstairs, and access to
these rooms was by an open teak stair, like a ship's
ladder.

Jock stood at the foot of these and called, "Roddy!"
Roddy's footsteps creaked across the floorboards
over Jock's head. In a moment his brother's bulk appeared, and Roddy peered down at him over the rail
of the stairhead.

"Oh, it's you," said Roddy, as though it might be
anybody else.

"Brought the papers."

"Come on up. What a bloody awful day."

Jock mounted the stairs, and came out at the top in
the living room where Roddy spent his days. It was a
marvelous room, light and large, the ceiling gabled to
the shape of the roof, and one wall taken up by an
enormous picture window. This had been designed to
frame a view over the loch to the mountains, which, in
fine weather, took the breath away. But this morning
what could be seen was enough to chill the soul. Snow
and grey water, running before the wind and capped
in white; the hills on the far shore were lost in murk.

It was a man's room, and yet a room of taste and
even beauty; lined with books and cluttered with a
number of objects which, though worth little, were vis-
ually pleasing. A carved overmantel; a blue and white
jar filled with pampas grasses; a dangling mobile of
paper fishes, probably Japanese. The floorboards had
been sanded and polished and sparsely scattered with
rugs. Elderly armchairs and a sofa sagged invitingly.
In the cavern of a fireplace (which had had to be specially constructed at the time of the conversion, and
had proved to be the most costly item of all) a couple
of birch logs sizzled on a bed of peat. The room had

an extraordinary and quite unique smell about it. Compounded of cigar smoke, and peat smoke too, and the sharp aroma of linseed oil.

Roddy's old Labrador, Barney, lay supine on the heathrug. At Jock's appearance, he raised his grizzled nose, and then yawned and went back to sleep again.

Roddy said, "Have you been to the kirk?"

"Yes." Jock began to unbutton his overcoat with frozen fingers.

"Did you know the telephone's dead? There must be a line down somewhere." He gave his brother a long, measuring look. "You appear to be blue with cold. Have a drink." He moved ponderously towards the table where he kept his bottles and glasses. He had already, Jock noticed, provided himself with a large, dark whisky. Jock did not ever drink in the middle of the day. It was one of his rules. But somehow today, ever since the minister had mentioned that glass of sherry, he had been thinking about it.

"Have you got some sherry?"

"Only the pale kind. Dry as a bone."

"That'll do very nicely."

He took off his coat and went to stand in front of the fire. Roddy's mantelpiece was always littered with undusted bits and pieces. Curling photographs, old pipes, a mug of pheasant quills, and out-of-date invitations, probably unanswered. There was today, however, a sparkling new card propped against the clock, impressively copperplated, gold-edged and marvelously pretentious.

"What's this? Looks like a royal command."

"Nothing so splendid. A dinner at the Dorchester. Television awards. Best documentary of the year. God knows why I've been invited. I thought I'd been crossed off all the lists. Actually, apart from the tedium of the after-dinner speeches, I used to quite enjoy those occasions. Met a lot of new young writers, new faces. Interesting to talk to."

"Are you going to this one?"

"I'm getting too elderly to travel the length of the country for a free hangover." He had laid down his whisky, located the sherry, found a suitable glass, poured his brother's drink. Now he retrieved a smoldering, half-smoked cigar from an ashtray, picked up the two glasses and came back to the fireside. "If it were to take place somewhere civilized, like Inverness, I might deign to add tone to what will otherwise be a vulgar brawl. As it is . . ." He raised his glass. "Slainthe, old boy."

Jock grinned. "Slainthe."

Roddy was nine years Jock's junior. When they were young, Roddy had been the handsome one of the three brothers, the dallying charmer who had broken more hearts than could be decently counted, and who never lost his own. Women adored him. Men were never quite so sure. He was too good-looking, too clever, too talented at all the sorts of things that it was not considered manly to be talented at. He drew and he wrote and he played the piano. He could even sing.

On shoots he always seemed to get the prettiest girl of the party into his butt, and quite often forgot that the object of the exercise was to slay grouse. No sound, no blast would come from his butt, while the grouse sailed serenely over him in coveys, and at the end of the drive he would be found deep in conversation with his companion, his gun unfired, and his dog wheeking and frustrated at his feet.

Naturally brilliant, he had skimmed through his schooldays without apparently doing a stroke of work, and had gone on to Oxford in a blaze of glory. Trends were started by Roddy Dunbeath and fashions set. Where others sported tweed, he favored corduroy, and soon everybody was wearing corduroy. He was president of the OUDS and a renowned debater. Nobody was safe from his wit, which was usually gentle, but could be barbed.

When the war broke out, Jock was already a regular soldier with the Camerons. Roddy, impelled by a deep patriotism which he had always kept to himself, joined up the day that war was declared. He signed on, to everybody's surprise, with the Royal Marines, on account of, he said, they had such a pretty uniform; but in no time at all, he was training to be a Commando, struggling up precipitous cliffs on the end of a rope and hurling himself from training planes with tightly closed eyes and his hand clenched around the rip cord of his parachute.

When it was all over and the country was at peace again, it seemed to Jock Dunbeath that everyone who wasn't married, rushed to rectify the situation. There was a veritable epidemic of matrimony, and Jock himself had fallen prey to it. But not Roddy. Roddy picked up his life where he had left it in 1939 and went on from there. He made himself a home at Benchoile and started to write. *The Eagle Years* came out first, and then *The Wind In The Pines*, and then *Red Fox*. Fame embraced him. He went on lecture tours, he made after-dinner speeches, he appeared on television.

By now he was putting on weight. While Jock stayed thin and spare, Roddy became stout. Gradually his girth spread, his chin doubled, his handsome features were lost in heavy jowls. And yet, he was as attractive as ever, and when the gossip columns in the daily papers ran out of tidbits about the nobility, they would print blurred photographs of Roddy Dunbeath (*The Eagle Years*) dining with Mrs. So-and-So, who was, as everybody knew, a champion of wild life.

But youth had gone, lost somewhere over the years, and at last even his mild fame began to slip away. No longer feted in London, he returned, as he had always returned, to Benchoile. He occupied himself in writing short articles, the scripts for television nature films, even small items for the local newspapers. Nothing changed him. He was still the same Roddy, charming and witty, the engaging raconteur. Still willing to squeeze his bulk into his velvet jacket and drive himself for miles down dark country roads to make up the numbers at some remote dinner party. And—even more astonishing—somehow getting himself home again in the small hours of the morning, half-asleep and awash with whisky.

For he was drinking too much. Not uncontrollably nor offensively, but still he seldom seemed to have a glass out of his hand. He began to slow down. He, who had always been physically indolent, was now becoming chronically idle. He could scarcely make the effort to get himself into Creagan. His life had become encapsulated at Benchoile.

"What are the roads like?" he asked now.

"Passable. You wouldn't have got far in the MG."

"No intention of going anywhere." He took the cigar from his mouth and aimed it at the fireplace. It made a tiny flame. He stooped to lift more logs from the great basket that stood by the hearth, and toss them into the grey ashes of the peat. Dust rose in a cloud. The fresh logs flickered and caught fire. There was a small explosion, and one or two sparks flew out onto the aged hearthrug. The smell of burning wool filled Jock's nostrils, and Roddy trod them out with the sole of his brogue.

"You should have a fireguard," said Jock.

"Can't stand the look of the things. Besides, they keep all the heat in." He gazed thoughtfully down at his fireplace. "Thought I might get one of those chain curtains. Saw one advertised the other day, but now I can't remember where I saw it." He had finished his drink. He began to drift back towards the bottles on the table. Jock said, "You've hardly time for another. It's past one o'clock already."

Roddy looked at his watch. "Well, bless my soul, so it is. It's a wonder Ellen hasn't yet given us her weekly screech. I suppose you couldn't persuade her to use the old gong. She could bring it out into the stable yard and ring it there. It would be so much more in keeping if I could be summoned to Sunday lunch in the big house by the dignified rumble of a gong. Gracious living and all that. We mustn't let ourselves go, Jock. We must keep up appearances even if there is no person to appreciate our efforts. Think of those old empire builders, dining in the jungle in their starched shirts and black ties. There's backbone for you."

The glass of sherry had freed Jock's inhibitions a little. "This morning the minister told me that we need some young company at Benchoile," he told Roddy.

"Well, what a pretty thought." Roddy hesitated over the whisky bottle, thought better of it, and poured himself a small sherry instead. "Handsome lads and pretty lasses. What happened to all those young relations of Lucy's? The house used to be running with her nephews and nieces. They were all over the place. Like mice."

"They've grown up. Married. That's what happened to them."

"Let's stage a grand reunion and get them all back again. We'll put a notice in the personal column of the *Times*. 'The Dunbeaths of Benchoile require young company. All applications will be given consideration.' We might get some rather amusing replies."

Jock thought of the letter that he had written to John. He had not told Roddy about that letter. Cautiously, he had made up his mind that when a reply came from John, and not before, he would take Roddy into his confidence.

But now, he found that resolution wavering. He and

Roddy saw so little of each other, and it was seldom that they found themselves on such easy and companionable terms as they were at this moment. If he brought the business of John up now, then they could discuss it over Sunday lunch. After all, sometime, it all had to be thrashed out. He finished his sherry. He squared his shoulders. He said, "Roddy . . ."

But was interrupted by a banging on the door downstairs, and then a blast of icy air as it was opened. A voice, shrill and cracked, rose from the foot of the stairs.

"It's past one o'clock. Did you know that?"

Roddy looked resigned. "Yes, Ellen, we did."

"Have you got the colonel with you?"

"Yes, he's here."

"I saw the Landrover in the garage, but he's not been near the big house. You'd better both come over now, or the bird'll be ruined." Ellen had never been one for much formality.

Jock laid down his empty glass and went to collect his coat. "We're coming now, Ellen," he told her. "We're coming right away."

CHAPTER 6
Monday

The fact that the telephone lines were down and the phone not working was of small concern to Roddy Dunbeath. Where others tried six or seven times in a morning to make outside calls, jigged the receiver in empty exasperation, and finally trod out into the snow to the nearest functioning call box, Roddy remained unperturbed. There was no person with whom he wished to get in touch, and he actively enjoyed the sensation of being undisturbed and unreachable.

And so, when the phone on his desk suddenly began to ring at half past eleven on Monday morning, he was at first startled out of his skin and then irritated.

During the night the wind had died, having first blown all the clouds out of the sky, and the morning had dawned, late and clear and still. The sky was a pale, arctic blue. The sun, rising over the foot of the loch, turned the snowclad countryside first pink, and then a dazzling white. The lawn in front of the house was patterned with the random tracks of rabbits and hares. A deer had been there, too, feeding off the young shrubs that Jock had planted at the back end of the year and tree shadows lay like long, smokey blue bruises. As the sun climbed over the rim of the hills, the sky deepened in blue, and this was reflected in the waters of the loch. Frost glittered, and the icy air was so still that when Roddy opened his window to throw out a handful of crusts for his birds, he could hear the baa-ing of the sheep which grazed on the slopes at the far side of the water.

It was not a day for much activity. But, with a certain resolution, and a deadline hanging over his head, Roddy had managed to finish the first draft of his article for the *Scottish Field*. With this behind him, he succumbed once more to idleness and was sitting at his window with a cigar and his binoculars at the ready. He had seen greylags feeding on the worn stubble of the arable fields beyond the pines. Sometimes, in hard weather like this, they would settle in the thousands.

The telephone rang. He said, aloud, "Oh, bloody hell," and at the sound of his voice Barney raised his head from the hearthrug. Thump thump went his tail. "It's all right, old boy, it's not your fault." He laid down his binoculars, got up, and went, reluctantly to answer it.

"Roddy Dunbeath."

There came strange peeping sounds. For a moment Roddy felt hopeful that the tiresome instrument was still out of order, but then the peeping sounds stopped and a voice came on, and hope died.

"Is that Benchoile?"

"The Stable House, yes. Roddy Dunbeath here."

"Roddy. This is Oliver Dobbs."

After a little, Roddy said, "Who?"

"Oliver Dobbs." It was a pleasant voice, young, deep, vaguely familiar. Roddy dug about, without noticeable success, in his unreliable memory.

"I'm not with you, old boy."

"We met at a dinner in London a couple of years ago. Sat next to each other . . ."

Recollection dawned. Of course, Oliver Dobbs. Clever young man. A writer. Won some prize. They'd had a great crack together. "But of course." He reached behind him for a chair, settled himself for conversation. "My dear boy, how splendid to hear you. Where are you calling from?"

"The Lake District."

"What are you doing in the Lake District?"

"I'm taking a few days off. I'm driving up to Scotland."

"You're going to come here, of course."

"Well, that's what I'm calling about. I tried to ring you yesterday, but they said the phone lines were down. When we met, you issued an invitation to come and see you at Benchoile, and I'm afraid I'm taking it up."

"Nothing to be afraid of. I couldn't be more pleased."

"We thought perhaps we might be able to come and stay for a couple of days."

"Of course you must come." The prospect of a couple of days in the company of that lively and intelligent young man was quite stimulating. But, "Who's we?" asked Roddy.

"Well, there's the rub," said Oliver Dobbs. "We're a sort of family. Victoria and me and Thomas. He's only two, but he's quite undemanding and very well-behaved. Would there be room for us all, because if not Victoria says we can go to a pub if there's such a thing nearby."

"Never heard such rubbish." Roddy was quite indignant. Benchoile hospitality had always been legendary. True, during the last five years, since Lucy died, the entries in the battered leather-bound visitors book, which lived on the hall table in the big house, were few and far between, but that didn't mean that there wasn't still the warmest of welcomes for any person who wished to come and stay. "Of course you must come here. When will you arrive?"

"Perhaps about Thursday? We thought we'd drive up the West Coast. Victoria's never been to the Highlands."

"Come by Strome Ferry and Achnasheen." Roddy knew the Scottish highways like the back of his hand.

"And then down Strath Oykel to Lairg. You've never seen such country in your life."

"Have you got snow up there?"

"We've had a lot, but the good weather's back again. By the time you get here, the road should be clear."

"And you're sure you don't mind us coming?"

"Absolutely delighted. We'll expect you Thursday about lunchtime. And stay," he added with the expansiveness of a potential host who has no intention of being involved in the tedious necessities of airing sheets or dusting bedrooms or cooking meals, "stay as long as you like."

The telephone call, coming out of the blue as it had, left Roddy in a pleasurable state of mild excitement. After he had replaced the receiver, he sat for a little, finishing his cigar, and anticipating, with the satisfaction of a boy, the forthcoming visit.

He loved young people. Trapped in the spreading bulk and the balding head of approaching old age, he still thought of himself as young. Inside, he still felt young. He remembered with pleasure the instant rapport that had sprung up between himself and Oliver Dobbs. How they had sat through that dinner, serious-faced and boiling with suppressed laughter at the endless, cliché-ridden speeches.

At one point, Oliver had made some remark, thrown from the corner of his mouth, about the chest measurements of the lady across the table from them, and Roddy had thought, "You remind me of me." Perhaps that was it. Oliver was his alter ego, the young man Roddy had once been. Or perhaps the young man he would like to have been, if circumstances had been different, if he had been born to a different way of life, if there had been no war.

The pleasure had to be shared. Not only that, Ellen Tarbat had to be told. She would put on a face, shake her head, accept the tidings in martyred resignation.

This was customary and meant nothing. Ellen always put on a face, shook her head and looked martyred, even if one happened to be the bearer of delightful news.

Roddy stubbed out his cigar, and without bothering to put on a coat, got up out of his chair and started down the stairs. His dog followed him. They went out into the cold morning air together, crossed the icy cobbles of the stableyard, and let themselves in through the back door of the big house.

The passages that lay beyond were stone-floored, cold, and seemingly endless. Doors gave off to coal sheds, woodsheds, laundries, store rooms, cellars, pantries. He came at last through a green-baize-covered door, and emerged into the big hall of the old house. Here, the temperature rose by a few degrees. Sun poured in through long windows and the glassed inner front door. It sent long beams, dancing with dust motes, down the turkey-rugged staircase and quenched the fire, which smoldered in the immense grate, to a bed of dusty ashes. Roddy stopped to replenish this from the basket of peats which stood alongside and then went in search of his brother.

He found Jock, inevitably, in the library, sitting at the unfashionable roll-top desk, which had belonged to their father, and dealing with the endless accounts and paper work related to the management of the farm.

Since Lucy had died, the drawing room had, by wordless consent, been closed and shut away, and this was now the apartment in which Jock spent his days. It was one of Roddy's favorite rooms, shabby and worn, the walls lined with books, the old leather-covered chairs sagging and comfortable as old friends. Today this room too was filled with the pale sunlight of the winter's day. Another fire burned in the hearth, and Jock's two golden Labradors lay, drugged in the warmth.

As Roddy opened the door, Jock looked up, over the spectacles which habitually slid to the end of his long beak of a nose. Roddy said, "Good morning."

"Hello," He took off the spectacles, leaning back in his chair. "And what might you be wanting?"

Roddy came in and shut the door. He said, "I am the bearer of pleasing news." Jock sat politely, waiting to be pleased. "You might even say, I was some sort of a fairy godmother, granting all your wishes."

Jock still waited. Roddy smiled and let his weight cautiously down into the armchair nearest the fire. After his trek across the yard and down the arctic passages of Benchoile, his feet felt cold, so he toed off his slippers and wriggled his stockinged feet in the warmth. There was a hole in one of his socks. He would have to get Ellen to mend it.

He said, "You know, yesterday, you said that the minister at Creagan said that what we needed at Benchoile was some young company. Well, we're going to get it."

"Who are we going to get?"

"A delightful and bright young man called Oliver Dobbs and what he pleases to call his 'sort of family.' "

"And who is Oliver Dobbs?"

"If you weren't such an old reactionary, you'd have heard of him. A very clever young man with a string of literary successes to his name."

"Oh," said Jock. "One of those."

"You'll like him." That was the extraordinary thing, Jock probably would. Roddy had called his brother a reactionary, but Jock was nothing of the kind. Jock was a liberal, through and through. Beneath his chilling, eagle-proud appearance lay concealed the real man, gentle, tolerant, well-mannered. Jock had never disliked a man on sight. Jock had always been willing and ready, in his reserved and diffident way, to see the other man's point of view.

"And what," asked Jock mildly, "does the 'sort of family' consist of?"

"I'm not quite sure, but whatever it is, we may well have to keep it from Ellen."

"When are they coming?"

"Thursday. Lunchtime."

"Where are they going to sleep?"

"I thought over here, in the big house. There's more space."

"You'll have to tell Ellen."

"I am steeling myself to do that very thing."

Jock sent him a long amused look, and Roddy grinned. Jock leaned back in his chair and rubbed his eyes with the gesture of a man who had been up all night. He said, "What time is it?" and looked at his watch. Roddy, who was longing for a drink, said it was twelve o'clock, but Jock didn't notice the hint, or if he did he took no account of it, but said, instead, "I'm going out for a walk."

Roddy suppressed his disappointment. He would go back to his own house and pour himself a drink there. He said "It's a beautiful morning."

"Yes," said Jock. He looked out of the window. "Beautiful. Benchoile at its most beautiful."

They talked for a little and then Roddy departed, with conscious courage, kitchenwards, in search of Ellen. Jock got up from his desk, and with the dogs at his heel, went out of the room and across the hall to the gunroom. He took down a shooting jacket, shucked off his slippers, climbed into a pair of green rubber boots. He took down his cap, pulled it down over his nose. A muffler to wind round his neck. He found knitted mittens in the pocket of the jacket and pulled them on. His fingers protruded from the open ends, swollen and purple as beef sausages.

He found his stick, a long shepherd's crook. He let himself thankfully out of the house. The cold air hit him, the piercing chill of it biting deep into his lungs. For days he had been feeling unwell. He put it down to tiredness and the bitter weather, but all at once, in the meagre warmth of the February sun, he felt a little better. Perhaps he should get out and about more, but one needed good reason to make the required effort.

Tramping over the creaking snow towards the loch, he thought of the young people whom Roddy had invited to stay, and he was not dismayed, as many men of his age would have been, by the prospect. He loved young people as much as his brother, but somehow he had always been shy with them, had never been much good with them. He knew that his manner, and his upright, soldierly appearance, were off-putting, but what could you do about the way you looked? Perhaps, if he had had children of his own, it would have been different. With children of your own, there would be no necessity to break down the barriers of shyness.

People to stay. They would have to get the rooms ready, light fires, perhaps open the old nursery. He had forgotten to ask Roddy the age of the child who was coming to stay. A pity there would be no fishing, but the boat was laid up anyway, and the boathouse locked for the winter.

His mind strayed back to other house-parties, other children. He and his brothers when they were small. Their friends, and then Lucy's numerous young nephews and nieces. Rabbit's friends and relations he had called them. He smiled to himself. Rabbit's friends and relations.

He had reached the edge of the loch. It stretched before him, edged with ice from which the winter-pale rushes grew in straggling clumps. A pair of peewits flew overhead, and he raised his head to watch their passing. The sun in his eyes was blinding, and he put up a hand as shade from the dazzle. His dogs nuzzled into the snow, scenting exciting smells. They inspected the ice, in small nervous darts, but were not brave, or perhaps foolhardy, enough to venture out onto the shining surface.

It was indeed a beautiful day. He turned back to look at the house. It lay, a little above him, across the snow-covered slope; familiar, loved, secure. Sunlight glinted on windows, smoke issued from chimneys, rising straight up in the still air. There was a smell of moss, of peat, and the resin of the spruces. Behind the house, the hills rose to meet the blue sky. His hills. Benchoile hill. He felt immensely content.

Well, the young company were coming. They would be here on Thursday. There would be laughter, voices, footsteps on the stairs. Benchoile was waiting for them.

He turned away from the house and set out once more upon his walk, his stick in his hand, his dogs at his heel, his spirit untroubled.

When he did not put in an appearance for his midday meal, Ellen became worried. She went to the front door to look for him, but saw only the single line of footprints that led to the edge of the loch. He had been late many times before, but now her Highland instincts were dark with foreboding. She went to find Roddy. He rang Davey Guthrie and in a moment Davey appeared in his van and the two men set out together to look for Jock.

It was not a difficult search, for the prints of him and his dogs lay clear in the snow. They found the three of them in the lea of dry-stone dike. Jock lay quietly, his face serene and turned up to the sun. The dogs were wheeking and anxious, but it was instantly clear that their master would never know anxiety again.

CHAPTER 7
Tuesday

Thomas Dodds, wearing new red rubber boots, squatted at the water's edge, fascinated by this strange new phenomenon that had suddenly come into his life, and staring at it with the mesmerized, unblinking gaze of some old seafarer. It was all bigger and brighter and wetter than anything he had ever before encountered in his short life, and there were, as well, the added diversions of the little choppy waves, so sunlit and cheerful, the screaming of the sea birds which wheeled in the cold air over his head, and the occasional passing boat. Every now and then he dug up a handful of gritty sand and threw it into the sea.

Behind him, a few yards off, Victoria sat on the shingly beach and watched him. She wore thick, corduroy trousers and three sweaters, two of them her own and one borrowed from Oliver, and she sat huddled, with her knees pulled up and her arms wrapped around them for warmth. It was, indeed, extremely cold. But then, at ten o'clock on a February morning in the north of Scotland—well, nearly the north of Scotland—it would have been surprising if it had been anything else.

It wasn't even a proper beach, just a narrow strip of shingle between the wall of the hotel garden and the water. It smelt fishy and tarry, and was littered with scraps of debris from the boats that plied up and down the long sea loch on their way to and from the fishing grounds. There were bits of string, an old fish-head or

two, and a damp furry object, which on investigation
proved to be a rotting doormat.

"The back of beyond," Oliver had said yesterday
evening as the Volvo topped the pass and began the
long gradual descent to the sea, but Victoria thought
that the isolation was beautiful. They were now much
further north than they had intended to come, and so
far west that if you took another step, you fell into the
sea; but the views, the sheer size and grandeur of the
country, the colors, and the brilliance of the sparkling
air had made the long drive more than worthwhile.

Yesterday morning they had woken to a Lake District
streaming in rain, but as they drove up into Scotland
a wind had sprung up from the west, and the clouds
had been blown away. All yesterday afternoon, and this
morning again, the sky was clear, the air piercing cold.
Snow-covered peaks of distant hills glittered like glass,
and the waters of the sea loch were a dark indigo blue.

The loch, Victoria had discovered, was called Loch
Morag. The little village, with its tiny shops and fleet
of fishing boats tied up at the sea wall, was also called
Loch Morag, and the hotel was the Loch Morag Hotel. (Oliver said that he expected the manager was
called Mr. Lochmorag and his wife, Mrs. Lochmorag.) Built for the sole purpose of catering to fish-
ermen—both freshwater and sea fishing, the brochure
boasted, was on their doorstep—it was large and ugly,
constructed of some strange stone the color of liver,
and much crenellated, towered and turreted. Indoors,
it was furnished with worn turkey carpets and unin-
spired wallpaper the color of porridge, but there were
peat fires burning in the public rooms and the people
were very kind.

"Would the wee boy like high tea?" had asked the
comfortable lady in the mauve dress who appeared, in
this quiet season, to have taken on the duties not only
of head waitress and barmaid, but receptionist as well.
"Maybe a boiled egg, or a wee bit oatcake?" Thomas

stared at her, unhelpfully. "Or a jeely. Would you like a jeely, pet?"

In the end they had settled for a boiled egg and an apple, and the kind lady (Mrs. Lochmorag?) brought it up to his bedroom on a tray, and sat with Thomas while Victoria had a bath. When she emerged from the bathroom, she found Mrs. Lochmorag playing with Thomas and the pink and white calico pig that they had bought him in London before they left, along with a wardrobe of clothes, a toothbrush and a pot. Victoria had wanted to buy an endearing teddy bear, but Oliver informed her that Thomas did not like fur, and chose the pig himself.

The pig was called Piglet. He wore blue trousers and red braces. His eyes were black and beady and Thomas approved of him.

"You've got a lovely wee boy, Mrs. Dobbs. And what age is he?"

"He's two."

"We've made friends, but, mind, he hasn't said a word to me."

"He . . . he doesn't talk very much."

"Oh, he should be talking by now." She heaved Thomas onto her knee. "What a lazy wee boy, not saying a word. You can say Mummy, now, can't you? Are you not going to say Mummy? Are you not going to tell me the name of your pig?" She took Piglet and jigged him up and down, making him dance. Thomas smiled.

"He's called Piglet," Victoria told her.

"That's a bonny name. Why does Thomas not say Piglet?"

But he did not say Piglet. He did not indeed say anything very much. But this in no way detracted from his charm. In fact, it added to it, because he was such a cheerful and undemanding child that four days of his company had been nothing but pleasure. In the car, during the long drive north, he sat on Victoria's knee, hugging his new toy, and gazing out of the window at passing lorries, fields, towns; obviously enjoying all the new and strange sights, but seeing no reason to comment upon them. When they stopped for meals or to stretch their legs, Thomas joined them, eating bacon and eggs or drinking milk or munching the slices of apple that Oliver peeled and cut up for him. When he became tired or bored, he plugged his mouth with his thumb, settled himself with endearing confidence in Victoria's arms, and either slept or sang to himself, with eyes drooping and dark lashes silky against his round red cheeks.

"I wonder why he doesn't talk more?" she had said to Oliver once, when Thomas was safely asleep on her lap and could not overhear the discussion.

"Probably because nobody's ever talked to him. Probably they were all too busy sterilizing the house and manicuring the garden, and boiling his toys."

Victoria did not agree with Oliver. No child, so well-adjusted and content, could have been neglected in the smallest way. Indeed, his behavior and his sunny disposition gave every indication that he had spent his short life enveloped in affection.

She said as much and instantly aroused Oliver's ire. "If they were so marvelous with him, then how come he doesn't seem to be missing them? He can't have been particularly fond of them if he hasn't asked for them once."

"He hasn't asked for anything," Victoria pointed out. "And most likely his being so confident and unafraid is all to do with the way he's been brought up. Nobody's ever been unkind to him, so he doesn't expect unkindness. That's why he's being so good with us."

"Balls," said Oliver shortly. He could not stand a single good word being said on the Archers' behalf.

Victoria knew he was being unreasonable. "If Thomas howled for his grandparents all the time, and complained, and wet his pants and generally behaved like most children would under the same circumstances, I suppose you'd have blamed that on the Archers, too."

"You're talking in hypothetical circles."

"I'm not." But she didn't know what a hypothetical circle was, and so couldn't argue further. Instead, she lapsed into silence. *But we must ring up Mrs. Archer,* she thought. Or write to her or something. Oliver must let her know that Thomas is all right. Some time.

It was, perhaps, their only quarrel. Otherwise, the entire undertaking, which could have been, and even deserved to be, disastrous, was proving an unqualified success. Nothing had gone wrong. Everything had proved simple, easy, delightful. The winter roads were fast and empty; the scenery, the open skies, the stunning countryside, all contributed to their pleasure.

In the Lake District it had rained, but they had put on waterproofs and walked for miles, with Thomas, cheerful as ever, atop his father's shoulders. There had been fires burning pleasantly in their bedrooms at the little lakeside hotel, and boats moored at the jetty that lay at the end of the garden, and in the evening a kindly chambermaid had watched over Thomas while Oliver and Victoria dined by candlelight, on grilled trout and rare beefsteaks that had never seen the inside of a deep freeze.

That night, lying in the soft darkness, in feather-bedded warmth, in Oliver's arms, she had watched the curtains stirring at the open window and felt the cool damp air on her cheeks. From the quiet darkness beyond the window came the sounds of water and the creak of the boats tied up at the jetty, and there had come a distrust of such perfect content. Surely, she told herself, it could not go on. Surely something would happen that would spoil it all.

But her apprehension was unfounded. Nothing happened. The next day was even better, with the road pouring north to Scotland and the sun coming out as they crossed the border. By the afternoon, the great peaks of the Western Highlands lay ahead of them, iced in snow, and at the foot of Glencoe they stopped at a pub for tea and ate homemade scones dripping with butter. And after that the countryside grew more and more magnificent, and Oliver told Victoria that it was called Lochaber, and he began to sing "The Road to the Isles."

"Sure by *Tummel* and Loch *Rannoch* and Locha-*ber* we will go . . ."

Today Loch Morag. Tomorrow, or perhaps the next day, Benchoile. Victoria had lost all sense of time. She had lost all sense of anything. Watching Thomas, she hugged herself more tightly and rested her chin on her knees. Happiness, she decided, should be tangible. A thing you could take hold of and put somewhere safe, like a box with a lid or a bottle with a stopper. And then, later, sometime when you were miserable, you could take it out and look at it and feel it and smell it, and you would be happy again.

Thomas was tiring of throwing sand into the sea. He straightened up on his small legs and looked about him. He spied Victoria, sitting there, where he had left her. He grinned, and began to stump unsteadily towards her up the littered little beach.

Watching him filled her heart with an almost unbearable tenderness. She thought, if I can feel like this about Thomas, after only four days, how does Mrs. Archer feel, not even knowing where he is?

It didn't bear thinking about. Basely, cowardly, she pushed the idea to the back of her mind and opened her arms to Thomas. He reached her and she hugged him. The wind blew her long hair across his cheek, and tickled. He began to laugh.

While Victoria and Thomas sat on the beach and

waited for him, Oliver was telephoning. The previous night had been the first performance of *Bent Penny* at Bristol, and he couldn't wait to hear what the critics had said in the morning papers.

He was not exactly on tenterhooks, because he knew that the play was good—his best, in fact. But there were always elements and reactions that were apt to take one unawares. He wanted to know how the show had gone, how the audience had responded, and whether Jennifer Clay, the new little actress getting her first big chance, had justified the faith that the producer and Oliver had put in her.

He was on the telephone to Bristol for nearly an hour, listening while the ecstatic reviews were read aloud to him along six hundred miles of humming wires. The critics from the *Sunday Times* and the *Observer*, he was told, were coming down to see the play at the end of the week. Jennifer Clay was on the brink of being swept to stardom, and there had already come interested noises from a couple of important West End managements.

"In fact, Oliver, I think we've got a hit on our hands."

Oliver was gratified, but he had watched the show in rehearsal, and he was not particularly surprised. The Bristol call finally finished, he rang his agent, and all the good news was confirmed. As well, there had been feelers from New York about his play *A Man In The Dark,* which had done so well in Edinburgh a summer ago.

"Would you be interested?" the agent asked.

"What do you mean, 'interested'?"

"Would you be prepared to go to New York if you have to?"

Oliver loved New York. It was one of his favorite places. "I'd be prepared to go even if I didn't have to."

"How long are you going to be away?"

"Couple of weeks."

"Can I get in touch with you?"

"After Thursday, I'll be at Benchoile, in Sutherland. Staying with a guy called Roddy Dunbeath."

"Eagle Years Dunbeath?"

"The very man."

"What's the phone number?"

Oliver reached for his leather diary, thumbed through it. "Creagan two three seven."

"OK, I've got it. If I have any fresh news I'll call you."

"You do that."

"Good luck, then Oliver. And congratulations."

His agent rang off. After a little, though reluctant to put an end to such a momentous conversation, Oliver replaced his own receiver, and sat looking at it for a moment or two, while slowly, relief flooded through him. It was over. *Bent Penny* was launched, like a child sent out into the world. A child conceived with passion, brought to life in the most agonizing birth pains, nursed and coaxed to maturity, and bludgeoned into shape, it was, at last, no longer Oliver's responsibility.

All over. He thought of the production, the rehearsals, the personality problems, the temperaments, the tears. The chaos, the panics, the rewriting, the total despair.

I think we've got a hit on our hands.

It would make him, probably, a lot of money. It might even make him rich. But this was of small account compared to the easement of his spirit, and the sense of freedom that existed now that it was all behind him.

And ahead . . .? He reached for a cigarette. There was something waiting for him, but he wasn't sure what. He only knew that the subconscious edge of his imagination, the part that did all the work, was already filling with people. People living in a certain place, a certain style. Voices had conversations. The dialogues had a form and a balance all their own, and the words, and the faces of the individuals who spoke them, swam up, as they always did, out of his prodigious memory.

These first stirrings of life made everyday existence, for Oliver, as intense and dramatic as it is for most men when they fall in love. This, for him, was the best part of writing. It was the same as the anticipation of waiting in a darkened theatre for the curtain to go up on the first act. You didn't know what was going to happen, but you knew that it would be marvelous and tremendously exciting and better—much better—than anything you had ever seen before.

He got up off the bed and went to the window and flung it open to the icy morning air. Gulls wheeled and screamed over the funnel of a weather-beaten fishing boat as she butted her way, against the western wind, out to the open sea.

On the far side of the dark blue water the hills were frosted in white, and below him was the hotel garden and the scrap of a beach. He looked down upon Victoria and his son Thomas. They did not know he was watching. As he observed them, Tom grew tired of his game of throwing sand into the water, and turned and made his way up the beach to Victoria's side. She opened her arms to him and drew him close, and her long fair hair blew all over his red and chubby face.

The combination of this delightful scene and his own euphoric frame of mind filled Oliver with an unfamiliar content. He knew that it was ephermeral; it might last a day or even an hour or two. But all at once it seemed that the world was a brighter and a more hopeful place; that the smallest incident could take on immense significance; that affection would turn to love, and love—that humdrum word—to passion.

He closed the window and went downstairs to tell them his good news.

CHAPTER 8
Thursday

Miss Ridgeway, that impeccable private secretary of undetermined years, was already at her desk when, at a quarter to nine in the morning, John Dunbeath emerged from the lift onto the ninth floor of the new Regency House Building and the opulent, elegant offices of the Warburg Investment Corporation.

She looked up as he came through the door, her expression, as always, polite, pleasant and impassive.

"Good morning, Mr. Dunbeath."

"Hi."

He had never before had a secretary whom he did not call by her Christian name, but sometimes the formality of "Miss Ridgeway" stuck in his throat. They had, after all, worked together for some months. It would have been so much easier to call her Mary or Daphne or whatever her name was, but the truth of the matter was that he hadn't even found this out, and and there was something so strictly formal about her manner that he had never plucked up the courage to ask.

Sometimes, watching her as she sat there, with one shapely leg crossed over the other, taking down his letters in her faultless shorthand, he pondered on her private life. Did she care for an aged mother and take an interest in good works? Did she go to concerts at the Albert Hall and spend her holidays in Florence? Or did she, like a secretary in some film, remove her spectacles and shake loose her mouse pale hair, receive lovers and indulge in scenes of unbridled passion?

He knew that he would never know.

She said, "How was the trip?"

"OK. But the plane was late getting in yesterday evening. We got held up in Rome."

Her eyes moved over his dark suit, his black tie. She said, "You got the cable all right? The one from your father?"

"Yes. Thanks for that."

"It came on Tuesday morning. I thought you'd want to know. I sent a copy through to Bahrain right away. The original is on your desk with some personal mail . . ." John moved through to his own office, and Miss Ridgeway rose from her chair and followed him. ". . . and yesterday's *Times* that the announcement was in. I thought you'd like to see it."

She thought of everything. He said, "Thank you," again and opened his briefcase and took out the report, the twelve pages of foolscap, covered with his own neat writing, that he had composed in the airplane during the flight back to London.

"You'd better get one of the typists on to this right away. The vice president will want to see it as soon as possible. And when Mr. Rogerson gets in, tell him to give me a buzz." He glanced at his desk. "And this morning's *Wall Street Journal?*"

"I have it, Mr. Dunbeath."

"And the *Financial Times* as well. I didn't have time to pick one up." She started out of the office, but he called her back. "Hang on a moment." She returned and he dealt out more papers. "I want the file on this. And if you can can, find me some information on a Texas company called Albright; they've been drilling in Libya. And this has to be telexed through to Sheikh Mustapha Said, and this . . . and this . . ."

After a little, "Is that all?" asked Miss Ridgeway.

"For the moment." He grinned. "Except that I'd appreciate a large cup of black coffee."

Miss Ridgeway smiled understandingly, becoming quite human. He wished that she would smile more. "I'll get it," she said, and left him, closing the door, without a sound, behind her.

He sat at his gleaming desk and debated for a moment as to what he should do first. His In tray was piled high, letters neatly clipped to their relevant files, and, he knew, arranged in their order of priority, with the most urgent documents on the top. The three personal letters had been placed in the middle of his blot ter. The blotting paper was, as it was every day, new and pristine white. There was also the copy of yesterday's *Times*.

He reached for the green telephone to make an internal call.

"Mr. Gardner please."

He tucked the receiver under his chin and opened the newspaper to the back page.

"John Dunbeath here. Is he in yet?"

"Yes, he's in, Mr. Dunbeath, but he's not in the office right now. Shall I get him to call you?"

"Yes, do that." He replaced the receiver.

DUNBEATH. Suddenly, on February 16th at Benchoile in Sutherland, Lt. Col. John Rathbone Dunbeath, D.S.O., J.P., late Cameron Highlanders, in his 68th year. Funeral Service in the Parish Church, Creagan, 10:30 a.m. Thursday February 19th.

He remembered the old boy, tall and lean, every inch a retired soldier; his pale glare and his prow of a nose; his long legs striding easily up the hill through knee-high heather; his passion for fishing, for shooting grouse, for his land. They had never been close, but there was still an empty sense of loss, as there must be when a man, bound close by family and blood, dies.

He laid down the paper and took his father's cable from the envelope in which Miss Ridgeway had protectively placed it. He read what he had already read, in Bahrain, two days previously.

YOUR UNCLE JOCK DIED RESULT OF A HEART ATTACK BENCHOILE MONDAY 16th FEBRUARY STOP FUNERAL CREAGAN 10:30 THURSDAY MORNING 19th FEBRUARY STOP WOULD BE GRATEFUL IF YOU COULD REPRESENT YOUR MOTHER AND MYSELF STOP FATHER

He had sent cables from Bahrain. To his parents in Colorado, explaining why he would not be able to comply with his father's request. To Benchoile, to Roddy, he had sent sympathy and more explanations, and before he left Bahrain, he had found the time to write Roddy a letter of condolence, which he had posted by first-class mail on his arrival at Heathrow.

The other two letters waited for his attention, one envelope hand-written, the other typed. He picked up the first and began to open it, and then stopped, his attention caught by the writing. An old-fashioned pen nib, black ink, the capitals strongly defined. He looked at the postmark and saw "CREAGAN." The date was the tenth of February.

He felt his stomach contract. *A ghost going over your grave* his father used to say when John was a small boy and scared by the unknown. *That's what it is. A ghost going over your grave.*

He slit the envelope and took out the letter. His suspicions were confirmed. It was from Jock Dunbeath.

Benchoile,
Creagan,
Sutherland.
Wednesday,
9th February.

Dear John,

Your Father tells me that you are now back in this country and working in London. I do not know your address, so I am sending this to your office.

It seems a long time since you stayed with us. I looked it up in the visitors' book and it seems to be ten years. I realize that you are a very busy man, but if you are able to get a little time off, perhaps you would think about making the journey north and spending a few days at Benchoile. It is possible to fly to Inverness or to catch a train from Euston in which case either I or Roddy would come to Inverness to meet you. There are trains to Creagan, but they are few and far between and involve several hours delay.

We have had a mild winter, but I think cold weather is on the way. Better now than in the Spring when late frosts play havoc with the young grouse.

Let me know what you think and when it might be convenient for you to visit us. We look forward to seeing you again.

With best wishes,

Affectionately,

Jock

The arrival, out of the blue, of this extraordinary invitation; the coincidence of timing, the fact that it had been written only days before Jock's fatal heart attack, were intensely disturbing. John sat back in his chair and read the letter through again, consciously searching for some inner meaning between the carefully penned and characteristically stilted lines. He could find none.

It seems to be ten years.

It was ten years. He remembered himself at eighteen with Wellington behind him and all the joys of Cambridge ahead, spending part of the summer holidays with his father at Benchoile. But he had never gone back.

Now, it struck him that perhaps he should feel guilty about this lapse. But too much had happened to him. Too much had been going on. He had been at Cambridge, then New York, and then Harvard, spending all his vacations in Colorado, either at his father's ranch, or else skiing at Aspen. And then Lisa had come into his life, and after that all his spare energy had been spent in simply keeping up with her. Keeping her happy, keeping her amused, keeping her in the high style which she was convinced was her due. Being married to Lisa meant the end of vacations in Colorado. She was bored by the ranch and too fragile to ski. But she adored the sun, so they went to the West Indies, to Antigua, the Bahamas, where John missed the mountains and tried to work off his physical needs in scuba diving or sailing.

And after the divorce, he had buried himself so deeply in his work that somehow there didn't even seem to be time to get out of the city. It was his president in New York who had finally read the riot act, and had him posted to London. Not only was it a promotion, he told John, but it would make a vital and necessary change of pace. London was quieter than

New York, the rat race not so frantic, the ambience generally more easy-going.

"You'll be able to get North and see Jock and Roddy," his father had said over the telephone when John had called to give him the news, but somehow with one thing and another John had never got around to doing this. Now, it struck him that he should feel guilty about this lapse. But the truth was that Benchoile, though undoubtedly beautiful, held no irresistible lure for John. Having been brought up in the heart of the Rockies, he had found the hills and glens of Sutherland peaceful, but somehow tame. There was fishing, of course, but fishing in Colorado, in the trubutaries of the mighty Uncompahgre, which ran through his father's spread, was unsurpassable. Benchoile had a farm, but again, that seemed small compared to the endless ranges of the ranch, and the grouse shooting, with its rules and shibboleths, its traditions of butt and beat, had left the young John totally cold.

Even as a boy, he had rebelled against slaughtering wildlife, and had never gone hunting, for mule deer or elk, with the other men, and there seemed no reason, just because he was staying in Scotland and it was expected of him, to give up the habits and convictions of a lifetime.

Finally, and this was the most important reason of all, he had never thought that his Uncle Jock liked him very much. "He's just reserved. He's shy," John's father had assured him, but still, try as he could, John had never been able to work up a rapport with his father's eldest brother. Conversations between the two of them, he remembered, had never done more than creak painfully along, like wagon wheels in need of a good greasing.

He sighed, and laid the letter down, and picked up the last envelope. This time he slit it open without inspecting it first, and with his mind still brooding over the letter from Jock, he unfolded the single sheet of paper. He saw the old-fashioned letterhead, the date.

> McKenzie, Leith & Dudgeon,
> Solicitors, Writers to
> The Signet.
> 18 Trade Lane,
> Inverness.
> Tuesday, 17th February.

John Dunbeath, Esq.,
Warburg Investment Corporation,
Regency House,
London.

John Rathbone Dunbeath Deceased

Dear Mr. Dunbeath,

I have to inform you that under the terms of the Will of your Uncle, John Rathbone Dunbeath, you have been bequeathed the Benchoile Estate in Sutherland.

I suggest that you take an early opportunity to come north and see me in order to make practical arrangements for the management and future of the property.

I shall be happy to see you at any time.

Yours sincerely,

Robert McKenzie.

When Miss Ridgeway came back into the room, bearing his black coffee in a fine white Wedgwood cup, she found John sitting, motionless at his desk, an elbow on his blotter, the bottom half his face covered by his hand.

She said, "Here's your coffee," and he looked up at her, and the expression in his dark eyes was so somber that she was moved to ask if he was all right, if anything had happened.

He did not reply at once. And then he sat back in his chair, letting his hand fall to his lap, and said that yes, something had happened. But after a long pause, during which he showed no signs of wishing to elucidate on this remark, she laid the cup and saucer beside him, and left him alone, closing the door between them with her usual tactful care.

CHAPTER 9
Thursday

As they drove east, up and away from the mild-mannered sea lochs of the West of Scotland, leaving the farms and villages and the smell of sea wrack behind them, the countryside changed character with dizzying abruptness, and the empty road wound upwards into a wilderness of desolate moorland, apparently uninhabited except for a few stray sheep and the occasional hovering bird of prey.

The day was cold and overcast, the wind from the east. Grey billows of cloud moved slowly across the sky, but every now and then there came a break in the gloom, a ragged scrap of pale blue appeared, and a gleam of thin wintry sunshine, but this only seemed to accentuate the loneliness rather than do anything to alleviate it.

The undulating land stretched in all directions, as far as the eye could see, patchworked in winter-pale grasses and great tracts of dark heather. Sometimes this was broken by a gaping peat-pit or the somber black of bog. Then scraps of snow began to appear, like the white spots on a piebald horse, and lay where it had been trapped in corries and ditches and in the lea of low drystone dikes. As the gradient steepened, the snow grew thicker, and at the head of the moor—the roof-ridge, as it were, of the country—it was all about them, a blanket of white six inches deep or more, and the road was ice-rutted and treacherous beneath the wheels of the Volvo.

It was like finding oneself in the Arctic, or on the moon. Certainly in some place that one had never even remotely imagined visiting. But then, just as abruptly, the wild and desolate moor was behind them. They had crossed the watershed, and, imperceptibly, the road began to slope downhill once more. There were rivers and waterfalls and stands of larch and fir. First appeared isolated cottages, and then hill farms and then villages. Presently they were running alongside an immense inland loch, and there was the great rampart of a hydroelectric dam and beyond this a little town. The main street ran by the water's edge, and there was a hotel and a number of small boats pulled up on the shingle. A signpost pointed to Creagan.

Victoria became excited. "We're nearly there." She leaned forward and took from the cubbyhole on the dashboard the Ordnance Survey map that Oliver had bought. With Thomas's dubious help, she opened it out. One corner spread out over the driving wheel, and Oliver flipped it back. "Watch it, you'll blind me."

"It's only about another six miles to Creagan."

Thomas, using Piglet as a weapon, struck the map a blow and knocked it from Victoria's hands and onto the floor.

Oliver said, "Put it away before he tears it to pieces." He yawned and shifted in his seat. It had been a hard morning's drive.

Victoria rescued the map and folded it up and replaced it. The road ahead of them wound steadily downhill, between steep banks of bracken and copses of silver birch. A small river kept them company, chuckling and sparkling on its way in a series of little pools and waterfalls. The sun, obligingly, came out from behind a cloud; they turned a final corner, and ahead, glinting and silvery, lay the sea.

She said, "It's really amazing. You leave one coast behind you, and you drive up and over the moor and through the snow, and then you come to another sea. Look, Thomas, there's the sea."

Thomas looked, but was unimpressed. He was getting tired of driving. He was getting tired of sitting on Victoria's knee. He put his thumb in his mouth and flung himself backwards, striking her a resounding blow on the chest with the back of his bullet-hard head.

His father snapped, "Oh, for God's sake, sit still."

"He has sat still," Victoria was moved to point out in Thomas's defense. "He's been a very good boy. He's just getting bored. Do you suppose there's a beach at Creagan? I mean a proper sandy one. We haven't found a proper sandy beach yet. All the ones on the West seemed to be covered in stones. If there was one I could take him."

"We'll ask Roddy."

Victoria thought about this. Then she said, "I *do* hope he isn't going to mind us all turning up like this. I hope it isn't going to be difficult." She had never quite got rid of this apprehension.

"You've already said that a dozen times, at regular intervals. Stop being so anxious."

"I can't help feeling that you cornered Roddy. Perhaps he didn't have time to think up an excuse."

"He was delighted. Jumped at the chance of a little lively company."

"He knows you, but he doesn't know Tom and me."

"In that case, you'll both have to be on your best behavior. If I know Roddy, he won't care if you've got two heads and a tail. He'll just say how do you do, very nicely, and then, I hope and believe, will hand me an enormous gin and tonic."

Creagan, when they reached it, proved a surprise. Victoria had expected the usual small Highland township with its single narrow main street, flanked by rows of plain stone houses built flush on the pavement. But Creagan had a wide, tree-lined street, with deep cobbled sidewalks on either side. The houses, which stood back from the road and were separated from it by quite large gardens, were all detatched and remarkably attractive, with the simple proportions and elegant embellishments associated with the best period of Scottish domestic architecture.

In the middle of the town the main street opened up into a wide square, and in the center of this, sitting on a sward of grass, rather as though it had been set carefully down in the middle of a green carpet, rose the granite walls and slate-capped tower of a large and beautiful church.

Victoria said, "But it's lovely! It's like a French town."

Oliver, however, had noticed something else. "It's empty."

She looked again, and saw that this was true. A stillness brooded over Creagan, like the pious gloom of a Sabbath. Worse, for there was not even the cheerful clangor of bells. As well, there seemed to be scarcely anybody about, and only a few other cars. And . . . "All the shops are shuttered," said Victoria. "They're closed and all the blinds have been pulled down. Perhaps it's early closing."

She rolled down the window on her side of the car to let the icy air blow in on her face. Thomas tried to put his head out, and she pulled him back onto her knee. She smelled the salt of the sea and the tang of sea wrack. Overhead a gull began to scream from a rooftop.

"There's a shop open," said Oliver.

It was a small newsagent, with plastic toys in the window and a rack of colored postcards at the door. Victoria rolled up the window again, for the blast of cold air was bitter. "We can go and buy postcards there."

"What do you want postcards for?"

"To send to people." She hesitated. Ever since that morning by Loch Morag, her conscience had been constantly troubled by the nagging awareness of Mrs. Archer's anxiety and distress for Thomas. The opportunity to confide in Oliver had not, so far, presented itself, but now . . . She took a deep breath and went on with the bold determination of one intent upon striking while the iron is hot. "We can send one to Thomas's grandmother."

Oliver said nothing.

Victoria took no notice of this lack of response. "Just a line. To let her know he's safe and sound."

Oliver still said nothing. This was not a good sign. "Surely it couldn't do any harm." She could hear the pleading note in her own voice, and despised herself for it. "A postcard, or a letter or *something*."

"How you do bang on."

"I'd like to send her a postcard."

"We're not sending her a bloody thing."

She could not believe that he could be so blinkered. "But why be like that? I've been thinking . . ."

"Well, stop thinking. If you can come to no conclusion more intelligent than that one, then simply make your mind a blank."

"But . . ."

"The whole point of coming away was to get away from the Archers. If I'd wanted them on my doorstep, hounding me with lawyer's letters and private detectives, I'd have stayed in London."

"But if she *knew* where he was . . ."

"Oh, shut up."

It was not so much what he said as the tone of voice that he used to say it. A silence grew between them. After a little, Victoria turned her head and looked at him. His profile was stony, his lower lip jutted, his eyes narrowed, and staring straight at the road ahead. They had left the town behind them, and the car was picking up speed when they turned a corner and came all at once, upon the signpost, pointing inland, to Benchoile and Loch Muie. Oliver was caught unawares. He braked abruptly, and swung the car around with a screech of tires. They started up the single-track road, heading for the hills.

Unseeing, Victoria gazed ahead. She knew that Oliver was wrong, which was perhaps one of the reasons that he was being so stubborn. But Victoria could be stubborn, too. She said, "You've already told me that she hasn't got a leg to stand on, legally. That she can't do anything to get Thomas back. He's your child, and your responsibility."

Again, Oliver said nothing.

"So if you're so certain of yourself, there can be no reason not to let her know that he's all right."

He still was silent, and Victoria played her final card. "Well, you may not intend telling Mrs. Archer that Thomas is safe and well, but there's nothing to stop me writing to her."

Oliver spoke at last. "If you do," he said quietly. "If you so much as pick up a telephone, I promise you, I'll batter you black and blue."

He sounded as though he actually meant it. Victoria looked at him in astonishment, searching for some sign to put her mind at rest, to convince herself that this was simply Oliver, using words as his strongest weapon. But she found no reassurance. The coldness of his anger was devastating, and she found herself trembling as though he had already struck her. His stony features blurred as her eyes filled with sudden, ridiculous tears. She looked away, quickly, so that he should not notice them, and later, surreptitiously, wiped them away.

So it was that, with the sourness of the quarrel between them, and Victoria struggling not to cry, that they came to Benchoile.

Jock's Dunbeath's funeral had been a big and important affair, as befitted a man of his position. The church was full and later the graveyard, crowded with somberly clad men, from all walks of life, who had come—some many miles and from all directions—to pay their respects to an old and much-liked friend.

But the wake that followed was small. Only a few close colleagues made the journey to Benchoile, there to gather about the blazing fire in the library and to partake of Ellen's homemade shortbread, washed down with a dram or two of the best malt whisky.

One of these was Robert McKenzie, not only the family lawyer, but as well a lifetime friend of Jock Dunbeath. Robert had been Jock's best man when Jock married Lucy, and Jock was godfather to Robert's eldest boy. Robert had driven up that morning from Inverness, appeared in the church wearing his long black overcoat that made him look like one of the undertakers, and afterwards had acted as pallbearer.

Now, with his duties behind him, and a drink in his hand, he had become once more his usual brisk and businesslike self. In the middle of the proceedings, he drew Roddy aside.

"Roddy, if it's possible, I'd like a word with you sometime."

Roddy sent him a keen glance, but the other man's long face was set in its usual professional lines, and gave nothing away. Roddy sighed. He had been expecting something like this, but scarcely so soon.

"Anytime, old boy. What do you want me to do, nip down to Inverness? Beginning of next week, maybe?"

"Later, perhaps that would be a good idea. But I'd rather have a moment or two now. I mean, when this is over. It won't take more than five minutes."

"But of course. Stay and have a bit of lunch. It won't be more than soup and cheese, but you're more than welcome."

"No, I won't do that. I have to get back. I've a

meeting at three o'clock. But if I could just stay on after the others have gone?"

"Absolutely. No trouble at all . . ." Roddy's eyes wandered away from the lawyer. He spied an empty glass in somebody's hand. "My dear fellow, another dram for the road . . ."

It was not a gloomy gathering. Indeed, there were nothing but happy memories to recall, and soon there were smiles and even laughter. When the guests finally took themselves off, driving away in Range Rovers, or estate cars, or battered farm vans, Roddy stood outside the open front door of Benchoile and saw them on their way, feeling a little as though he were saying good-bye to the guns at the end of an enjoyable day's shoot.

The simile pleased him, because it was so exactly the way that Jock would have liked it. The last car made its way down through the rhododendrons, over the cattle grid, and out of sight around the corner. Only Robert McKenzie's old Rover remained.

Roddy went back indoors. Robert waited for him, standing in front of the mantelpiece, with his back to the fire.

"That went very well, Roddy."

"Thank God it didn't rain. Nothing worse than a funeral in a downpour." He had had only two whiskies. Robert still had a bit in his glass, so Roddy poured himself another small one. "What was it you wanted to talk to me about?"

"Benchoile," said Robert.

"Yes, I imagined it was that."

"I don't know if Jock told you what he intended doing with the place?"

"No. We never discussed it. There never seemed to be any pressing need to discuss it." Roddy considered this. "As things have turned out, perhaps we should have."

"He never said anything about young John?"

"You mean Charlie's boy? Never a word. Why?"

"He's left Benchoile to John."

Roddy was in the act of pouring water into his tumbler. A little of it spilled onto the tray. He looked up. Across the room his eyes met Robert's. Slowly he laid down the water jug. He said, "Good God."

"You had no idea?"

"No idea at all."

"I know Jock meant to talk it over with you. Had every intention of doing so, in fact. Perhaps the opportunity never came up."

"We didn't see all that much of each other, you know. More or less lived in the same house, but didn't see that much of each other. Didn't really talk . . ." Roddy's voice trailed off. He was confused, confounded.

Robert said gently, "Do you mind?"

"Mind?" Roddy's blue eyes widened in astonishment. "Mind? Of course I don't mind. Benchoile was never mine, the way it was Jock's. I know nothing about the farm; I have nothing to do with the house or the garden; I was never particularly interested in the stalking or the grouse. I simply roost in her. I'm the lodger."

"Then you didn't expect you'd be taking over?" Robert was considerably relieved. One could never imagine Roddy Dunbeath being disagreeable about anything, but he might well have been disappointed. Now, it appeared, he was not even that.

"To tell you the truth, old boy, I never even thought of it. Never thought of Jock dying. He always seemed such a tough old thing, walking the hill, and bringing the sheep down with Davey Guthrie, and even working in the garden."

"But," Robert reminded him, "he had had a heart attack."

"A very mild one. Nothing to worry about, the doctor said. He seemed to be all right. Never complained.

But then, of course, Jock was never a man to complain. . . ." Once more the sentence drifted to silence. Even for Roddy Dunbeath, thought the lawyer, his thought processes seemed more than usually vague.

"But Roddy, since Jock died, surely you must have wondered what was going to happen to Benchoile?"

"To tell you the truth, old boy, I haven't had much time for wondering. Hell of a lot to organize, you know, when something like this happens. I've been waking up in a cold sweat in the middle of the night, trying to remember what it is I've forgotten to do."

"But . . ."

Roddy began to smile. "And of course, half the time I haven't forgotten it at all."

It was impossible. Robert abandoned Roddy's future, and brought the discussion sharply back into line.

"About John, then. I've written to him, but I haven't yet had a reply to my letter."

"He's been in Bahrain. I had a cable from him. That's why he wasn't here this morning."

"I've invited him to come up and see me. The future of the property will have to be discussed."

"Yes, I suppose it will." Roddy thought about this. He said, with some conviction, "He won't want to live here."

"What makes you so certain?"

"Just that I can't imagine he would have the smallest interest in the place."

"Jock didn't seem to think that."

"It was hard to know, sometimes, exactly what Jock was thinking. I never thought he particularly liked Charlie's boy. They were always so intensely polite to each other. It's not a good sign, you know, when people are too polite. Besides, John Dunbeath has a career of his own. He's a clever, cool, successful young man, wheeling and dealing and making a lot of money. Not that he needs to make a lot of money, because he's always had it through his mother. And that's another thing, he's an American."

"Half American." Robert permitted himself a smile. "And I'd have thought you'd be the last man in the world to hold that against him."

"I don't hold it against him. I have nothing against John Dunbeath. I mean that. He was an exceptional boy and extremely intelligent. But I don't see him as the laird of Benchoile. What would he do with himself? He's only twenty-eight." The more Roddy thought about it, the more preposterous the idea became. "I shouldn't think he knows one end of a sheep from the other."

"It doesn't take much intelligence to learn."

"But why *John*?" The two men looked at each other glumly. Roddy sighed. "I know why of course. Because Jock had no children and I had no children and there wasn't anybody else."

"What do you think will happen?"

"I suppose he'll sell it. It seems a pity, but for the life of me, I can't think what else he'd do with the place."

"Let it? Come here for holidays?"

"A weekend cottage with fourteen bedrooms?"

"Well then, keep the farm in hand and sell the house?"

"He'd never get rid of the house unless he let the shooting and the stalking rights go with it, and Davey Guthrie needs that land for his sheep."

"If he does sell Benchoile, what will you do?"

"That's the sixty four thousand dollar question, isn't it? But I've lived here, on and off, all my life, and perhaps that's too long for any man to stay in one place. I shall move away I shall move abroad. Somewhere distant." Robert had visions of Roddy in Ibiza, wearing a panama hat. "Like Creagan," he finished, and Robert laughed.

"Well, I'm glad you know," he said, and finished

his drink and set down the empty glass. "And I hope, between us all, we'll be able to sort it all out. I . . . I expect John will want to come here sooner or later. To Benchoile, I mean. Will that be all right?"

"Right as rain, old boy. Anytime. Tell him to give me a ring."

They moved towards the door.

"I'll be in touch."

"You do that. And Robert, thank you for today. And for everything."

"I'll miss Jock."

"We all will."

He drove away, headed for Inverness and his three o'clock meeting, a busy man with much to think about. Roddy watched the Rover disappear, and then he was all alone, and he knew that now it was really over. And successfully over, which was so surprising. No small mishaps had occurred, and the funeral had passed in an orderly and soldierly fashion, just as if Jock had organized it himself, and not his singularly disorganized brother. Roddy drew a long sigh, part relief and part sadness. He looked up at the sky, hearing the chatter of greylags high above the clouds, but they stayed out of sight. A thin wind moved up the glen from the sea, and the slate grey surface of the water shivered beneath its touch.

Jock was dead and Benchoile now belonged to young John. So perhaps this day was not only the end of the beginning, but also, if John decided to sell it all, the beginning of the end. The idea would take some getting used to, but in Roddy's book, there was only one way to tackle such gargantuan problems, and that was as slowly as possible, a single step at a time. This meant no anticipation and no precipitant action. Life would move quietly on.

He looked at his watch. It was now half past twelve. His thoughts moved ahead to the remainder of the day, and he suddenly remembered the approaching

car, and the young family coming to spend a few days
at Benchoile. Oliver Dobbs and some female or other
and their child. It occurred to Roddy that Oliver was
the sort of man who would always have some female
or other in tow.

They would be arriving at any moment, and the
prospect lifted his spirits. The day was a sad one, but,
thought Roddy, where God closes a window, he opens
a door. What this old saw had to do with Oliver
Dobbs, he couldn't be sure, but it helped one to realize
that there could be no time for useless grieving, and
Roddy found this comforting.

Thinking of comfort brought him sharply back to
an awareness of the physical agony that he had en-
dured all morning.

It was to do with his kilt. He had not worn this
garment for two years or more, but for the laird's funeral, it had seemed appropriate to put it on. Accordingly, this morning he had taken it, reeking of camphor, from the cupboard, only to discover that he had
put on so much weight that the kilt would scarcely go
round him, and after struggling with it for five minutes or more, he had been forced to take himself over
to the big house and enroll the aid of Ellen Tarbat.

He found her in the kitchen, dressed in the inky
black that she kept for funerals, and with her gloomi-
est hat—and none of Ellen's hats were very cheerful—
already skewered to her head by an immense jet-
headed hat pin. Ellen's tears for Jock had been shed
privately, decently, behind the closed door of her bedroom at the top of the house. Now, dry-eyed and tight-
lipped, she was engaged in polishing the best tumblers
before setting them out on the damask-covered table
in the library. When Roddy appeared, clutching his
kilt about him like a bathtowel, she said, "I told you
so," as he had known she would, but she laid down the
tea towel and came manfully to his aid, heaving her
puny weight on the leather straps of the kilt, like a

tiny groom trying to tighten the girth of some enormous, overfed horse.

Finally, by brute force, the pin of the buckle went
into the last hole of the leather strap.

"There," said Ellen triumphantly. She was quite red
in the face, and a few stray white hairs had escaped
from her bun.

Roddy held his breath. Now, he let it out cautiously. The kilt tightened across his belly like a pair
of tightly laced stays, but the straps, miraculously,
held.

"You've done it," he told her.

Ellen tidied her hair. "If you were to ask me, I'd say
it was about time you went on a diet. Or else you'll
need to take your kilt into Inverness and get the man
to let it out. Otherwise you'll be giving yourself a sei-
zure, and it's yourself we'll be burying next."

Infuriated, Roddy strode from the kitchen. The kilt
straps had held, somehow, all morning, but now, grate-
fully, he realized he need suffer no longer, and accordingly he made his way back to the Stable House, took
off his finery and climbed into the most comfortable
clothes he owned.

He was just shrugging himself into his old tweed
jacket when he heard the approaching car. From his
bedroom window, he saw the dark blue Volvo approaching up the drive between the rhododendrons
and come to a halt at the edge of the grass in front of
the house. Roddy gave a cursory glance in the mirror,
smoothed down his ruffled hair with his hand, and
went out of the room. His old dog Barney hauled himself to his feet and followed. He had spent the morning shut up and alone, and was not going to risk being
left behind again. The two of them emerged from the
stable yard just as Oliver climbed out from behind the
driving wheel of the car. He saw Roddy and slammed
the car door shut behind him. Roddy went towards

him, feet crunching over the gravel, his hand outstretched in welcome.

"Oliver!"

Oliver smiled. He looked just the same, Roddy thought, with some satisfaction. He did not like people to change. At the television dinner Oliver had worn a velvet jacket and a flamboyant tie. He was now in faded corduroys and a huge Norwegian sweater, but otherwise he seemed just the same. Same coppery hair, same beard, same smile.

Oliver came towards him, and they met in the middle of the gravel. The very sight of him, tall and young and handsome, gave Roddy new heart.

"Hello, Roddy."

They shook hands, Roddy taking Oliver's hand in both his own, so pleased was he to see him.

"My dear fellow, how are you? How splendid you were able to make it. And right up to time, too. Did you have trouble finding us?"

"No trouble at all. We bought an Ordnance Survey map in Fort William and simply followed the red lines." He looked about him, at the house, the slope of the lawn, the grey waters of the loch, the hills beyond. "What a fantastic place."

"Yes, it's lovely, isn't it?" Side by side they regarded the view. "Not much of a day to see it on, though. I'll have to arrange some better weather for you."

"We don't mind about the weather. However cold it is, all Victoria seems to want to do is sit on beaches." This reminded Oliver of the other occupants of his car. He seemed to be about to do something about them, but Roddy stopped him.

"Look . . . just a minute, old boy. I think we should have a word first." Oliver looked at him. Roddy scratched the back of his neck, searching for the right words. "The thing is . . ." But there seemed no way of getting around it, so he brought it straight out. "My brother died at the beginning of the week.

Jock Dunbeath. His funeral was this morning. In Creagan."

Oliver was horrified. He stared at Roddy, taking this in, and then he said, "Oh, God," and there was everything in his voice; distress and sympathy and a sort of agonized embarrassment.

"My dear fellow, please don't feel badly about it. I wanted to tell you right away, so that you'd understand the situation."

"We came through Creagan. We saw all the shutters down, but we didn't know the reason."

"Well, you know how it is. People like to pay their respects in this part of the world, 'specially when it's a man like Jock."

"I'm so dreadfully sorry. But, when did this happen?"

"Monday. About midday. Just about this time. He was out with the dogs and he had a heart attack. We found him in the lea of one of the dikes."

"And you couldn't get in touch with me and tell us not to come, because you didn't know where I was. What a ghastly situation for you."

"No, I didn't know where you were, but even if I had, I wouldn't have got in touch with you. I've been looking forward to seeing you, and I should have been most disappointed if you hadn't come."

"We can't possibly stay."

"Of course you can stay. My brother is dead, but the funeral is over, and life must go on. The only thing is, I'd originally planned that you should sleep in the big house. But it struck me that without Jock there, it might be a little depressing for you, so if you don't mind rather close quarters, you'll be staying in the Stable House with me. Ellen, Jock's housekeeper, and Jess Guthrie from the farm have made up the beds and lit the fires, so everything's ready for you."

"Are you sure you wouldn't rather we just took ourselves off again?"

"My dear boy, it would make me miserable. I've been looking forward to a little young company. Don't get nearly enough of it these days . . ."

He glanced across at the car, and saw that the girl, perhaps tiring of sitting there while the two men talked, had got out of it, and now she and the little boy were making their way, hand in hand, down the slope of the grass towards the water's edge. She was dressed more or less as Oliver was dressed, in trousers and a thick sweater. She had tied a red and white cotton scarf around her head, and the red of the scarf was the same as the little boy's dungarees. In such a setting, they made a charming picture, investing the grey, brooding scene with color and a certain innocence.

"Come and meet them," said Oliver, and they began to walk slowly back towards the car.

"Just one thing more," said Roddy. "I'm taking it for granted that you're not married to this girl?"

"No, I'm not." Oliver's expression was amused. "Do you mind?"

The inference that Roddy Dunbeath's attitudes might well be out of date and out of touch made Roddy feel mildly indignant. "Heavens, no. I don't mind in the very least. Anyway, it's nothing to do with me, it's your affair entirely. There is just one point, though. It would be much better if the people who work at Benchoile believe you to be married. It sounds old-fashioned, I know, but people are old-fashioned up here, and I wouldn't want to offend them. I'm sure you understand."

"Yes, of course."

"Ellen, the housekeeper would probably have a heart attack and pass out on me if she knew the wicked truth, and God knows what would happen to Benchoile if that happened. She's been here forever, longer than most people can remember. She arrived in the first instance, fresh from some remote Highland croft, to look after my younger brother, and she's remained, immovable as a rock, ever since. You'll meet her, but don't expect a devoted, smiling, gentle old dear. Ellen is as tough as old boots and can be twice as unpleasant! So you see, it's quite important not to offend her."

"Yes, of course."

"Mr. and Mrs. Dobbs, then?"

"Mr. and Mrs. Dobbs," Oliver agreed.

Victoria, with Thomas's fat hand held firmly in her own, stood by the reedy margins of Loch Muie and struggled with a terrible conviction that she had come to a place where she had no business to be.

It is better to travel hopefully than to arrive. Arrival, it seemed, had brought nothing but a sense of desolation and disappointment. This was Benchoile. But the Benchoile that Victoria had imagined was the Benchoile seen through the eyes of the ten-year-old boy that Roddy Dunbeath had been. *The Eagle Years* was a saga of summertime, of blue skies and long golden evenings and hills purple with heather. An idyll that boore no relation to this windswept and foreboding scene. It seemed to Victoria unrecognizable. Where was the little rowing boat? Where was the waterfall where Roddy and his brothers had picnicked? Where the children, running barefoot?

The answer was simple. Gone forever. Shut away between the covers of a book.

This now, was Benchoile. So much sky, so much space, so quiet. Only the sough of the wind in pine branches and the lap of grey water on the shingle. The size and the silence of the hills was unnerving. They enclosed the glen, rose sheer from the opposite shore of the loch. Victoria's eyes followed their slope, upwards, past great bastions of rock and scree, over swelling shoulders dark with heather, to distant summits weiled in the scudding grey sky. Their very size, their watchfulness, had an obliterating effect. She felt shrunk, dwarfed, insignificant as an ant. Incapable of dealing with anything, least of all the sudden deterioration of her relationship with Oliver.

She tried to call it a silly quarrel, but knew that it was more than that, a breach both bitter and unexpected. That it had blown up at all was Victoria's own fault. She should have kept quiet about sending the stupid postcard to Mrs. Archer. But at the time it had seemed important, an issue worth fighting for. And now everything was spoiled, and not a word had either of them spoken since Oliver's last violent outburst. And perhaps that was Victoria's fault too. She should have stood up for herself, given threat for threat, and, if necessary, threatened blow for blow. Proved to Oliver that she had a will of her own instead of sitting mesmerized like a rabbit, and with her eyes so full of tears she couldn't even see the road ahead.

She felt overwhelmed. By the quarrel, by Benchoile, by a physical tiredness that made her ache, by the uncomfortable feeling that she had mislaid her own identity. Who am I? What am I doing in this outlandish place. How did I ever get here?"

"Victoria." She had not heard them approaching across the grass, and Oliver's voice startled her. "Victoria, this is Roddy Dunbeath."

She turned to face a man huge and shabby as a much-loved teddy bear. His clothes looked as though they had been thrown at him, his sparse grey hair blew in the wind, his features were lost in fat. But he was smiling at her. His blue eyes were warm with friendliness. Before them, Victoria's depression, her first fearful impressions of Benchoile, abated a little.

She said, "Hello." They shook hands. He looked down at Thomas. "And who's this?"

"This is Tom," She stooped and lifted him up to her shoulder. Tom's cheeks were intensely red, and he had mud on his mouth where he had been tasting pebbles.

"Hello, Tom. How old are you?"

"He's two," Oliver told him, "and you'll be delighted to hear that he scarcely ever utters a word."

Roddy considered this. "Well, he appears to be quite healthy, so I don't suppose you've got anything to worry about." He looked back at Victoria. "I'm afraid Benchoile isn't at its best today. There's too much cloud about."

There was an old black Labrador at his heels. Thomas caught sight of him, and wriggled, wanting to be put down so that he could go and pat the dog. Victoria set him back on his feet, and he and the dog looked at each other. Then Thomas touched the soft, grizzled muzzle

"What is he called?" asked Victoria.

"Barney. He's very old. Almost as old as I am."

"I thought you'd probably have a dog."

"Victoria," Oliver explained, "is one of your fans, Roddy." He sounded quite cheerful and ordinary again, and Victoria wondered if the quarrel that had blown up that morning was, for the time being, forgotten.

"How splendid," said Roddy. "Nothing I like better than having a fan about the place."

Victoria smiled. "I was looking for the waterfall."

"Even on a fine day you can't see it from here. It's hidden behind an outcrop. There's a little bay. Perhaps if the weather clears and I can find the key to the boathouse, we'll get over one day and you can see it for yourself." A gust of wind, with a cutting edge like a knife, keened down upon them. Victoria shivered and Roddy was galvanized into hostly action. "Now, come along, we'll all get pneumonia standing here. Let's get your cases out of the car and get you all settled in."

Again, it was like nothing that Victoria had imagined. For Roddy led them, not into the big house, but through the archway into the stableyard, and so on to what was obviously his own little house. The bedrooms were on the ground floor. "This is for you and Oliver," said Roddy, going ahead of them like a welltrained hotel porter. "And there's a dressing room off it, where I thought you could put the child; and here's the bathroom. It's all pretty cramped I'm afraid, but I hope you'll be comfortable."

"I think it's perfect." She set Tom down on the bed, and looked about her. There was a window facing out over the water, and a deep windowsill, upon which stood a little jug of snowdrops. She wondered if it was Roddy who had put them there.

"It's a funny sort of house," he told her. "The living room and the kitchen are upstairs, but I like it that way. Now, when you've unpacked and made yourselves comfortable, come up and we'll have a drink and something to eat. Does Thomas like soup?"

"He likes anything."

Roddy looked suitably amazed. "What an accommodating child," he remarked, and went off and left her.

Victoria sat on the edge of the bed, and lifted Thomas onto her knee and began to divest him of his little jacket. And all the time her eyes went around the room, loving it because it was so right, whitewashed and simply furnished, and yet containing all that any person could possibly need. It even had a fireplace, built across one corner of the room, in which a stack of peats was smoldering, and there was a basket containing more peat alongside the hearth, so that one could replenish it oneself, keep it going all night if need be. She thought of going to sleep by firelight, and it seemed, all at once, the most romantic thing in the world. Perhaps, she told herself cautiously, perhaps after all, everything was going to be all right.

Oliver appeared behind her, bearing the last of the suitcases. He put this down and shut the door behind him.

"Oliver . . ."

But, abruptly, he interrupted her. "Something ghastly's happened. Roddy's brother died at the beginning of the week. That was his funeral in Creagan this morning. I mean, that's why all the blinds were down."

Victoria stared at him, over the top of Thomas's head, in horrified disbelief. "But why didn't he let us know?"

"He couldn't. He didn't know where we were. And anyway, he swears he wanted us to come."

"He's just saying that."

"No, I don't think he is. In a way, I think we're probably the best thing that could happen to him. You know, give him something to think about. Anyway, we're here now. We can't go away again."

"But . . ."

"And there's another thing. We're Mr. and Mrs. Dobbs like in the hotel register. Apparently, there's a string of old retainers who'll all give notice if they know the terrible truth." He began nosing around, opening cupboards and doors, like a great, long cat making itself at home. "What a fantastic setup. Is this where Thomas is sleeping?"

"Yes. Oliver, perhaps we should only stay one night."

"What do you mean? Don't you like it here?"

"I love it, but . . ."

He came to drop a kiss on her open, protesting mouth, and Victoria was silenced. The quarrel still lay between them. She wondered if the kiss was meant as an apology, or whether she was going to have to be the first to say she was sorry. But before she was able to make up her mind about this, one way or the other, he had kissed her again, patted Thomas on the head, and left them. She heard him running upstairs, heard his voice mingling with Roddy's. She sighed, and lifted Thomas off the bed and took him to the bathroom.

It was midnight and very dark. Roddy Dunbeath, steeped in brandy, had taken a torch and whistled up his dog, and gone the rounds of the big house, to make sure, he explained to Oliver, that the doors and windows were all securely closed, and that old Ellen, up in her attic bedroom, was safe for the night.

Oliver wondered, safe from what? They had been introduced, formally, to Ellen during the course of the evening, and she had seemed to him not only older than God but just as formidable. Victoria had long since gone to bed. Thomas was sleeping. Oliver lit the cigar that Roddy had given him and took it out of doors.

The silence that greeted him was immense. The wind had dropped and there was scarcely a sound. His footsteps crunched as he went across the gravel, and then fell silent when he reached the grass. He could feel its cold dampness through the soles of his shoes. He reached the loch and began to walk along the edge of the water. The air was icy. His light clothes—the velvet jacket and the silk shirt—were no protection, and the cold washed over his body like a freezing shower. He reveled in the shock of it and felt refreshed and stimulated.

His eyes grew accustomed to the darkness. Slowly, the massive presence of the surrounding hills began to take shape. He saw the translucent shimmer of the loch. From the trees behind the house, an owl hooted. He came to the little jetty. Now, his footsteps sounded hollow on the wooden planking. At the end, he stopped, and threw the butt of the cigar into the water. It sizzled and then was dark.

The voices were there. The old woman. *It's not the way your father would have done it.* She had been living in his head for months, but she was Ellen Tarbat. And yet she was not Ellen from Sutherland. She was called Kate and she came from Yorkshire. *Your father didn't do things that way, not that way at all.* She was embittered, she was worn, she was indestructible. *He was always a man to pay his way. And proud. When I buried him, I did it with ham. Mrs. Hackworth buried her man, but she's that mean, she did it with nobbut buns.*

She was Kate, but she was Ellen too. This was the way it happened. Past and present, fantasy and reality, all spun together like a steel rope, so that he did not know where one ended and the other began. And this thing inside him would begin to grow, like some tumor, until it took over altogether, and he would become possessed by it, and by the people who fought to get out of the inside of his head; to get down on paper.

And for weeks, perhaps months, he would exist in a shambling vacuum, incapable of anything except the most basic and essential of bodily functions; like sleeping, and ambling around the corner to the pub, and buying cigarettes.

The anticipation of this state filled him with trembling excitement. Despite the cold, he found that the palms of his hands were sweaty. He turned and looked back at the dim bulk of the house. A light burned in the attic, and he imagined old Ellen pottering about, putting her teeth into a tumbler, saying her prayers, getting into bed. He saw her, lying, staring at the ceiling, her nose sticking up over the edge of the sheet, waiting for the fitful sleep of old age.

There were other lights. From Roddy's sitting room, from behind drawn curtains. From the bedroom below it where Victoria slept.

He made his way, slowly, back to the house.

She was asleep, but she woke when he came in and turned on the light by their bed. He sat beside her, and she turned on the pillow and yawned, and saw who it was and said his name. She wore a nightdress of thin white lawn, edged with lace, and her pale hair spread on the pillow like strands of primrose-colored silk.

He pulled off his tie and undid the top button of his shirt, and she said, "Where have you been?"

"Out."

"What time is it?"

He kicked off his shoes. "Late." He leaned across and took her head between his hands. Slowly, he began to kiss her.

He slept at last, but Victoria lay awake in his arms for an hour or more. The curtains were drawn back and the cold night air flowed in through the open window. In the hearth the peat fire burned steadily, and its flicker and glow were reflected in patterns of light on the low, white ceiling. The quarrel of the morning had been dissolved in love. Victoria was reassured. She lay there in the tranquil knowledge—as calming as a sedative—that nothing this perfect could possibly go wrong.

CHAPTER 10
Friday

She was suddenly, intensely, wide awake, disoriented, with no idea where she was meant to be. She saw the wide window, and beyond it, the sky—pale, pristine, cloudless. The outline of the hills was sharp as glass, the topmost peaks touched by the first rays of the rising sun. Benchoile. Benchoile, possibly at its best. It looked as if it were going to be a beautiful day. Perhaps she could take Thomas to the beach.

Thomas. Thomas's grandmother. Mrs. Archer. Today she was going to write to Mrs. Archer.

Just like that, while she slept, her mind, perhaps realizing that Victoria was capable of dithering about this problem, indefinitely, had apparently made itself up. The letter would be written this morning, posted at the earliest opportunity. She would find out the address by going to the post office in Creagan and asking for the relevant telephone directory. Woodbridge was in Hampshire. It was only a small place. There would not be many Archers living in such a small place.

The form of the letter began to frame itself. *I am writing to let you know that Thomas is well and very happy.*

And Thomas's father? Beside her Oliver slumbered soundlessly, his head turned away from her, his long arm stretched outside the covers, the palm of his hand turned up, the fingers curled and relaxed. Victoria raised herself on her elbow and looked down at his

untroubled face. He seemed, in that moment, defense-
less and vulnerable. He loved her. Love and fear could
not share the same bed. She was not afraid of Oliver.

And anyway—cautiously she lay back on her pillows—Oliver need never know. *Oliver did not want
me to write to you,* she would put, *so perhaps it would
be better if you do not acknowledge this letter or try
to get in touch.*

She could not think why this harmless deception
had not occurred to her before. Mrs. Archer would understand. All she would want was reassurance about
her missing grandson. And Victoria would promise, at
the end of the letter, to write again, to keep in touch.
It would seem that it was going to be quite a corre-
spondence.

From the next room, from beyond the closed door,
came sounds of Thomas stirring. A strange sound,
"Meh, meh, meh," disturbed the morning quiet.
Thomas, singing. She imagined him sucking his
thumb, thumping Piglet against the wall by his bed.
After a little the singing stopped, there were scuffling
sounds, the door opened and Thomas appeared.

Victoria pretended to be asleep, lay with her eyes
closed. Thomas climbed up onto the bed and lay on
top of her, forcing her eyelids open with a stubby
thumb. She saw his face, only inches from her own, the
blue eyes alarmingly close, his nose nearly touching
her own.

She had not yet written to his grandmother, but today she was going to, and the knowledge freed Victoria
of guilt and filled her with tenderness towards
Thomas. She put her arms around him and hugged
him, and he laid his cheek on hers and thoughtfully
kicked her in the stomach. After a little, when it became obvious that he was not going to be still for a
moment longer, she got out of bed. Oliver still slept,
undisturbed. She took Thomas into his room and
dressed him, and then dressed herself. They left Oliver

sleeping, and hand-in-hand climbed the stairs to forage for breakfast.

The domestic arrangements at Benchoile appeared to be fluid—the two establishments, the big house and the Stable House running, as it were, in harness. Yesterday they had lunched on soup and cheese in Roddy's cheerful, littered living room, eating off a table drawn up to the window, the meal as informal as a picnic. Dinner, on the other hand, was a quite different affair, served in the immense dining room of the big house. By some unspoken agreement, they had all changed for this occasion. Oliver had put on his velvet jacket, and Roddy wore a straining doublet made of tartan, with a cummerbund filling the gap between his shirt and the dark trousers, which would no longer do up around his waist. A fire had burned in the grate, there were candles in the silver candlesticks, and tall, dim portraits of varied Dunbeaths looked down upon them from the paneled walls. Victoria had wondered which was Jock, but didn't like to ask. There was something vaguely unnerving about the empty chair at the head of the table. She felt as though they were all intruding, as though they had walked into another man's house, without permission, and at any moment the owner was going to walk in and find them there.

But she, apparently, was the only one of them troubled by this uneasy guilt. Oliver and Roddy talked incessantly, of their world of writers, publishers, producers, about which Victoria knew nothing. The conversation flowed, well-oiled by an abundance of wine. And even the old woman, Ellen, had seemed to see nothing amiss in such good spirits on the very night of the laird's funeral. To and fro she trod in her worn-down shoes, her best apron over her black dress, handing the heavy ashets through the hatch that led to the kitchen, and taking away the used plates. Victoria had made signs that she would like to help, but Roddy had stopped her. "Jess Guthrie's in the kitchen, giving Ellen a hand. She'll be mortally offended if you so much as rise from your chair," he had told Victoria when Ellen was out of earshot, and so she sat, against all her better instincts, and let herself be waited on with the others.

At one point during the course of the meal Ellen had taken herself off for ten minutes or more. When she returned with the coffee tray, she had announced, without preamble, that the wee boy was sleeping like an angel, and Victoria realized that she had made the journey down the long stone passages and across the stable yard, to check on Thomas, and was touched.

"I was just going to look at him myself," she told Ellen, but Ellen's mouth had bunched up, as though Victoria had said something indecent. "And why should you be getting up from your dinner, when there's me here to see to the child?" Victoria felt reprimanded.

Now, the following morning, she struggled with the inconsistencies of another person's kitchen, but, by the lengthy expedient of opening one door after another, she ran to earth eggs, bread, a jug of milk. Thomas was no help at all, and always seemed to be under her feet. She found suitable plates and mugs, knives and forks. Some butter and a jar of instant coffee. She laid the small plastic-topped table, set Thomas up on a chair, tied a tea towel around his neck, took the top off his egg. He settled down, silently, to demolish it.

Victoria made herself a cup of coffee and pulled up a chair to face him. She said, "Would you like to go to the beach today?"

Thomas stopped eating and looked at her, the egg yolk running down his chin. She wiped it away. As she did this the door that led into the house from the stable-yard opened and shut. Footsteps came slowly up the stairs. The next moment Ellen appeared at the open kitchen door.

"Good morning," said Victoria.

"Yes, and you're up and about already. You're an early starter, Mrs. Dobbs."

"Thomas woke me."

"I came over to see if you'd like me to give him his breakfast, but I see you've already seen to that yourself."

Her manner was disconcerting, because you could never tell by her voice whether you were doing the right thing or not. And it was no help looking at her face, because her expression was one of constant disapproval, the faded eyes cold and beady and her mouth pursed as though someone had run a string around it and then pulled it tight. Her hair was thin and white, dragged back from her temples and screwed into a tight little bun. Beneath it her scalp gleamed pinkly. Her figure seemed to have shrunk with age, so that all her clothes—her ageless and seemly clothes—appeared to be a size too big. Only her hands were large and capable, red with scrubbing, the joints swollen and twisted like old tree roots. She stood with these folded across her stomach, over the flowered apron, and looked as though, in her long life, she had never once stopped working. Victoria wondered how old she was.

She said, tentatively, "Perhaps you'd like a cup of coffee?"

"I never touch the stuff. It doesn't agree with me at all."

"A cup of tea, then?"

"No, no. I've had my tea."

"Well, why don't you sit down? Take the weight off your feet?"

For a moment, she thought that even this mild overture of friendliness was going to be rejected, but Ellen, perhaps seduced by Tom's unblinking stare, reached for a chair, and settled herself at the head of the table.

"Eat up your egg, then," she said to Thomas, and then to Victoria, "He's a beautiful child." Her Highland voice turned this into, "He's a peautiful chilt."

"Are you fond of children?"

"Oh, yes, and there used to be so many of them at Benchoile, all over the place." She had come, it was obvious, to see Thomas and have a gossip. Victoria waited, and inevitably the old voice rambled on. "I came here to look after Charlie when he was a baby. Charlie was the youngest of the boys. I looked after the others as well, but I had Charlie all to myself. Charlie's in America now, you know. He married an American lady." Casually, as though they could not help themselves, her hands went out to spread Thomas's toast with butter, to cut the toast into fingers for him.

Victoria said, "I feel so badly, us arriving to stay so soon after . . . I mean, we didn't know, you see . . ."

She stopped, lost in confusion and wishing that she had never started, but Ellen was quite unperturbed.

"You mean, the laird dying so suddenly like that, and the funeral only yesterday?"

"Well, yes."

"It was a beautiful funeral. All the grand people were there."

"I'm sure."

"Mind, he was a lonely man. He had no children of his own, you see. It was a great sorrow to Mrs. Jock that she was never able to have any babies. 'There you are Ellen,' she used to say, 'and there's the empty nursery upstairs, waiting for the babies, and it doesn't look as though there's going to be a single one.' And, indeed, there wasn't."

She put another finger of toast into Thomas's hand.

"What happened to her?"

"She died. Five years ago or more. She died. She was a beautiful lady. Always laughing." She told Thomas, "Yes, yes, you are eating a splendid breakfast."

"Didn't your baby . . . didn't Charlie ever have any children?"

"Oh, yes, Charlie had a boy, and what a bright little lad he was. They used to come over for the summers, all three of them, and what good times those were. Picnics up the hill or on the beach at Creagan. "I've too much to do in the house to come for picnics," I used to tell him, but John would say, 'But Ellen, you must come too, it'll not be a proper picnic without you.' "

"He was called John."

"Yes, he was named for the Colonel."

"You must have missed him when he had to go back to America."

"Oh, the place seemed empty after they had gone. Like a tomb."

Victoria, watching Ellen, suddenly liked her very much. She stopped, feeling intimidated or even shy. She said, "I knew a little bit about Benchoile before I got here yesterday, because I'd read all Roddy's books."

"Those were the best times of all, when the boys were young. Before that war."

"He must have been a funny little boy with all his strange pets."

Ellen clicked her tongue and held up her hands in horror at the memory. "I sometimes thought he'd be the death of me. Just a wee devil. He looked like an angel, mind, but you never knew what Roddy would be up to next. And when it came to washing his clothes, as likely as not the pockets would be filled with mealy worms."

Victoria laughed. "That reminds me," she said, "I wonder if there's somewhere I could do some washing. We've been traveling for four days and I haven't been able to wash anything, and soon we're all going to run out of clothes."

"You can put them in the washing machine."

"If I brought it all over to the big house after breakfast, perhaps you could show me where the washing machine is, and how to use it."

"Now, you don't worry about that. I'll see to the washing. You don't want to spend your holiday doing washing. And . . ." she added, with cunning innocence ". . . if you should want to be away on a wee outing with your husband, I could keep an eye on the child for you."

She was obviously longing to get her hands on Thomas, to get him to herself. Victoria thought of the letter she was going to write. "I ought to do some shopping, in that case. We seem to have run out of toothpaste, and Oliver's bound to want cigarettes. If I took our car to Creagan this morning, would you really look after Thomas for me? He doesn't like shopping very much."

"And why should he like shopping? It's a dull occupation for a little man." She leaned forward, nodding her head at Thomas as though already they had some sort of a conspiracy going between them. "You'll stay with Ellen, won't you pet? You'll help Ellen with the washing?"

Thomas stared at the small brown winkled face bobbing up and down so close to his own. Victoria watched for his reaction to this in some anxiety. It would be embarrassing if he screamed and hurt Ellen's feelings. But Thomas and Ellen recognized each other. They were years apart in age, but they both belonged to the same world. Thomas had finished his breakfast. He got off his chair and rescued Piglet from the floor by the refrigerator and took him to show Ellen.

She took the pig and bounced him up and down on the table as though he were dancing.

> Kitty Birdy had a pig
> She could do an Irish jig

sang Ellen in her cracked old voice. Thomas smiled. He laid his hand on her knee, and her own gnarled hand came down to close on the fat fingers.

It was amazing how simple, how straightforward, things became as soon as you had reached a decision. Problems ironed themselves out, difficulties dissolved. Ellen bore Thomas and the washing away, thus relieving Victoria, in a single stroke, of two of her most pressing commitments. Roddy and Oliver, probably sleeping off the brandy they had consumed the evening before, had still not appeared. Victoria, in seach of writing paper, went into Roddy's living room and found the curtains still undrawn and the atmosphere thick with stale cigar smoke. She drew the curtains and opened the windows and emptied the ashtrays into the remains of last nights fire.

In the letter rack on Roddy's littered desk, she found writing paper both plain and headed. She hesitated for a moment, debating which to use. If she used the plain paper, and wrote no address, then Mrs. Archer would still not know where to find them. But surely this smacked a little of secrecy, as though she and Oliver really had something to hide.

Besides, the headed paper, thickly embossed, had a certain opulence about it, which would in itself be reassuring. "BENCHOILE, CREAGAN, SUTHERLAND." She imagined Mrs. Archer being impressed by the very simplicity of this. So she took a sheet of the headed paper, and found an envelope lined with dark blue tissue. She found, in a tarnished silver mug, a ball-point pen. It was as though some person had arranged it all, ready for her, making it even easier.

Dear Mrs. Archer,

I am writing to let you know that Thomas is well

and very happy. Ever since we left London, he has been very good, hardly cried at all, and has never woken up at nights. He is eating well, too.

She paused, chewing the pen, debating whether she should tell Mrs. Archer that not once had Thomas asked for his grandmother. She finally decided that this would not be tactful.

As you can see we are now in Scotland and the sun is shining, so maybe we will be able to take Thomas to the beach.

She paused again, and then went on to the final and most tricky bit of all.

Oliver does not know I am writing to you. We did discuss it, but he was very against the idea. So perhaps it would be better if you do not acknowledge this letter or try to get in touch. I will write later again and let you know how Thomas is.

With best wishes,

Yours sincerely,

Victoria . . . Victoria what? She was not Victoria Dobbs and she no longer felt like Victoria Bradshaw. In the end she wrote just her Christian name and left it at that. She put the letter in its envelope and put the envelope into her cardigan pocket. Downstairs, she crept into the bedroom and collected her handbag with her money in the wallet. Oliver hadn't moved. She let herself out again, and got into the Volvo, and drove herself to Creagan.

Roddy Dunbeath, wearing a large blue-and-white striped apron which made him look like a successful pork butcher, stood at the counter in his little kitchen, chopped vegetables for the lunchtime pot of soup, and tried, at the same time, to disregard the fact that he was suffering from a hangover. At twelve o'clock he was going to pour himself a sustaining, medicinal horse's neck, but it was only now a quarter to twelve, and so he was filling in the time—and so managing to resist jumping the gun—with a little soothing culinary activity. He liked cooking. Was, in fact, an excellent chef, and it made it all the more enjoyable having a little house party to cook for besides himself.

The house party in question, whether by private arrangement, or by chance, was happily living up to Benchoile traditions, and had taken itself off. By the time Roddy had prized himself out of bed this morning, the girl Victoria and the child had disappeared. Roddy was thankful for this. He had a horror of visitors hanging about and looking bored, and he needed peace and quiet in which to attend to his small domestic duties.

But he went through to the big house to make a few polite inquiries, and was told by Ellen that Victoria had taken the Volvo and gone to Creagan. The little boy was with Ellen, helping her to hang washing on the line, and playing with the basket full of pegs.

Oliver, when he finally put in an appearance, seemed unperturbed by all this independent activity on the part of his family. In fact, thought Roddy, if anything he appeared relieved to be shed of them for an hour or two. Together, he and Roddy had eaten an enormous breakfast, and together had hatched a plan to drive, that afternoon, up to Wick. There, a friend of Roddy's, tiring of the rat race in the south, and the endless commuting, had started a small printing business, specializing in limited editions of beautifully hand-bound books. Roddy, interested in anything that smacked of genuine craftsmanship, had been meaning for some time to go and see the presses working, and to be shown around the bindery, and Oliver, when the idea was put to him, was equally enthusiastic.

"What about Victoria?" Roddy asked.

"Oh, she'll probably want to do something with Thomas."

The telephone call to Wick was made, and the visit arranged. Whereupon Oliver, after a bit of restless prowling, admitted that he wanted to do some work, so Roddy lent him a scribbling pad and sent him off to the library in the big house, where, with a bit of luck, Oliver had spent the morning, undisturbed.

In the meantime Roddy, left to himself, had lit a roaring fire, written a couple of letters, and was now making soup. The air was filled with the crisp, sharp smell of celery, sunlight streamed through the window, Vivaldi burbled from his transistor. The telephone started to ring.

Roddy swore, and went on cutting celery, as though the telephone would somehow answer itself. But of course it didn't, so he laid down the knife and wiped his hands on a tea towel and went through to the living room.

"Roddy Dunbeath."

"Roddy. It's John Dunbeath."

Roddy sat down. Luckily there was a chair behind him. He could not have been more astonished. "I thought you were in Bahrain."

"No, I got back yesterday morning. Roddy I'm so dreadfully sorry about Jock. And that I couldn't make the funeral."

"My dear boy, we quite understood. Good of you to send the cable. Where are you calling from? London? You sound as though you're in the next room."

"No, I'm not in London. I'm in Inverness."

"*Inverness?*" Roddy's thought processes, blunted by last night's cognac, were not working in what you would call top gear. "How you do get around. When did you get to Inverness?"

"I caught the Highlander last night, I was here this morning. I've spent the morning with Robert McKenzie. He said it would be OK if I rang you . . . if I came to Benchoile."

"But of course. How *splendid*. Stay for a few days. Stay for the weekend. When can we expect you?"

"Well, this afternoon sometime. I'm hiring a car. Would it be all right if I came this afternoon?"

"Marvelous . . ." Roddy started to say, and then remembered the complications. He struck his forehead with the heel of his hand, a theatrical gesture of recall, totally wasted when there was no person to observe it. "Oh, damn, except that I won't be here. I've arranged to go up to Wick. I've got a chap staying and we're going to go there and look at a printing press. But that doesn't matter. We'll be back sometime, and Ellen'll be here."

"How is Ellen?"

"Indestructible. Puts us all in the shade. I'll tell her you're coming. I'll tell her to expect you."

"I hope I'm not putting you out."

Roddy remembered that he had always been an intensely well-mannered person. "Not putting us out at all." He added, because there seemed no point in not doing so, "Besides, it's your house now. You don't have to ask yourself to stay."

There was a tiny silence. Then, "Yes," said John and he sounded thoughtful. "Yes. That's one of the things I want to talk to you about. There's an awful lot to discuss."

"We'll have a good old chin-wag after dinner," Roddy promised him. "Anyway, see you later. I'm really looking forward to it. It's been too long, John."

"Yeah," said John, suddenly sounding very American. "I guess it's been too long."

Victoria returned ten minutes or so later, just as Roddy had finished the soup, tidied the kitchen, and poured himself the longed-for brandy and ginger ale. He was sitting by the window, watching a flock of black-and-white shelduck which had settled down to feed by the edge of the loch, when he heard the sound of the returning car. A moment or so later the downstairs front door opened and shut.

He called, "Victoria!"

"Hello."

"I'm up here. All on my own. Come and join me."

Obediently, she came running up the stairs, and saw him at the far end of the room, sitting in solitary state, with only Barney for company.

"Where is everybody?" she asked, coming over to join him.

"Oliver's in the big house, closeted in the library and working. And Thomas is still with Ellen."

"Perhaps I should go and get him."

"Don't be ridiculous. He's perfectly all right. Sit down. Have a drink."

"No, I don't want a drink." But she sat beside him, pulling off her scarf. He thought, all at once, how pretty she was. Yesterday, when he had first seen her, he had not thought her pretty at all. She had seemed to him both shy and colorless; dull, even. At dinner she had scarcely said a word, and Roddy had been hard put to understand what Oliver saw in her. But this morning, she was a different person. Shining eyes, pink cheeks, a mouth all smiles. Now, Roddy found himself wondering why Oliver didn't marry the girl. Perhaps it had something to do with her background. How old was she? Where had he met her? How long had they been together. She looked ridiculously youthful to be the mother of a two-year-old boy, but then young people these days seemed to plunge into relationships when they were scarcely out of school, committing themselves to domesticity in a manner that the young Roddy would have found intensely frustrating. She had, he noticed, beautiful teeth.

He said, "You're looking very bright eyed and bushy tailed. Something good must have happened in Creagan."

"It's just that it's such a beautiful morning. You can see for miles, and everything's all sparkly and bright. I didn't mean to be so long. I only went to buy some toothpaste and cigarettes and things, but Ellen said she didn't mind looking after Thomas, and Creagan is so pretty, I just stayed there and looked around, and I went into the church, and into that house they call The Deanery, but it's a craft shop now."

Her enthusiasm was endearing. "Did you buy anything?"

"No, but I might go back and buy something. They've got beautiful Shetland sweaters. And then I went and looked at the beach. I can't wait to take Thomas. You'd have thought it would be cold, but it wasn't. The sun was quite warm."

"I'm glad you had a good morning."

"Yes." She met his eyes, and some of the brightness went out of her face. "I somehow didn't get the chance to say anything last night, but . . . Well, Oliver told me about your brother, and I was so sorry. I just feel so awful about us all being here."

"You mustn't feel awful. You're good for me."

"It's just something else for you to worry about. I've been feeling guilty all morning because I should have been helping you or Ellen, instead of simply abandoning Thomas."

"Do you good to get away from Thomas for an hour or so."

"Well, as a matter of fact, it was rather nice." They smiled, in complete understanding. "Did you say that Oliver was working?"

"That's what he said."

Victoria made a little face. "I didn't realize that he wanted to work."

"Probably wants to get some idea down on paper

before it goes out of his head." He remembered the projected trip to Wick that afternoon and told her about it. "We'll take you with us if you like, but Oliver thought you'd want to do something with Tom."

"I'd rather stay here."

"In that case, you can do something for me. There's a young man arriving some time during the afternoon. He's going to stay for a day or two. So if we're not back, perhaps you could look after him, pour the tea, generally make him welcome."

"Yes of course. But where's he going to sleep? We seem to have filled your house."

"He's going into the big house. I've already had a word with Ellen and she's alight with excitement; linen sheets on the bed, everything scoured and polished."

"I'd have thought she already had enough to do without more visitors arriving."

"Ah, but you see, this young man is Ellen's precious baby. In fact, he's my nephew John Dunbeath."

Victoria stared at Roddy in astonishment. "John Dunbeath. You mean your brother Charlie's boy? Ellen told me about him this morning at breakfast. But I thought he was in America."

"No, he's not. In fact, he's just telephoned me from Inverness."

"Ellen must be over the moon."

"She is. Not just because he's coming to stay, but because John is the new laird of Benchoile. My brother Jock has left Benchoile to John."

Victoria was confused. "But I thought you were the new laird."

"Heaven forbid."

She smiled. "But you'd be such a wonderful laird."

"You're very kind, but I'd be a useless one. I'm too old, too set in my evil ways. Better a new young broom to sweep us all clean. When I told Ellen the news a

gleam came into her beady eye, but whether it was a
tear or a glitter of triumph I wouldn't be able to say."

"Don't be horrid about her. I like her."

"I like her too, but one day she'll drive me into a
nuthouse." He sighed and looked down at his empty
glass. "Are you *sure* you wouldn't like a drink?"

"Quite sure."

"In that case, be a good girl and go and run Oliver
and that little boy of yours to earth, and tell them
lunch will be ready in about ten minutes." He heaved
himself off the window seat and went to throw more
logs onto his dying fire. As usual they sparked vio-
lently, and as usual Roddy tramped the glowing embers to death on his long-suffering hearthrug.

Victoria went to do as he had asked. At the top of
the stairs, she paused.

"Where did you say I'd find Oliver?"

"In the library."

She left him, clattering down the open treads like an
eager child. Alone, Roddy sighed again. He debated,
and finally succumbed. He poured himself another
drink, and took it through to the kitchen where he
inspected his fragrant soup.

Victoria put her head around the door. "Oliver."

He was not writing. He sat at the desk in the window, with his arms hanging loose and his legs outstretched, but he was not actually writing.

"Oliver."

He turned his head. It took a second or two for him
to recognize her. Then his blank eyes came to life. He
smiled, as though she had just woken him up. He put
up a hand to rub the back of his neck.

"Hi."

"It's lunchtime."

She closed the door behind her. He held out a long
arm and she went over to him, and he drew her close,
burying his face in her thick sweater; nuzzling, like a

child, into its warmth. Memories of last night filled
her with sweetness. She laid her chin on the top of his
head, and looked down at the desk and sheets of paper, covered with scribbles and doodles and Oliver's
narrow, tight writing.

She said again, "It's time for lunch."

"It can't be. I've only been here five minutes."

"Roddy says you've been here since breakfast."

"Where did you get to?"

"Creagan."

"What were you doing there?"

"Shopping." He put her away from him, and looked
up into her face. Coolly, Victoria met his eyes, and repeated herself. "Shopping. I bought you cigarettes. I
thought you'd soon be running out."

"Marvelous girl."

"And there's someone else coming to stay; arriving
this afternoon."

"Who's that?"

"John Dunbeath. Roddy's nephew." She put on a
spurious Highland accent. "The new young laird of
Benchoile."

"Good God," said Oliver. "It's like living in a novel
by Walter Scott."

She laughed. "Do you want some lunch?"

"Yes." He pushed the scribbling pad away from
him, and stiffly, stood up. He stretched and yawned.
"But I want a drink first."

"Roddy's longing for someone to have a drink with
him."

"Are you coming too?"

"I'll find Thomas first." They moved towards the
door. "Ellen's had him all morning."

"Bully for Ellen," said Oliver.

John Dunbeath, driving the hired Ford, came
through Eventon, and the road swung east. To his
right lay the Cromarty Firth beneath the cloudless

winter sky; blue as the Mediterranean and in all the extravagance of a flood tide. Beyond it, the peaceful hills of the Black Isle drew a skyline sharp as a razor in the clear, glittering light. Rich farmland swept down to the edge of the water, sheep grazed on the upper slopes, and scarlet tractors, minimized to toys by the distance, were out ploughing the rich dark earth.

The dazzling brightness of the day came as an unexpected bonus. John had left London cloaked in grey rain, and boarded the Highlander in a state of unrelieved exhaustion. Weary from forty-eight hours of ceaseless activity, suffering from jet lag, and still in a mild state of shock occasioned by Jock Dunbeath's unthought of bequest, he had drunk two enormous whiskies, and fallen into a sleep so deep that the sleeping car attendant had had to come and shake him awake, and inform him that the train had actually arrived at Inverness Station five minutes before.

Now, on his way to Benchoile, and with nothing but necessarily unhappy news to impart to all who lived there, he could not get rid of the feeling that he was going on holiday.

Part of this was due to association of ideas. The further he got from London and the closer to Benchoile, the clearer and more vivid became the memories. He knew this road. The fact that he had not driven it for ten years did not seem to matter at all. He felt that it could have been yesterday, and the only thing amiss was the fact that his father was not beside him, cheerful with anticipation, and anxious for John not to miss a single familiar landmark.

The road forked. He left the Cromarty Firth behind him and climbed up and over Struie and down to the further magnificence of the Dornoch Firth. He saw the wooded slopes on the distant shore, and behind these the snow-capped ramparts of the hills of Sutherland. Far to the east lay the open sea, still and blue as a day in summer. He rolled down the window of the

car and caught the smells, damp and evocative, of moss
and peat, and the sharp tang of the sea wrack washed
up on the shoreline far below him. The road sloped
away, and the Ford idled its way down the smoothly
cambered curves.

Forty minutes later, he was through Creagan. He
began to slow down in anticipation of the turning to
Benchoile. He came upon it and left the main road,
and now all was familiar in quite a different way. For
he was back on Benchoile land. Here was the path
that he had taken one grey day with his father and
Davey Guthrie, that led over the distant summit of the
hill and down into the desolate glen of Loch Feosaig.
There they had fished, and late in the evening, Jock
had driven around by the road to collect them and
bring them home.

Below him purled the river, and he passed the spot
where he had once stood for two hours or more, fighting a salmon. The first line of grouse butts swung into
view; the Guthries' farmhouse. The trodden garden
was cheerfully bannered with washing, and the teth-
ered sheepdogs raged at the passing car.

He rounded the final bend of the road. Before him
lay the long sweep of Loch Muie, and at the end of it,
slumbering, solitary in the late afternoon sunshine, the
old grey house.

This was the worst of all, but his heart was hard-
ened and his mind made up. *I shall sell it*, he had told
Robert McKenzie this morning, because, from the moment he had read the lawyer's letter, he had known
that there was nothing else that he could possibly do.

Whether she had been watching for the car or not,
John had no idea, but Ellen Tarbat appeared almost
instantly. He had only time to open the boot of the
Ford and take out his suitcase before she was there,
coming out of the front door, down the steps towards
him. A little tottery about the legs, smaller than he
remembered her, strands of white hair escaping from

her bun, her red, knotted old hands flung wide in welcome.

"Well, well, and you are here. And what a delight to see you again after all these years."

He laid down his suitcase and went to embrace her. He had to bend almost double to receive her kiss and her frailness, her lack of substance, were unnerving. He felt that he should urge her indoors before she was caught up by a breath of wind and blown away. And yet she had pounced on his suitcase and had started to try to lug it indoors before he could stop her, and he had to forcibly wrest it from her grasp before she would let it go.

"What do you think you're doing? I'll carry that."

"Well, let's get in, away from the cold."

She led the way back up the steps and into the house, and he followed her and she closed the big doors carefully behind her. He walked into the big hall and was assailed by a smell made up of peat smoke and pipe smoke and floor polish and leather. Blindfolded, or drunk, or dying, he would have known by that smell that he was back at Benchoile.

"And did you have a good journey? What a surprise when Roddy told me this morning that you were coming. I thought you were away with all those Arabs."

"Where's Roddy?"

"He and Mr. Dobbs have gone to Wick. But he'll be back this evening."

"Is he all right?"

"He seems to be bearing up very well. It was a terrible thing your uncle dying, and such a shock to us all . . ." She had begun to lead the way upstairs, very slowly, one hand on the bannister. ". . . but I had a premonition. When he did not come in for his lunch, I was certain that something had happened. As, indeed, it had."

"Perhaps it was a good way for him to go."

"Yes, yes, you are right. Out on a walk, with his

dogs. Enjoying himself. But it is a terrible thing for the folk who are left behind."

She had reached the turn of the stair. She paused, to sigh, to draw fresh breath for the next flight. John shifted his suitcase from one hand to the other. They went on up.

"And now you have come to Benchoile. We wondered, Jess and I, what would happen with the colonel dying so suddenly, but it didn't seem very fitting to start enquiring. So when Roddy came to tell me this morning, you can imagine my delight. 'Why,' I said to him, 'that is the right person for Benchoile. Charlie's boy! There was never anybody like Charlie.' "

He did not want to continue this line of conversation. He changed the subject firmly. "And how about yourself, Ellen? How have you been keeping?"

"I am not getting any younger, but I manage to keep busy."

Knowing the size of the house, he wondered how she would manage to do anything else. They had now, at last, reached the landing. John wondered where he was sleeping. He had a ghastly suspicion that Ellen might have put him in his uncle's bedroom; it was just the sort of horror she would be capable of springing on him, and he was thankful when she led him towards the best spare bedroom where, before, his father had stayed. She opened the door to a flood of sunlight and a gust of cold, fresh air. "Oh," said Ellen, and went to close the windows, and John, following her into the room, saw the high, wide beds with their white starched cotton covers, the dressing table with the curly framed mirror, the velvet-covered chaise longue. Even the blast of fresh air could not dispel the smell of polish and carbolic. Ellen, it was obvious, had been busy.

"You won't find anything changed." Having closed the windows Ellen pottered about, straightening a starched linen mat, opening the immense wardrobe to

check on coat hangers, and letting out a wave of camphor. John laid down his suitcase on the luggage rack
at the foot of one of the beds, and went to the window.
The sun was beginning to slip out of the sky and a
rosy flush stained the hilltops. The mown grass of the
lawn spread as far as a shrubbery, and beyond this to a
copse of silver birch, and as he stood there, two figures
appeared through these trees, making their way slowly
towards the house. A girl, and a little boy. Behind
them, looking more exhausted than they, an old black
Labrador. "And the bathroom's just through that
door, I've put clean towels out, and . . ."

"Ellen. Who's that?"

Ellen joined him at the window, peering with her
old eyes.

"That is Mrs. Dobbs and her little boy Thomas. The
family is staying with Roddy."

They had emerged from the trees and were now out
in the open. The child, tagging behind his mother,
suddenly spied the water, and began to make for the
loch's edge. The girl hesitated, and then resignedly,
followed him.

"I thought that you and she could have tea together
in the library, and Thomas can have his tea with me."
She went on, tempting him, "There's a batch of scones
in the oven and heather honey on the tray." When
John neither spoke, nor turned from the window, Ellen was a little put-out. After all, she had opened the
heather honey especially for him. "I've put towels on
the rail, so that you can wash your hands," she reminded him, with some asperity.

"Yes. Sure." He sounded abstracted. Ellen left him.
He heard her slow descent of the staircase. The girl
and the child seemed to be having a small argument.
Finally, she stopped and picked him up and started to
carry him up towards the house.

John left the window and went out of the room and
downstairs, and out of the front door. They saw him

at once, and the girl, perhaps startled by his sudden appearance, stood still. He crossed the gravel and started down the slope of the lawn. He could not tell the exact moment of her recognition. He only knew that he had recognized her instantly, as soon as she appeared through the trees.

She wore jeans and a brilliant green sweater with suede patches on the shoulders. Her face, and the child's face, so close, observed his approach. The two pairs of wide blue eyes were ridiculously alike. There were freckles on her nose that had not been there before.

Mrs. Dobbs. With, doubtless, the child who had been making such a hullaballoo the night John drove her home. Mrs. Dobbs.

He said, "Hello, Victoria."

She said, "Hello."

Now, there were four of them around the dinner table, and the empty chair at its head was no longer empty.

Victoria wore a caftan of soft blue wool, the neck and the edges of the sleeves threaded with gold. She had, for the evening, put up her hair, but the arrangement seemed to John Dunbeath to have been ineptly contrived. It trailed one or two pale strands of hair, and served, instead of making her look sophisticated, only to enhance her air of extreme youth. The exposed back of her long neck seemed, all at once, as vulnerable as a child's. Her eyes were darkened, her beautiful mouth very pale. The shut-away, secret expression was still there. For some reason, this pleased John. It came with some satisfaction to realize that if he had not been able to break down the barrier, then neither had Oliver Dobbs.

"They're not married," Roddy had told him over a drink before dinner, when they were waiting for the

Dobbses to appear. "Don't ask me why. She seems a charming little thing."

Charming, and reserved. Perhaps in bed, in love, those defenses came down. His eyes moved from Victoria to Oliver, and he was annoyed to discover that from these pretty images his instincts shied like a nervous horse. Firmly, he brought his attention back to what Roddy was saying.

". . . the great thing is to keep investing capital in the land. Not only money, but resources and time. The aim is to make one good blade of grass grow where nothing grew before; to keep up employment for the local people; to stop the endless drift of the country population to the big cities."

This was Roddy Dunbeath, revealing a totally unexpected side to his character. Victoria, helping herself to an orange from the bowl in the middle of the table, wondered how many people had heard him expound thus on a subject that was obviously close to his heart. For he spoke with the authority of a man who had lived in Scotland all his life, who recognized its problems, and was prepared to argue to the hilt against any easy solution that he believed to be inadequate or impractical. People seemed to lie at the root of it all. Everything came back to people. Without people there could be no sort of community. Without communities there could be no sort of future, no sort of life.

"How about forestry?" asked John Dunbeath.

"It depends how you go about it. James Dochart, who farms Glen Tolsta, planted a stretch of hill with woodland, maybe four hundred acres . . ."

She began to peel the orange. He had been at Benchoile for about five hours. She had had five hours in which to get over the shock of his sudden appearance, but she still felt bewildered. That the young American she had met in London, and John Dunbeath, nephew to Roddy and only son of Ellen's beloved Charlie, should be one and the same person, still seemed impossible; unacceptable.

He sat now, at the end of the softly candle-lit table, relaxed and attentive, his eyes on Roddy, his expression somber. He wore a dark suit and a very white shirt. His hand, on the table, slowly turned his glass of port. The candlelight gleamed on the heavy gold of his signet ring.

". . . but he did it in a way that meant those four hundred acres still support some cows and four hundred sheep, and his lambing has improved. But forestry, the way the state goes about it, is no answer to the hill-farmer's problem. A solid mass of stitka spruce, and you're left with a three percent return on capital and another shepherd out of a job."

Mrs. Dobbs. She wondered if Roddy had told him that she wasn't married to Oliver, or whether he had guessed this for himself. Either way, he seemed to take it for granted that Thomas was her child. She told herself that this was a good thing. She and Oliver had come beyond justifications and explanations. This was the way she wanted it to be. She had wanted to belong to somebody, to be needed, and now she belonged to Oliver and she was needed by Tom. She began to break the orange into segments. Juice dripped over her fingers, and onto the delicately trellised Meissen plate.

"How about the tourist industry?" John was asking. "Highlands and Islands."

"Tourism is very tempting, very nice, but it's also dangerous. There is nothing more dismal than a community depending on tourists. You can convert holiday cottages, you can build log-cabin chalets, you can even open your house to summer visitors, but given one bad summer and the wet and the cold frighten the ordinary family man away. All right, if he's a fisherman or a hill walker or a bird watcher, he probably won't object to a bit of rain. But a woman with three children, trapped in a small cottage for a long, wet

fortnight, is going to insist on being taken to Torre-
molinos next summer. No, any population must have
jobs for men, and it's their jobs that are being lost."

Oliver sighed. He had had two glasses of port and he
was becoming sleepy. He listened to the conversation,
not because it was of much interest to him, but because he found himself fascinated by John Dunbeath.
The epitome, one would have thought, of the quiet,
well-bred, Down-Easter, with his Brooks Brothers
shirt, and elusive mid-Atlantic accent. As he talked,
Oliver observed him covertly. What made him tick?
What were the motivations behind that polite, reserved façade? And what—most intriguing of all—did
he think about Victoria?

That they had already met in London, he knew.
Victoria herself had told him this evening, while
Oliver soaked in a bath, and she brushed her hair, and
they talked through the open door.

"So extraordinary," she had said, in her lightest and
most casual of voices. He knew that voice. It was Victoria's keep-out sign, and always aroused his avid curiosity. "He was the man who brought me home from
the party that evening. Do you remember? When Tom
was crying."

"You mean John Hackenbacker of Consolidated
Aloominum? Well, I never did. How extraordinary."
This was fascinating. He mulled it over, squeezing
spongefuls of peat-brown water over his chest. "What
did he say when he saw you again?"

"Nothing really. We had tea together."

"I thought he was flying off to Bahrain."

"He was. He's flown back again."

"What a little bird of passage he is. What does he do
when he's not flying hither and yon?"

"I think he's in banking."

"Well, why isn't he in London, where he should be,
cashing people's cheques?"

"Oliver, he's not that sort of a banker. And he's got

a few days leave to try and sort out his uncle's estate."

"And how does he feel about being the new young laird of Benchoile?"

"I didn't ask him." She sounded cool. He knew he was annoying her, and went on with his teasing.

"Perhaps he fancies himself in a kilt. Americans always adore dressing themselves up."

"That's a stupid generalization."

There was now a definite edge to her voice. She was, Oliver realized, sticking up for the new arrival. He got out of the bath and wrapped a towel around himself and came through to the bedroom. Victoria's anxious blue eyes met his through her mirror.

"That's a very long word for you to use."

"Well, he's not that sort of an American at all."

"What sort of an American is he?"

"Oh, I don't know." She laid down her comb and picked up her mascara brush. "I don't know anything about him."

"I do." Oliver told her. "I went and talked to Ellen while she was bathing Tom. Get on the right side of her, and she's a mine of the most delicious morsels of gossip. It seems that John Dunbeath's father married a veritable heiress. And now he's been landed with Benchoile. To him who has shall be given. He's obviously been walking about with a silver spoon sticking out of his mouth since the day he was born." Still wrapped in the bath towel, he began to prowl around the bedroom, leaving wet footmarks on the carpet.

She said, "What are you looking for?"

"Cigarettes."

To he who has shall be given. Roddy had given Oliver a cigar. He leaned back in his chair, and through its smoke, through narrowed eyes, he watched John Dunbeath. He saw the dark eyes, the heavy, tanned features, the closely cut pelt of black hair. He looked, Oliver decided, like a tremendously wealthy young Arab, who had just climbed out of his djellabah and into a Western suit. The malice of the simile pleased him. He smiled. John looked up at that moment and saw Oliver smiling at him, but although there was no antagonism in his face, he did not smile back.

"What about the oil?"

"The oil, the oil." Roddy sounded like Henry Irving intoning "The bells, the bells!"

"Do you reckon it belongs to Scotland?"

"The nationalists think so."

"How about the private millions that British and American companies have invested before the oil could be discovered? If it hadn't been for that, the oil would still be under the North Sea, and nobody would know about it."

"They say this is what happened in the Middle East . . ."

Their voices faded to a soft murmur. Their words became indistinguishable. The other voices moved in, the real voices. Now the girl was there, sullen and pushy.

And where do you think you're going?

I'm going to London. I'm going to get a job.

What's wrong with Penistone? What's wrong with getting a job in Huddersfield?

Oh, Mum not that sort of a job. I'm going to be a model.

A model. Tarting up and down some street with no knickers on, more like.

It's my life.

And where are you going to live?

I'll find somewhere. I've got friends.

You move in with that Ben Lowry, and I'm finished with you. I tell you straight, I'm finished . . .

". . . soon there won't be any real craftsmen left. And I mean real ones, not the wierdos who come from God knows where and set themselves up in windswept sheds to print silk scarves that no one in their right minds would ever buy. Or to weave tweed that looks like dishcloths. I'm talking about the traditional craftsmen. Kiltmakers and silversmiths, being seduced away by the big money to be earned in the rigs and the refineries. Now, take this man we went to see today. He's got a good business going. He started with two men, and now he's employing ten, and half of them are under twenty."

"What about his markets?"

"This is it. He'd already contacted his market outlets before he came north." Roddy turned to Oliver. "Who was that publisher he worked for before—when he was in London? He told us the name, but I can't remember it."

"Umm?" Oliver was dragged back into the conversation. "Sorry, I wasn't really paying attention. The publisher? Hacket and Hansom, wasn't it?"

"Yes, that's it, Hackett and Hansom. You see . . ."

But then Roddy stopped, suddenly aware that he had been holding forth for far too long. He turned to Victoria to apologize, but at this instant, to her obvious horror, she lost herself in an enormous yawn. Everybody laughed, and she was covered in confusion.

"I'm not really bored, I'm just sleepy."

"And no wonder. We're behaving abominably. I am sorry. We should have saved it for later."

"It's all right."

But the damage was done. Victoria's yawn had broken up and ended the discussion. The candles were burning down and the fire was nearly out, and Roddy looked at his watch and realized that it was half past ten. "Good heavens, is that the time?" He put on an impeccable Edinburgh accent. "How it flies, Mrs. Wishart, when you're enjoying yourself."

Victoria smiled. "It's the fresh air," she said, "that makes you sleepy. Not the lateness of the hour."

Oliver said, "We're not used to it." He leaned back in his chair and stretched.

"What are you going to do tomorrow?" Roddy asked. "What are we all going to do tomorrow. You can choose, Victoria. What would you like to do? It's going to be a good day, if we can rely on the weather forecast. How about the waterfall. Shall we take a picnic over to the waterfall? Or has anybody got a better suggestion?"

Nobody had. Pleased with his notion, Roddy enlarged on the plan. "We'll take the boat across if I can find the key to the boathouse. Thomas would like a boat trip, wouldn't he? And Ellen will pack us a nosebag. And when we get over there we'll light a fire to keep us warm."

This seemed to meet with everybody's approval, and on this note, the evening began to come to an end. Oliver finished his port, stubbed out his cigar, and stood up.

"Perhaps," he said, mildly, "I should take Victoria off to bed."

This suggestion was made to the company in general, but as he said it, he looked at John. John's face remained impassive. Vcotoria pushed back her chair, and he got to his feet and came around the table to hold it for her.

She said, "Good night, Roddy" and came to kiss him.

"Good night."

"Good night John." She did not kiss John. Oliver went to open the door for her. As she went through it he turned back to the dusky room, and said with his most charming smile, "See you in the morning."

"See you," said John.

The door closed. Roddy threw more peat on the fire, stirred it to life. Then he and John drew chairs up to its warmth and resumed their discussion.

CHAPTER 11
Saturday

The weather forecasters had been only partially correct. The sun indeed was shining, but intermittent clouds blew across its face, driven by a western wind, and the very air had a liquidity about it, so that hills, water, sky, all looked as though they had been painted by a huge sodden brush.

The house and the garden were sheltered by the curve of the hills, and only the smallest of breezes had shaken the trees as they waited to embark themselves and an immense amount of equipment into the old fishing boat, but they had no sooner moved forty yards or so from the shore, when the true force of the wind made itself felt. The surface of the beer-brown water was flurried and driven with quite large waves, foam-crested and splashing over the gunwales. The occupants of the boat huddled into the various waterproof garments that had been gleaned from the Benchoile gunroom and handed around at the start of the voyage. Victoria wore an olive drab oilskin with enormous toggle-fastened poacher's pockets, and Thomas had been wrapped in a shooting jacket of immense antiquity, lavishly stained with the blood of some long-defunct bird or hare. This garment restricted him considerably, and Victoria was thankful for this, because it made the task of holding him still less difficult, his one idea apparently being to cast himself bodily overboard.

John Dunbeath, without any spoken agreement, had

taken the oars. They were long and heavy, and the sound of creaking rowlocks, the faint piping of the wind, and the splash of breaking waves against the side of the boat were the only sounds. He wore a black oilskin that had once belonged to his uncle Jock, and a pair of green shooting boots, but his head was bare, and his face wet with spray. He rowed expertly, power-fully, the swing of his body driving the prow of the balky old boat through the water. Once or twice he shipped his oars in order to look over his shoulder and judge how far the wind and the run of the water were carrying them off course, and to get his bearings. He looked very much at home, at ease. But then he had done this thing, and come this way, many times before.

Amidships, on the center thwart, sat Roddy and Oliver. Roddy with his back to Victoria, and with his dog Barney secure between his knees; Oliver astride the thwart, leaning back with his elbows propped on the gunwale. Both men had their eyes on the ap-proaching shore, Roddy scanning the hillside through his binoculars. From where she sat, Victoria could see only the outline of Oliver's forehead and chin. He had turned up the collar of his jacket, and his long legs, straddled in their faded jeans, ended in a pair of aged sneakers. The wind caught his hair and blew it back from his face, and the skin, fine-drawn over his cheek-bones, was burned russet with the wind.

In the bottom of the boat, pools of water, inevita-bly, slopped. Every now and then, when he thought about it, Roddy would lower his binoculars on their leather strap and bail absent-mindedly, dipping the water up with an old tin bowl and emptying it over-board. It didn't seem to make much difference. Any-way, the picnic baskets, the box of kindling, the bun-dles of tarpaulins and rugs had all been stowed with care, out of reach of the puddles. There seemed to be enough food to feed an army, and various vacuum flasks and bottles had a special basket to themselves, with divisions, so that they did not bang together and break.

Roddy, having finished with a little bit of bailing, took up his binoculars again, and began to cover the hill.

"What are you looking for?" Oliver asked.

"Deer. It's amazing how hard they are to see on a hill face. Last week when we had the snow you could pick them out from the house, but there don't seem to be any about today."

"Where will they be?"

"Over the hill, probably."

"Do you get a lot here?"

"Sometimes as many as five hundred. Deer and does. In cold weather they come down and eat the fodder we put out for the cattle. In the summer they bring their young down, after dark, to graze in the pastures and drink from the loch. You can drive up the old cattle road from the foot of the loch. Keep the headlights of the car turned off, and you take them unawares. Then turn the lights onto them, and it's a beautiful sight."

"Do you shoot them?" Oliver asked.

"No. Our neighbour over the hill has the stalking rights. Jock let them to him. However, the deep freeze at Benchoile is full of haunches of venison. You should get Ellen busy on it before you take yourselves off again. It can be dry and tough, but Ellen's a way with venison. It's delicious." He lifted the leather strap over his head and handed the binoculars to Oliver. "Here, you have a look, see if you can spot anything with your young eyes."

Now, in the magical way that such things come about, the other shore, their destination, drew nearer and began to reveal its secrets. No longer was it a landscape blurred by distance, but a place of rocky outcrops, emerald green swards, white pebble beaches. Bracken, dense as fur, coated the lower slopes of the hill. Higher up, this gave way to heather and the occa-

sional lonely Scots pine. The distant skyline was edged
by the uneven outline of a drystone dike, the march
wall between Benchoile land and the neighboring
property. In places this dike had broken, leaving a gap
like a missing tooth.

But there was still no sign of the waterfall. Holding
Thomas in the circle of her arms, Victoria leaned forward, meaning to ask Roddy about this, but at that
moment the boat swept past a great promontory of
rock, and the little bay was revealed before them.

She saw the white shingle beach, and purling down
the hillside, the burn, tumbling and twisting through
heather and bracken, until, twenty feet or so above the
beach, it leaped out over a ledge of granite and
spouted down into the pool at its base. White as a
mare's tail, dancing in the sunlight, fringed with
rushes and moss and fern, it lived up to all Victoria's
expectations.

Roddy turned to smile at her face of openmouthed
delight.

"There you are," he told her. "Isn't that what you
came all this way to see?"

Thomas, as excited as she was, lurched forward and
escaped from her hold. Before she could catch him, he
had stumbled, lost his balance, and fallen forward
against his father's knee.

"Look!" It was one of his few words. He banged
Oliver's leg with his fist. "Look!"

But Oliver was still engrossed with Roddy's binoculars, and either did not notice Thomas, or else paid no
attention. Thomas said, "Look," again, but in the
throes of trying to get his father to listen to him, he
slipped and fell, bumping his head on the thwart and
finishing up in the bottom of the boat, sitting in three
inches of icy water.

He began, not unnaturally, to cry, and the first wail
was out before Victoria, scrambling forward, could rescue him. As she picked him up, and lifted him back

into her arms, she looked up and saw the expression on John Dunbeath's face. He was not looking at her, he was looking at Oliver. He was looking as though, quite happily, he could have punched Oliver in the nose.

The keel ground up onto the shingle. John shipped his oars and climbed overboard, and heaved the prow of the boat up onto the dry beach. One by one they alighted. Thomas was carried to safety by Roddy. Oliver took the forward painter and tied it up to a large, concrete-embedded spike, which was, perhaps, for this very purpose. Victoria handed out picnic baskets and the rugs to John, and finally, herself jumped ashore. The single of the beach crunched beneath the soles of her shoes. The sound of the waterfall filled her ears.

There seemed to be a strict protocol for Benchoile picnics. Roddy and Barney led the way up the beach, and the others followed, a straggling, laden procession. Between the waterfall pool and the tumbledown walls of the ruined croft was a sward of grass, and here they set up camp. There was a traditional fireplace, a ring of blackened stones and charred wood bearing witness to previous picnics, and it was very sheltered, although high above, the clouds still raced. The midday sun blinked in and out, but when it shone, it shed a real warmth, and the dark waters of the loch took on the blue of the sky and danced with sun pennies.

The group shed their bulky waterproofs. Thomas set off by himself to explore the beach. John Dunbeath took up a stick and began to scrape together the ashes in the fireplace. From the drink basket Roddy took two bottles of wine, and stood them at the edge of the pool, to cool. Oliver lit a cigarette. Roddy, his wine safely dealt with, stopped to watch a pair of birds, twittering and anxious, circling a rock ledge at the edge of the waterfall.

"What are they?" asked Victoria.

"Dippers. Water ouzels. It's early for them to be nesting." He began to climb the steep bank in order to investigate this. Oliver, with the binoculars still dangling around his neck, watched for a moment, and then followed him. John was already searching for kindling for the fire, gathering handfuls of dry grass and charred heather stalks. Victoria was about to offer her help, when she spied Thomas, heading for the loch and the pretty waves. She ran after him, jumping down onto the beach, and catching him up, just in time, into her arms.

"Thomas!" She held him close and laughed into his neck. "You can't go into the water."

She tickled him and he chuckled, and then arched his back protesting and frustrated. "Wet!" he shouted into her face.

"You're wet already. Come along, we'll find something else to do."

She turned and carried him back up the beach, to where the pool overflowed to a shallow stream that ran over the pebbles to the loch. Beside this she set Thomas, and stooping, picked up a handful of stones, and began to throw them, one by one, into the water. Thomas was diverted by the little splashes they made. After a little he squatted down on his haunches and began to throw pebbles for himself. Victoria left him and went back to the picnic place, and removed the plastic mug from the top of a vacuum flask. She took this back to Thomas.

"Look." She sat beside him and filled the mug with stones. When it was full, she poured them out into a heap. "Look, it's a castle." She gave him the mug. "You do it."

Carefully, one at a time, with starfish hands, Thomas filled the mug. The occupation absorbed him. His fingers, red with cold, were clumsy, his perseverance touching.

Watching him, filled with the tenderness that was by now becoming familiar, Victoria wondered about maternal instincts. Was one meant to have them, if one didn't have a child of one's own? Perhaps, if Thomas had not been such an engaging person, she would never have experienced this basic, unreasonable surge of protective affection. But there it was. Like a child in some sentimental old film, he seemed to have found his way into her heart, made himself snug and was there to stay.

The whole situation was odd to say the least of it. When he had first told Victoria about stealing Thomas from the Archers, Victoria, although shocked at Oliver, had also been moved. That Oliver Dobbs, of all people, should be so aware of his own parenthood as to take this extraordinary step was somehow a marvelous thing.

And to begin with, he had seemed both amused and involved; buying Thomas a toy, carrying him around on his shoulders, even playing with him in the evenings before Victoria put him to bed. But, like a child quickly bored by a new diversion, his interest seemed to have waned, and now he took little notice of Thomas.

The incident in the boat was typical of his attitude. Against all Victoria's better instincts, it was becoming impossible not to suspect that Oliver's impulsive removal of his son had not been prompted by fatherly pride and a real sense of responsibility, but that in his own oblique way he was simply getting back at his parents-in-law. The taking of Thomas from them sprang more from reasons of spite than reasons of love.

It really didn't bear thinking about. Not just because of the slur this cast upon Oliver's motivations and so upon his character, but because it rendered Thomas's future—and indirectly her own—miserably precarious.

Thomas banged her with his fist and said, "Look."

Victoria looked, and saw the tumbled pile of pebbles and his beaming, grubby face, and she pulled him up onto her knee and hugged him.

She said, "I love you. Do you know that?" and he laughed as though she had made some tremendous joke. His laughter eased everything. It would all be all right. She loved Thomas and she loved Oliver, and Oliver loved Victoria, and obviously—in his own undemonstrative way—loved Thomas as well. With so much loving around the place, surely nothing could destroy the family that they had become.

Behind her, she heard the crunch of footsteps coming down the beach towards them. She turned and saw John Dunbeath. Beyond him, the fire now blazed, plumed with blue smoke. The other two men had disappeared. She searched for them, and saw their distant figures, more than halfway up towards the march wall, and still climbing.

John said, "I guess we won't get our lunch for another hour. They've gone up to search for the deer."

He reached her side, and stood a moment, looking out across the water, to the distant sunlit blur of the house, half hidden in the trees. From here it looked infinitely desirable, like a house in a dream. Smoke rose from a chimney, a white curtain blew, like a flag, from an open window.

Victoria said, "It doesn't matter. About lunch, I mean. If Thomas gets hungry we can always feed him something to stave off his pangs till the others get back."

He sat beside them, leaning back with his elbows in the shingle. "You're not hungry, are you?" he asked Thomas.

Thomas said nothing. After a bit, he clambered off Victoria's knee and went back to his game with the plastic cup.

Victoria said, "Don't you want to go and look for deer too?"

"Not today. Anyway I've seen them before. And that's quite a climb. I didn't realize Oliver would be so energetic and interested in wildlife."

There was no hint of criticism in his voice, but even so Victoria sprang to Oliver's defense. "He's interested in everything. New experiences, new sights, new people."

"I know it. Last night after you'd gone to bed, Roddy finally got round to telling me that he's another writer. It was funny, because when I was introduced to him, I thought 'Oliver Dobbs, I know that name,' but the associations eluded me. And then when Roddy told me, the penny dropped. I've read a couple of his books, and I saw one of his plays on television. He's a very clever man."

Victoria's heart warmed towards him. "Yes, he is clever. He's just had a new play put on in Bristol. Its called *Bent Penny*. The first night was on Monday, and his agent says he's got a hit on his hands. It's probably going to the West End, just as soon as they can find a threatre."

"That's great."

She went on extolling Oliver, as though praise of him could in some way obliterate the memory of the fleeting expression she had caught on John Dunbeath's face when Thomas fell in the boat. "He hasn't always been successful. I mean, it's a notoriously difficult business to get started in, but he never wanted to do anything else, and I don't think he ever got discouraged or lost faith in himself. His parents practically disowned him because he didn't want to go into the army, or be a lawyer, or do anything like that. So, at the beginning, he really didn't have any security at all."

"How long ago was that?"

"I suppose from the moment he left school."

"How long have you known him?

Victoria leaned forward and picked up a handful of

pebbles. So close to the waters edge they were wet and shining and cold to touch. "About three years."

"Was he successful then?"

"No. He used to take dreadful, undemanding jobs, just to earn enough money to buy the groceries and pay the rent. You know, like barrowing bricks and mending roads and washing dishes in a fish-and-chips shop. And then a publisher began to take interest in him, and he got a play on television. And since then things have just snowballed, and he's never looked back. He and Roddy met through television, I expect Roddy told you. That's why we came to Benchoile. I read *The Eagle Years* when I was at school, and I've reread it at regular intervals ever since. When Oliver told me he knew Roddy and we were coming here to stay, I could hardly believe it was true."

"Has it lived up to its expectations?"

"Yes. Once you get used to it not being summer all the time."

John laughed. "It certainly isn't that." She thought he looked much younger when he laughed.

The sun had, for the last moment or so, been hidden behind a cloud, but now it came racing out again, and its brightness and warmth were so welcome, that Victoria lay back on the beach, and turned her face up to the sky.

She said, "The only thing that spoiled coming here was being told about your uncle dying. I felt we should have turned right round and gone away again, but Roddy wouldn't hear of it."

"It's probably the best thing in the world that could have happened. A bit of company for him."

"Ellen told me you used to come here when you were a little boy. I mean, when you weren't in Colorado."

"Yes. I used to come with my father."

"Did you love it?"

"Yes. But it was never home. Colorado and the ranch were my real home."

"What did you do when you used to come here? Did you slay deer and grouse and do manly things like that?"

"I used to fish. But I don't like shooting. I never have. It made life a little difficult."

"Why?" It was hard to imagine life for John Dunbeath ever being difficult.

"I suppose because I was the odd man out. Everybody else did it. Even my father. My uncle Jock didn't understand it at all." He grinned. "Sometimes I thought he didn't even like me very much."

"Oh, I'm sure he liked you. He wouldn't have left Benchoile to you if he hadn't liked you."

"He left it to me," John told her flatly, "because there wasn't anybody else."

"Did you guess he was going to leave it to you?"

"It never entered my head. That probably sounds crazy to you, but its true. I got back from Bahrain and found this lawyer's letter waiting for me on my desk." He leaned forward to pick up a handful of pebbles and started to pitch them, with deadly accuracy, at a lichened rock which jutted from the edge of the loch. He said, "There was another letter as well, from Jock. I guess he wrote it just a couple of days before he died. It's a funny feeling getting a letter from a person who's already dead."

"Are . . . are you going to come and live here?"

"I couldn't, even if I wanted to."

"Because of your job?"

"Yes. That and other reasons. I'm based in London just now, but I may be sent back to New York at the drop of a hat. I have commitments. I have my family."

"Your family?" She was taken by surprise. But, on consideration, why should she be so surprised? She had met John in London, at a party, as a single man, but that did not mean that he had not left a wife and chil-

dren behind him in the States. Businessmen all over
the world were forced to lead such lives. There was
nothing unusual about such a situation. She imagined
his wife; pretty and chic as all young American women
seemed to be, with a space-age kitchen and a station
wagon in which to fetch the children from school.

He said, "By family, I mean my mother and father."

"Oh," Victoria laughed, feeling foolish. "I thought
you meant you were married."

With immense care, he pitched the last stone. It hit
the rock and fell into the water with a miniature
splash. He turned to look at her. He said, "I was married. Not any more."

"I'm sorry." There didn't seem to be anything else
to say.

"That's all right." He smiled reassuringly and she
said, "I didn't know."

"Why should you know?"

"No reason. It's just that people have been talking
about you, telling me about you. Roddy, and Ellen I
mean. But nobody said anything about your being
married."

"It only lasted a couple of years, and they never met
her anyway." He leaned back on his elbows and
looked out across the loch towards the hills and the
old house. He said, "I wanted to bring her to Benchoile. Before we were married I used to tell her about
it, and she seemed quite enthusiastic. She'd never been
to Scotland and she had all sorts of romantic imagin-
ings about it. You know, skirling pipes and swirling
mists and Bonnie Prince Charlie draped in tartan. But
ater we were married . . . I don't know. There never
seemed to be time to do anything."

"Was . . . the divorce why you came to live in
London?"

"One of the reasons. You know, a clean break, all
the rest of it."

"Did you have children?"

"No. Just as well, the way things turned out."

She knew then that she had been wrong about John. Meeting him for the first time, he had impressed her as being self-contained, self-reliant, and totally cool. Now she realized that beneath that smooth veneer was a person just like anybody else; vulnerable, capable of being hurt, probably lonely. She remembered that he had been meant to have a girlfriend with him that evening, but for some reason she had let him down. And so he had asked Victoria to have dinner with him, and Victoria had refused. Thinking of this, she now felt, in some obscure way, as though she had let him down.

She said, "My parents got divorced. When I was eighteen. You'd have thought I'd have been old enough by then to cope with the situation. But it does something to your life. Nothing's ever quite the same again. Security is lost forever." She smiled. "Now, that's something that Benchoile has got and to spare. Security oozes out of the walls. I suppose it's something to do with the people who've lived in the house, and the way people live there now, as though nothing has changed in a hundred years."

"That's right. It certainly hasn't altered in my life time. It even smells the same."

She said, "What will happen to it now?"

He did not answer at once. And then he told her. "I shall sell it."

Victoria stared at him. His dark eyes, unblinking, met hers, and beneath their steady regard, she slowly realized that he meant what he said.

"But, John, you *can't*."

"What else can I do?"

"Keep it on."

"I'm not a farmer. I'm not a sportsman. I'm not even a true-blooded Scot. I'm an American banker. What could I do with a place like Benchoile?"

"Couldn't you run it . . . ?"

"From Wall Street?"

"Put a manager in."

"Who?"

She cast about for some person, and came up, inevitably, with, "Roddy?"

"If I'm a banker, then Roddy is a writer, a dilettante. He's never been anything else. Jock, on the other hand, was the strong pillar of the family and an exceptional man. He didn't just stride around Benchoile with a dog at his heels and a string of instructions. He worked. He went up the hill with Davey Guthrie and brought the sheep down. He helped with the lambing and the dipping. He went to the market in Lairg. As well, it was Jock who kept an eye on the forestry, took care of the garden, mowed the grass."

"Isn't there a gardener?"

"There's a pensioner who cycles up from Creagan three days a week, but keeping the kitchen garden in vegetables and the house in logs seems to take up most of his time."

But Victoria was still unconvinced. "Roddy seems to know so *much* about everything. Last night . . ."

"He knows a lot, because he's lived here all his life, but what he can actually *do* is another matter altogether. I'm afraid that without Jock, supporting him and giving him a shove every now and then, Roddy is in mortal danger of simply sinking into the ground."

"You could give him a chance."

John looked regretful, but he shook his head. "This is a big property. There's twelve thousand acres of hill to be farmed, fences to be kept up, a thousand or more sheep to be reared. There's cattle involved, and crops, and expensive machinery. All that adds up to a lot of money."

"You mean you don't want to risk losing money?"

He grinned. "No banker wants to risk that. But in fact, it isn't that. I could probably afford to lose a bit; but no property is worth holding onto, unless it's a viable proposition and capable, at least, of washing its own face."

Victoria turned away from him, sitting up with her arms wrapped around her knees, looking back across the water to the old house. She thought of the warmth of that house, of its hospitality, of the people who lived there. She did not think of it as a viable proposition.

She said, "What about Ellen?"

"Ellen is one of the problems. Ellen and the Guthries."

"Do they know you're going to sell Benchoile?"

"Not yet."

"Does Roddy?"

"I told him last night."

"What did he say?"

"He wasn't surprised. He said he hadn't expected me to do anything else. And then he poured himself the biggest cognac you've ever seen and changed the subject."

"And what do you suppose will happen to Roddy?"

"I don't know," said John, and for the first time he sounded miserable. She turned her head over her shoulder, and once more their eyes met. His own were bleak and somber, and she was moved to sympathy for him in his dilemma.

She said, impulsively, "He drinks too much. Roddy, I mean."

"I know it."

"I love him."

"I love him, too. I love them all. That's why it's so ghastly."

She felt impelled to try to cheer him. "Perhaps something will turn up."

"Who are you, Mr. Micawber? No, I'm going to sell it. Because I have to. Robert McKenzie, he's the lawyer in Inverness, he's fixing an advertisement for me. It'll go into all the big national newspapers around the middle of the week. Desirable Highland Sporting Property For Sale. So you see, I can't go back now. I can't change my mind."

"I wish I could make you."

"You can't, so don't let's talk about it anymore."

Thomas was getting bored with his game. He was also getting hungry. He had dropped his plastic mug, and now he came to climb onto Victoria's knee. John looked at his watch. He said, "It's nearly one o'clock. I think you and I and Thomas should go and find something to eat . . ."

They got slowly to their feet. Victoria brushed shingle from the seat of her jeans. She said, "What about the others?" and turned to look up the hill, and saw Oliver and Roddy already on their way down, moving a great deal faster than they had on the way up.

"They're feeling hungry, too, and thirsty as well, no doubt," said John. "Come along . . ." he stooped and hoisted Thomas up into his arms, and led the way back to where his fire smoldered ". . . . let's see what Ellen's put in the picnic baskets."

Perhaps because of the picnic—which had been so successful—and the memories of former happy parties that this had evoked, the conversation that night at dinner did not concern the literary world of London, nor the problems of the future of Scotland, but became instead, a feast of reminiscence.

Roddy, sated with fresh air, flushed by wine and good food, and relentlessly prompted by his nephew John, was in his element, carried along on an unstoppable flood of anecdotes that reached far back into the past.

Around the polished, candle-lit table, old retainers, eccentric relations, domineering dowagers, most of them long since defunct, came back to life. There was the story of the Christmas house party when the tree caught fire; the grouse-shoot at which a universally

disliked young cousin peppered the guest of honor
with shot and was sent home in disgrace; the long-
forgotten winter when the blizzards cut the house off
for a month or more, and its occupants were reduced
to boiling snow to make the porridge and playing endless charades to keep themselves amused.

There were the sagas of the overturned boat, the
sheriff's Bentley, which, inadvertently left with its
hand brake off, had finished up in the bottom of the
loch; and the gentle-woman of reduced circumstances,
who had come to stay for a weekend, and remained
firmly installed in the best guest room two years later.

It took a long time to run out of stories, and even
when he did, Roddy remained inexhaustible. Just as
Victoria was about to suggest that perhaps it was time
to retire to bed (it was now past midnight) he pushed
back his chair, and led them all purposefully away
from the table and across the hall to the deserted, dust-
sheeted drawing room. There stood the grand piano,
draped in an old sheet. Roddy turned this back,
pulled up a stool to the keyboard, and started to play.

The room was piercingly cold. The curtains had
long since been taken down, and the windows shuttered, and the old melodies echoed like cymbals
against the empty walls. High above, descendant from
the center of the lavishly decorated ceiling, a crystal
chandelier of immense proportions sparkled like a
cluster of icicles, and scattered facets of colored light
that were reflected in the bars of the brass fender that
stood before the white marble fireplace.

Roddy sang songs from before the war. Noel Cow-
ard at his most sentimental, and Cole Porter.

> I get no kick from champagne,
> Mere alcohol doesn't thrill me at all,
> So tell me, why should it be true . . .

The rest of the party grouped themselves about him.

Oliver, his dramatic senses stirred by the turn that the evening had so unexpectedly taken, leaned against the piano and smoked a cigar, watching Roddy as though he could not bear to miss a single nuance of the other man's expression.

John had crossed to the fireplace, and stood before it, with his hands in his pockets and his shoulders propped against the mantelpiece. Victoria had found a chair in the middle of the room, draped in faded blue gingham, and had perched herself on one of its arms. From where she sat, Roddy had his back to her, but above him, flanking a centrally hung mirror, were two tall portraits, which she knew, without being told, were of Jock Dunbeath and his wife Lucy.

With her ears full of the nostalgic tinkling music, she looked from one to the other. Jock had been painted in the full dress kilt of his regiment, but Lucy wore a tartan skirt and a bracken-brown sweater. She had brown eyes and laughter on her mouth, and Victoria wondered if it was she who had decorated this room, and chosen the pale carpet with its swags of roses, or whether she had inherited it from her mother-in-law, and liked it just the way it was. And then she found herself wondering if Jock and Lucy knew that Benchoile was going to be sold. Whether they were sad about it, or angry, or understood John's dilemma. Looking at Lucy, Victoria decided that she probably understood. But Jock . . . Jock's face above the high collar, the golden epaulettes, was carved into an expression of suitable blankness. The eyes were deep-set and very pale. They would reveal nothing.

She realized that she was slowly freezing. She had put on, that evening, for some reason, a most unsuitable dress, sleeveless and far too light for a winter evening in Scotland. It was the sort of dress meant to be worn with suntanned arms and bare sandals, and in it she knew that she looked thin and colorless and cold.

You're the cream in my coffee,
You're the milk in my tea . . .

Victoria shivered, and rubbed her arms with her hands, trying to warm herself. From across the room, John Dunbeath's voice came quietly, "Are you cold?" and she realized that he had been watching her, and this made her self-conscious. She put her hands back in her lap and nodded, but made a secret face to let him know that she did not want to disturb Roddy.

He took his hands out of his pockets and left the fireplace and came over to her side, on the way gathering up a dustsheet, revealing the French rosewood chair that it had been protecting. He folded the dustsheet like a shawl, and bundled it around her shoulders, so that she was swathed in folds of soft, old cotton, very comforting to the touch.

He did not go back to the fireplace, but settled himself on the other arm of her chair, with his arm lying along its back. His nearness was somehow as comforting as the dustsheet that he had wrapped around her, and after a little she did not feel cold anymore.

Roddy stopped at last for breath, and to refresh himself from the glass that stood on top of the piano. "I think that's probably enough," he told them all. But John said, "You can't stop yet. You haven't played 'Will Ye Go, Lassie, Go.' "

Over his shoulder Roddy frowned at his nephew. "When did you ever hear me play that old song?"

"I suppose when I was about five years old. But my father used to sing it, too."

Roddy smiled. "What a sentimental guy you are, to be sure," he told him, but he turned back to the piano, and the old Scottish tune, in the three-four time of a slow waltz, filled the empty, haunted room.

O the summer time is coming
And the trees are sweetly blooming

And the wild mountain thyme
Grows around the blooming heather.
Will ye go, lassie, go?

I will build my love a tower
Near yon pure crystal fountain
And on it I will pile
All the flowers of the mountain.
Will ye go, lassie, go?

If my true love, she were gone,
I would surely find another
Where wild mountain thyme
Grows around the blooming heather
Will ye go, lassie, go?

CHAPTER 12
Sunday

It was ten o'clock on the morning of the Sabbath. Once more the wind had come round to the northeast, swirling in from the sea, clean and bitterly cold. The sky, overcast with high, sailing clouds, glimpsed through, blue as a robin's egg, only occasionally, and it was hard to believe that only yesterday they had been picnicking at the waterfall, sitting in the sunshine with pleasant anticipatory thoughts of the approaching spring.

John Dunbeath sat by the fire in the Guthrie's kitchen and drank a cup of tea. The kitchen was snug as a nest. A fire burned redly in the stove, and thick walls and tightly closed windows defied the blustering wind. The air was filled with the smell of burning peat, overlaid by the fragrance of simmering broth, and the table in the center of the room was already laid for the Guthrie's midday dinner.

Jess was going to church. At the sideboard, she took up her hat, and, sagging slightly at the knees, in order to see her reflection in the mirror, put it on. Watching her, and then looking back at Davey, John decided that of all the Benchoile people, the Guthries had changed the least. Jess was still slim, still pretty, with only a trace of grey in her springy fair hair, and Davey looked, if anything, even younger than John remembered him, with his bright blue eyes and tufty, sandy eyebrows.

"Now," Jess picked up her gloves and pulled them

on. "I must get away. You'll have to excuse me, but I promised I'd pick up Ellen Tarbat and give her a lift to the kirk." She glanced at the portentous clock in the middle of the mantelpiece. "And if you two are going to be up the hill and home again in time for your dinner, you'd better not be sitting here all day, drinking your tea."

She departed. A moment later there came a great crashing of gears and the revving of a hard-worked engine, and Davey's small grey van bounced down the bumpy path in front of the house and disappeared in the direction of Benchoile.

"She's a terrible driver," Davey observed mildly. He finished his mug of tea, set it down on the table and stood up. "But she's right. We should go." He went through to the little lobby and took down his waterproof jacket from the peg by the door, collected his deerstalker, his crook, his spyglass. The two golden Labradors, who had been lying, apparently asleep, by the fireside, now sprang into feverish action, scenting walks. They barged to and fro, nuzzling Davey's knees, tails going like pistons. They were, Jess had told John, Jock Dunbeath's dogs.

"Poor creatures, they were with him when he died. And afterwards they wandered about Benchoile like a pair of lost spirits. There was some talk of putting the old one down. She's nearly nine years old now. But we couldn't abide the idea. The colonel had been so fond of her, and she's a great lass to the gun. So they both came to live with us. Mind, we've never had a dog in the house. Davey would never have a dog in the house. But these two had never been in a kennel in their lives, and so he had to relent. They could have stayed at Benchoile, I suppose, but Mr. Roddy has his own dog, and Ellen has enough to do without caring for a couple of great babies like these two."

Now Davey opened the farmhouse door, and the two Labradors escaped into the windswept, scrubby garden, racing like puppies around the blowing grass beneath the washing line. At their appearance, Davey's sheepdogs, shut up in their pen, began dementedly to bark, racing to and fro in the netted run. "Shut your mouths, you silly bitches," Davey told them good-naturedly, but they went on barking, and could still be heard long after the two men and the two dogs had gone through the gate in the wall at the back of the house, and started the long walk up through the heather.

It took them over an hour to reach the march fence that separated the northern boundary of Benchoile from the desolate Glen Feosaig which lay beyond. A long, steady climb, taken at Davey Guthrie's unhurried pace, pausing only to point out some landmark, to scan the hill for deer, to watch the soaring, hovering flight of a kestrel. The dogs were kept well to heel, but even so, every now and then a pair of grouse would explode from the heather at their feet, and go wheeling away, their flight lying close to the slope of the hill; "go-back, go-back," they called.

It was immense country. Slowly, Benchoile sank below them, the loch a long ribbon of pewter grey, the house and trees concealed by the swelling contours of the land. To the north the summits were still snow-clad, and snow lay in deep corries as yet untouched by the low winter sun. As they climbed, Creagan itself came into view, reduced by distance to a cluster of grey houses, a strip of green that was the golf course, the tiny spire of the church. Beyond was the sea, the horizon blanketed in cloud.

"Yes, yes," observed Davey, "it is a dreich sort of a day."

At the crest of the hill there was not even heather underfoot; only pits of peat starred with strange mosses and lichens. The ground was boggy. Black water oozed up around their feet as they trod upwards, and the hoofprints and droppings of deer were everywhere. When they came at last to the straggling dike, the wind pounced on them from the north. It filled ears, nostrils, lungs; whistled through stormproof clothing and brought tears to John's eyes. He leaned against the wall and looked down into Feosaig. The loch at its foot lay black and deep, and there was no evidence of human habitation. Only the sheep and the kestrels, and showing white against the distant hill, a pair of gulls, working their way inland.

"Are those our sheep?" John asked, raising his voice against the wind.

"Yes, yes," Jim nodded, and then turned and sat himself down, out of the wind, with his back to the wall. After a little John joined him. "But that's not Benchoile land."

"And this is not Feosaig land, either, but we have many Feosaig sheep grazing with ours."

"What happens, do you have a roundup?"

"We start to gather them in, around the end of this month. We bring them down to the sheep folds in the fields by the farmhouse."

"When do the ewes start lambing?"

"About the sixteenth of April."

"Will it still be as cold as this?"

"It may well be colder. Some big storms can blow in April, and they can leave the hills as white as midwinter."

"That can't make your job any easier."

"Indeed, it does not. I have seen myself digging ewes, heavy with lamb, out of the ditches and drifts. Sometimes a mother will desert her lamb, and then there's nothing for it but to take it back to the farmhouse and hand rear it with a bottle. Jess is a great one with the sickly lambs."

Yes, I'm sure she is, but that doesn't solve the problem of how you're going to cope with all this on your own. Roddy's told me how much my uncle did at the lambing. You're going to need another man, probably two, to help you during the next six weeks."

"Yes, that is indeed a problem," Davey agreed, not looking in the least perturbed. He felt in his pocket and came out with a paper bag. From this he extracted two large bread-and-butter sandwiches. He gave one to John and began to eat the other himself, munching at each mouthful like a ruminating cow. "But I have spoken to Archie Tulloch and he says that this year he will give me a hand."

"Who's he?"

"Archie is a crofter. He farms a few acres down the road to Creagan. But he is an old man—seventy years or more—and he won't be able to carry on with the crofting much longer. He has no son. A month or so before your uncle died, he spoke to me about Archie's croft. He had the idea that he would buy the place from Archie, and take it in with Benchoile. We can always use more land for the arable, and he has a fine cattle pasture down by the river."

"Would Archie be agreeable?"

"Yes, yes. He has a sister in Creagan. He has talked for some time of going to live with her."

"So we'd have more land and another house."

"Your uncle thought we would maybe take on another man, and put him to live in the croft. Your uncle was a fine man, but after that first heart attack he had begun to realize that, like the rest of us, he was not immortal."

He took another mouthful of bread and munched some more. A movement on the side of the hill caught the attention of his blue eyes. He laid down his half-eaten sandwich, drove his crook into the ground, and took out his spyglass. Using his crook and the thumb of his left hand as a steadier, he put the glass to his eye. There was a long silence, broken only by the buffet of the wind.

"A hare," said Davey. "Just a wee hare." He put the

spyglass back in his pocket, and reached for the crust of the sandwich. But the old Labrador had already wolfed it. "You are indeed a greedy bitch," he told her.

John leaned back against the wall. Awkward stones dug into his back. His body was warm from the hard exercise, and his face cold. Ahead of them a gap had appeared between the racing clouds. A gleam of sunshine broke across the gloom, and lay like a shaft of gold across the dark waters of Loch Muie. The bracken on the hill turned russet. It was very beautiful, and he realized in that instant, with some shock, that the land, for almost as far as he could see, belonged to him. This was Benchoile. And this . . . he took up a handful of black peaty soil, crumbling it between his fingers.

He was assailed by a sensation of timelessness. This was the way things had stayed for decades; tomorrow they would be no different, nor the weeks, nor the months that lay in the future. Action, of any kind, had all at once become distasteful, and this took him unawares, because apathy was a mood he had never suffered from. He had made his reputation, achieved a considerable personal success in his job, simply by means of swift and shrewd decision, immediate action, and a confidence in his own convictions that left no room for moral shilly-shallying.

He had arranged this morning's expedition with the sole intention of getting Davey on his own, and letting fall the information, as tactfully as possible, that by the middle of next week Benchoile would officially be up for sale. And yet now he found himself discussing its future policies with Davey, as though he had every intention of digging himself in for the rest of his life.

He was procrastinating. But did that matter so much? Was today, this morning, this moment, the right time to bring to an end everything that Davey Guthrie had worked for? Perhaps, he told himself, knowing that he was ducking the issue, it would be better to hold a sort of board meeting in the dining room at Benchoile, thus protecting himself from the human element of the problem by erecting a shield of business-like formality. He would get Ellen Tarbat around the table, and Jess as well, and Roddy, to lend a little moral support. Better still, he would ask Robert McKenzie, the lawyer, to come from Inverness and take the chair at this meeting. Then he could be given the job of breaking the bad news to them all at one fell swoop.

The sun went in. It was cold and dark again, but the silence between the two men remained companionable and totally unstrained. It occurred to John that the true Highlander like Davey Guthrie had much in common with the ranch hands who worked for his father in Colorado. Proud, independent, knowing that they were as good as any man—and probably better—they found no need to assert themselves, and so were the most straightforward of beings to deal with.

He knew that he must be straightforward with Davey. He said, breaking the silence, "How long have you been at Benchoile, Davey?"

"Nearly twenty years."

"How old are you?"

"Forty-four."

"You don't look it."

"It's the clean living that keeps a man healthy," Davey told him, without a smile. "And the good air. Do you not find working in London and New York and such big cities, that the air is very oppressive? Even if Jess and I have a day's shopping in Inverness, I cannot wait to get home and breathe the clean air of Benchoile."

"I suppose if you have a job in a place, you don't think too much about what you're breathing." He added, "Anyway, if I get to feel too stifled, I usually head back to Colorado. There, the air is so rarified that the first gasp is as intoxicating as a jigger of Scotch."

"Yes, yes, that ranch must be a fine place. And a great size, too."

"In fact, not as big as Benchoile. About six thousand acres, but of course we carry more stock. Six hundred acres of that is irrigated hay meadow, the rest is known as open range grazing."

"And what breed of cattle do you rear?"

"No particular breed. They vary from fine Hereford and Black Angus, all the way down to what's known in the West as Running Gear. If the snows have been heavy, and the high meadows are well irrigated and we don't have a killing frost in the late spring, we can graze a thousand head."

Davey ruminated on this, chewing on a blade of grass, and gazing peacefully ahead of him. After a little, he said, "There was a farmer from Rosshire, and he went to the bull-sales in Perth, and there he met one of those big cattlemen from Texas. And they got talking. And the Texan asked the farmer how much land he owned. And the farmer told him, 'two thousand acres.'"

At this point John realized that Davey was not continuing their dissertation on farming, but telling a joke. Anxious not to miss the punch line, or worse, to laugh at the wrong moment, he listened with sharpened attention.

"And then the farmer asked the Texan how much land he owned. And the Texan said to the farmer, 'You would not understand. You could not comprehend, if I told you how much of Texas I own. But I'll tell you this. If I got into my car and drove all day around my boundary fence, I still should not have circled my property.' And the farmer thought a little while, and then he said to the Texan, 'I had a car like that, once upon a time. I got rid of it.'"

There came a long pause. Davey continued to gaze

ahead. John stayed straight-faced as long as he could, and then the grin, unstoppable, crept up his face. Davey turned his head and looked at him. His blue eyes held a certain gleam, but otherwise he was as dour as ever.

"Yes, yes," he said, in his gentle Sutherland voice. "I thought that you would enchoy that. It is a very good choke."

Ellen Tarbat, dressed in her good Sunday black, pulled her hat down over her ears and pierced it to her bun with a formidable hat pin. It was a decent hat, only two years old, and trimmed with a buckle. There was nothing like a buckle for lending a bit of dignity to a hat.

She looked at the kitchen clock. It was a quarter past ten, and Ellen was going to church. She was giving them a cold lunch today instead of the usual roast. She had peeled the potatoes, and made a jam tart, and the dining room table was ready and laid. Now, she was ready for Jess to pick her up. Davey was not coming to church with them, because he and John Dunbeath had gone up the hill to look at the sheep. Ellen did not approve of such goings-on on the Sabbath and had said as much to John, but he had pointed out that he had not all the time in the world, and would soon have to go back to London. Ellen could not imagine why he should want to get back to London. She herself had never been to London, but her niece Anne had taken a trip a couple of years ago, and what she had told Ellen about it had left Ellen in no great hurry to follow her example.

Her hat settled, she picked up her coat. She had brought all her things downstairs earlier in the morning so as to save a trip up all those flights of stairs to her attic bedroom. Climbing stairs was one of the things that tired her. She hated being tired. She hated the way her heart thumped when she was tired. Sometimes she hated being old.

She put on her coat and buttoned it up, and adjusted the lapel where she had pinned her best Cairngorm brooch. She took up her bulging handbag, her black gloves. From the front of the house, the telephone rang.

She stook still, waiting, trying to remember who was in the house and who out of it. Mrs. Dobbs had taken the little boy out for a walk. John was with Davey. The telephone continued to ring, and Ellen sighed and laid down her bag and gloves and went to answer it. Out of the kitchen, across the hall, into the library. The telephone stood on the colonel's desk. Ellen picked up the receiver.

"Yes?"

There came a series of clickings and buzzings, distasteful to her ear. The telephone was another thing she hated. "Yes?" she said again, beginning to sound testy.

A final click, and a man's voice. "Is that Benchoile?"

"This is Benchoile."

"I want to speak to Oliver Dobbs."

"He's not here," said Ellen, instantly. Jess Guthrie would be at the door at any moment, and she did not want to keep her waiting.

But the caller was not so easily put off.

"Is there no way you can get hold of him? It's very important indeed."

The word *important* caught her attention.

It was splendid when important people came to stay and important things happened. It gave a body something to talk about that wasn't simply the price of lambs or the weather.

"He . . . he'll maybe be over at the Stable House."

"Could you go and get him?"

"It may take a moment or two."

"I'll hold on."

"The telephone is very expensive," Ellen reminded him sharply. Important or not, it was a sinful thing to waste good money.

"What?" He sounded taken aback, as indeed he might. "Oh. Well, never mind about that. I'd be grateful if you could get him. Tell him it's his agent."

Ellen sighed, and resigned herself to missing out on the first hymn. "Very well."

She laid down the receiver, and made the long journey down through the back of the house to the stable-yard. When she opened the back door the wind swirled and gusted and nearly pulled the doorknob out of her grasp. Bent against this, holding on her good hat, she crossed the cobbles and opened Roddy's front door.

"Roddy!" Her voice, raised, cracked a little.

There was a pause, and then footsteps crossed the floor above her, and Mr. Dobbs himself appeared at the head of the stairs, as tall, thought Ellen, as a lamp-post.

"He's not here, Ellen. He's gone to Creagan to get the Sunday papers."

"There's a telephone call for you, Mr. Dobbs. The man says he is your agent, and it is very important."

His face lit up. "Oh. Right." And he came helter-skelter down the stairs, so fast that Ellen was obliged to step sideways to avoid being knocked flat. "Thanks, Ellen," he said, as he shot past her.

"He's waiting at the other end of the telephone . . ." she raised her voice to his retreating back ". . . and the Lord himself knows what it's costing him."

But Mr. Dobbs was already out of earshot of her grumblings. Ellen made a face. Some people. She pulled her hat down, and followed him at her own pace. In the kitchen, she saw, through the window, the Guthrie's van, waiting for her, with Jess Guthrie at the wheel. She was flustered and halfway through the door before she realized that she had forgotten her gloves.

Oliver's telephone call from London lasted for more than half an hour, and by the time he got back to the Stable House, Roddy had returned from Creagan with all the Sunday papers, was ensconced in his deepest leather armchair in front of a furnace of a fire, and was already looking forward to the first gin-and-tonic of the day.

He laid down the *Observer*, and looked up over his spectacles as Oliver came bounding up the stairs two at a time.

"Hello," he said. "I thought I'd been deserted."

"I had a phone call." Oliver came to sit in the chair opposite to Roddy, with his hands hanging loose between his bony knees.

Roddy sent him a keen look. He sensed the suppressed, secret excitement. "Good news, I hope."

"Yes. Good. It was my agent. It's all fixed. The new play's moving to London when it's finished the run at Bristol. Same cast, same producer, everything."

"Fantastic." Roddy dropped the paper to the floor, reached up a hand to pull off his spectacles. "My dear boy, that really is the most splendid news."

"There are other goodies in the pipeline as well, but those can wait till later. I mean, they're not actually signed and sealed yet."

"I couldn't be more pleased." Roddy glanced at his watch. "The sun's not over the yardarm yet, but I think this calls—"

But Oliver interrupted him. "There's just one thing. Would you mind if I left Victoria and Thomas with you for a couple of days? I have to go to London. I have to go tomorrow. Just for one night. There's a plane from Inverness about five o'clock in the evening. I wondered, too, if someone would be able to drive me over to catch it."

"But of course. You can leave them here as long as you like. And I'll take you over in the MG."

"It's only for two days. I'll be coming back the next day. And after that I'll pack the others up and we'll make our way back south in the car."

The very idea of them all leaving made Roddy feel miserable. He dreaded being on his own again, not simply because he loved to have young company about the place, but because with Oliver and Victoria and little Thomas gone, he knew that there would no longer be an excuse not to face up to facts. And the facts were cold. Jock was dead. John was going to sell Benchoile. Ties and traditions would be broken forever. It was the end of a way of life. This was the last house party.

He said, with the vague notion of putting off the evil moment. "You don't have to go. You know you don't have to go."

"You know that we have to. As it is, you've been more than kind and marvelously hospitable, but we can't stay forever. Anyway, fish and guests stink after three days, and we've been here three already, so tomorrow we're going to start stinking."

"I'll miss you. We all will. Ellen has lost her heart to Thomas. It won't seem the same without you all around."

"You'll still have John."

"John won't stay longer than he has to. He can't. He's got to get back to London."

"Victoria tells me that he's going to sell Benchoile." Roddy was surprised. "I didn't realize he'd discussed it with Victoria."

"She told me last night."

"Yes. He's going to sell up. He really has no alternative. To be truthful, it's what I expected."

"What will happen to you?"

"It depends who buys the place. If it's a rich American with sporting instincts, perhaps I could get a job as ghillie. I rather see myself touching my cap and collecting massive tips."

"You should get married," said Oliver.

Roddy sent him another sharp look. "You're a fine one to be talking."

Oliver grinned. "I'm different," he said smugly. "I'm a different generation. I'm allowed to have a different set of morals and values."

"You certainly have those."

"Don't you approve?"

"It would make no difference whether I approved or not. I'm too idle a man to take up attitudes about matters which really don't concern me. Perhaps I was too idle to get married, because getting married was expected of me. I never really did anything that was expected of me. Not getting married was just part of the pattern. Like writing books and watching birds and drinking too much. My brother Jock despaired of me."

"I think it's a good way to be," said Oliver. "I suppose I've followed pretty much the same pattern myself."

"Yes," said Roddy, "but in my case I had a golden rule. I never got involved with anybody, because I knew that once I did I was in danger of hurting them."

Oliver looked at him, surprised. "You're talking about Victoria, aren't you?"

"She is very vulnerable."

"She is also intelligent."

"The heart and the head are two separate entities."

"Reason and emotion?"

"If you like."

Oliver said, "I can't be tied."

"You already are," Roddy pointed out. "You have the child."

Oliver reached for his cigarettes. He took one and lit it with a spill kindled from the fire. When it was alight, he tossed the spill onto the flames. He said, "In that case, isn't it a little late to start talking to me like a father?"

"It's never too late to rectify matters."

Across the hearthrug their eyes clashed, and Roddy recognized the coldness in Oliver's pale gaze. When he spoke, it was to change the subject. "Do you know where Victoria is?"

It was a sort of dismissal. Roddy sighed. "I think she took Thomas for a walk."

Oliver stood up. "In that case, I'd better go and find her. Tell her what's happening."

He went, running down the wooden staircase, and slamming the front door shut behind him. His footsteps rang across the cobbles of the stableyard. Roddy was left no wiser as to Oliver's intentions, suspecting that he had done more harm than good, and wishing that he had kept his mouth shut. After a little, he sighed again, hauled himself out of his chair and went to pour himself that longed-for gin-and-tonic.

Victoria, making her way back through the birch wood, saw Oliver emerge from beneath the stableyard archway, and walk out onto the gravel in front of the house. He was smoking a cigarette. She was about to call out to him, when he caught sight of her and Thomas, and came across the grass to meet them.

Thomas, whose legs had given out on him halfway home, was riding pickaback on Victoria's shoulders. When she saw Oliver coming towards them, Victoria bent down and let Thomas slip to the ground. He ran ahead of her and reached Oliver before she did, butting his father in the legs with his head and hobbling Oliver's knees with his arms.

Oliver did not pick him up, but stood there, penned, waiting until Victoria was within earshot.

"Where have you been?" he asked her.

"Just for a walk. We found another stream, but not

as pretty as the waterfall." She reached his side. "What have you been doing?"

"Telephoning," he told her. The walk, the cold air, had brought color to her cheeks. Her pale hair was blowing and tousled. She had found, somewhere, a clump of yellow aconites, and had picked one or two and put them in the buttonhole of her jacket. Oliver pulled her into his arms and kissed her. She smelled cool and fresh, of apples and the outdoors. Her lips were sweet and clean, her kiss tasted as innocent as clear water.

"Telephoning who?"

"I wasn't telephoning anybody. I was being telephoned."

"Who by?"

"My agent." He let her go, and stooped to disentangle Thomas from his legs. They began to walk towards the house, but Thomas protested, so Victoria went back to lift him up in her arms. When she was alongside Oliver once more, she asked, "What did he say?"

"Good things. *Bent Penny's* going to London."

She stopped dead. *"Oliver! But that's marvelous."*

"And I'm going to London too, tomorrow." Her face dropped. "I'm leaving you and Thomas behind."

"You can't mean it."

He laughed. "Don't look so tragic, you ninny. I'm coming back the next day."

"But why can't we come with you?"

"What's the point of coming to London for one day? Anyway, I can't talk business with you and Thomas under my feet all the time."

"But we can't stay here without you!"

"Why not?"

"I don't want to be left behind."

In a flash, Oliver became irritated. He stopped his good-natured teasing, and said, in some exasperation, "I'm *not* leaving you behind. I'm simply going to London for a night. I'm flying down and I'm flying

back. And when I get back, we're packing up and
we're getting into the car and we're all going south
again. Together. Now, does that make you happy?"

"But what am I going to do without you?"

"Exist, I imagine. It shouldn't be too difficult."

"I just feel it's so awful for Roddy. We dumped ourselves on him in the first place, and now . . ."

"He's fine. He's delighted at the idea of having you
and Thomas to himself for a day or two. And as for
dumping ourselves on him, he doesn't want us to go.
Once we've gone, he'll have to face reality, and he
doesn't relish that in the very least."

"That's a horrible thing to say about Roddy."

"OK, it's horrible, but it's true. OK, he's charming
and amusing, a character straight from the pages of
some old nineteen-thirties comedy. Rattigan, perhaps,
at his most fresh-faced. But I doubt if he's ever faced
an issue in his life."

"He was in the war. Anybody who went through the
war was bound to face issues. That was what it was all
about."

"I'm talking about personal issues. Not National
Emergencies. You can't hide from a National Emer-
gency by climbing behind a brandy and soda."

"Oh, *Oliver.* I hate it when you're like this. And I
still don't want you to go and leave Thomas and me
behind."

"Well, I'm going." She did not reply, and he put his
arm around her, and bent and kissed the top of her
head. "And you are not to sulk about it. And on Tuesday, when I fly back, you can jump into the Volvo
and come and meet me. And if you're particularly
charming, I shall take you out to dinner in Inverness.
And we'll eat haggis and chips and join in the folk
dancing. Can you think of anything more riveting?"

"I'd rather you didn't go." But she was beginning to
smile.

"I have to. Duty calls. I'm a successful man. Leaving

you behind is one of the prices I have to pay for being successful."

"Sometimes I wish you weren't."

He kissed her again. "You know what's wrong with you? You're never happy."

"That's not true."

He relented. "I know it isn't."

"I've been happy here," she told him, and she was suddenly shy. She hoped that Oliver would tell her that he had been happy too. But he did not say anything, and she heaved Thomas's weight from one arm to the other, and together, they walked back to the house.

CHAPTER 13
Monday

Roddy stood at the top of his staircase and called "Victoria!"

Victoria, who had spent the morning ironing shirts and handkerchiefs for Oliver, sorting out socks and sweaters, and finally packing a suitcase, straightened up from her task, pushed a lock of hair from her face, and went to open the bedroom door.

"I'm here!"

"John's here, and Oliver. Come and join us. We're having a drink."

It was nearly half past twelve, a bright, cold day and the sun was shining. Roddy and Oliver were leaving for the airport after lunch. A quarter of an hour previously, Ellen had appeared to take charge of Thomas and to get him ready for lunch, for lunch today was to be a substantial affair, cooked by Ellen and Jess Guthrie and eaten in the big dining room at Benchoile. This was Ellen's decision. She had always been of the opinion that no person should set out on a journey, however short, without a good meal inside him, and Oliver was, apparently, no exception. Accordingly, she and Jess had been busy all morning. Appetizing smells had wafted through from the big house, and there was a certain sense of occasion in the air, as though something important was happening, like a birthday, or the last day of the holidays.

Above her, in Roddy's sitting room, Victoria could hear the murmured conversation of the others. She closed the suitcase and snapped shut the locks. She went to the mirror and combed her hair, gave a final glance about the room to make sure that nothing had been forgotten, and then went upstairs to join the rest of the party.

Because of the sunshine and the brightness of the day, she found them gathered, not about the fireside, but at the huge window. Oliver and Roddy sat on the window seat with their backs to the view, and John Dunbeath on a chair that he had pulled back from the desk. When Victoria appeared, Roddy said, "Here she is, come along, we've been waiting for you," and John stood up and moved his chair to one side in order to make space for her. "What'll you have to drink?"

She considered this. "I don't think I really want a drink."

"Oh, come on," said Oliver. He held out a long arm, and drew Victoria to his side. "Don't be prissy. You've been beavering around all morning, being domestic. You deserve a drink."

"Oh, all right."

John said, "What would you like? I'll get it for you."

Still caught in the circle of Oliver's arm, she looked across at him. "A lager, perhaps?" And he smiled, and went through to Roddy's kitchen to collect her a can out of the fridge.

But there was scarcely time to open the can and pour the lager before they were interrupted by the sound of the front door opening, and Ellen's voice from the foot of the stairs, raised to tell them all that lunch was ready, it was on the table, it would spoil if they didn't come immediately.

Roddy said, sotto voce, "Drat the woman," but there was obviously nothing to be done about it, and so, carrying their various glasses, they all got to their feet and made their way downstairs and across the yard to the big house.

They found the dining room full of sunshine, the big table laid with a white cloth. A roast of beef steamed on the sideboard, dishes of hot vegetables stood on the hot plate, and Thomas was already installed, hungry and feedered, in an ancient wooden high chair that Jess Guthrie had brought down from the old nursery.

Ellen pottered to and fro on her unsteady legs, telling everybody where they were to sit, complaining that the roast was getting cold, and what was the point of cooking good meat if folks couldn't be on time for their meals?

John said, good-naturedly, "Now come on, Ellen, that's not true. We were off our backsides the moment you hollered up the stairs. Who's going to carve?"

"You," said Roddy instantly, and went to sit down with his back to the window, as far from the sideboard as possible. He had never been any good at carving. Jock had always done the carving.

John sharpened the horn-handled knife with all the élan of a master butcher, and got to work. Ellen took the first plate for Thomas, and herself dealt with it, cutting up the meat and squashing the vegetables and gravy into a mess like brown porridge.

"There he is, the wee man. You eat that up now, pet, and you'll turn into a great big boy."

"Not that we have too many problems," Roddy murmured when Ellen had departed and closed the door behind her, and everybody laughed because this morning Thomas's cheeks appeared to be fatter and rounder than ever.

They had finished their first course and were just starting in on Ellen's apple pie and baked custard, when the telephone started to ring. They all waited, as seemed to be the custom at Benchoile, for somebody else to go and answer it. Finally Roddy said, "Oh, damn."

Victoria took pity on him. "Shall I go?"

"No, don't bother." He took another leisurely mouthful of apple pie, and pushed back his chair and ambled from the room, still grumbling. "What a bloody stupid time to ring up." He had left the dining room door open, and they could hear his voice from the library. "Benchoile. Roddy Dunbeath here." Then a pause. "Who? What? Yes, of course. Hold on a moment and I'll go and get him." A moment later he reappeared, still holding the table napkin, which he had taken with him.

"Oliver, dear boy, it's for you."

'Oliver looked up from his plate. "Me? Who is it?"

"No idea. Some man or other."

He returned to his apple pie, and Oliver pushed back his chair and went to take the call. "I can't think," said Roddy, "why they can't invent some device so that when you sit down to a meal, you can stop the telephone ringing."

"You could always take it off the hook," John suggested mildly.

"Yes, but then I'd forget to put it back again."

Thomas was beginning to be bored with his pudding. Victoria picked up his spoon and began to help him. She said, "You could always just let it ring."

"I'm not strong-minded enough. I can let it ring for just so long, and then I can't bear it for another moment. I always imagine that someone is waiting to tell me something tremendously exciting, and I go cantering off to grab the receiver from the hook, only to find myself voice-to-voice as it were with the Inland revenue. Or else it's a wrong number."

John said, "If you're a wrong number, then why did you answer the phone?" which was somehow all the funnier, because he didn't often make jokes.

By the time Oliver returned, their meal was over. Roddy had lighted a cigar, and John brought the tray of coffee through from the kitchen. Victoria was peeling an orange for Thomas, because however much he ate, he always liked oranges more than anything. The orange was juicy and the task absorbed her, so that she did not look up when Oliver came back into the room.

"Good news, I hope," she heard Roddy say. The last of the peel fell away, and she broke the orange into sections and handed the first one to Thomas. Oliver did not reply. "Nothing serious?" Roddy now sounded concerned.

Still Oliver said nothing. The silence suddenly caught Victoria's attention. It grew longer, more strained. Even Thomas was stilled by it. He sat, with a piece of orange in his hand, and stared across the table at his father. Victoria's cheeks began to prickle. She realized that they were all looking at her. She looked at Roddy, and then up at Oliver. She saw his face, intensely pale, and his cold, unblinking eyes. She felt the blood drain from her own cheeks, and a reasonless sense of doom, like a sickness, knot her stomach.

She swallowed. "What is it?" Her voice sounded thin and insubstantial.

"Do you know who that was on the telephone?" Oliver asked her."

"I've no idea," but she could not keep her voice from trembling.

"It was Mr. Bloody Archer. Ringing up from Hampshire." *But I told her not to ring up. I said I'd write again. I explained about Oliver.* "You wrote to them."

"I . . ." Her mouth was dry, and she swallowed again. "I didn't write to him. I wrote to her."

Oliver advanced to the table, he laid the palms of his hands flat upon its surface, and leaned towards her.

"I told you not to write to her." Each word came out like a hammer blow. "I told you you were not to write to her, nor telephone her, to get in touch with her in any way at all."

"Oliver, I had to . . ."

"How did you know where to write, anyway?"

"I . . . I looked it up in the telephone directory."

"When did you write?"

"On Thursday . . . Friday . . ." She was beginning to be flustered. "I can't remember."

"What was I doing?"

"I . . . I think you were still asleep." It was beginning to sound so underhand, so secretive, that she was impelled to stand up for herself. "I *told* you I wanted to write to her. I couldn't bear her not knowing about Thomas . . . not knowing where he was." Oliver's expression softened not one whit. Victoria realized, with horror, that she was going to cry. She could feel her mouth shaking, the lump grow in her throat, her eyes begin to swim with terrible, shaming tears. In front of them all, she was going to start crying.

"She *knew* where he bloody was."

"No, she *didn't*."

"She knew he was with me. And that's all that bloody matters. He was with me and I am his father. What I do with him, and where I take him, is no concern of anyone else. Least of all, you."

Tears were now running down her face. "Well, I think——" she managed before he interrupted her.

"I never asked you to think. I simply told you to keep your stupid little mouth *shut*."

This was accompanied by Oliver's fist coming down in a massive blow on the dining room table. Everything on it shivered and bounced. Thomas, who had been stunned into silence by the unfamiliar violence of words that he did not know, but understood only too well, chose this moment to emulate Victoria, and burst into tears. His eyes screwed up, his mouth fell open, the remains of his half-chewed orange dribbled from his mouth down onto his feeder.

"Oh, for God's sake . . ."

"Oh, Oliver, *don't*." She sprang to her feet, her knees trembling, and tried to lift Thomas out of his chair, to comfort him. Thomas clung to her, burying his sticky face into her neck, trying to hide from the shouting. "Don't, in front of Thomas. *Stop!*"

But her anguished appeal was ignored. By now Oliver was past stopping. "You knew why I didn't want you to get in touch with the Archers. Because I guessed that as soon as they knew where we were, I'd be bombarded with maudlin appeals, and when they failed, threats. Which is precisely what has happened. The next thing we know, there'll be some black-coated little bastard on the doorstep delivering a letter from some lawyer or other . . ."

"But you said . . ." She couldn't remember what he had said. Her nose had started to run, and she could scarcely speak for crying. "I . . . I . . ." She scarcely knew what she was trying to say. *I'm sorry*, perhaps, but it was just as well that this final abasement was never uttered, because Oliver was in no mood to be placated by anything. Not his weeping son, nor his weeping mistress, nor all the apologies in the world.

"You know what you are? You're a deceitful little bitch."

And with this final broadside, Oliver straightened up from the table, and turned and stalked out of the room. Victoria was left, trapped by her own tears, with the weeping, hysterical child in her arms, with the appalled silence of the other two men, with the shambles of the ruined meal. Worst of all, with humiliation and shame.

Roddy said, "My dear," and got up from the table and came around to her side, and Victoria knew that she must stop crying, but she couldn't stop, or wipe away her tears, or even start looking for a handkerchief, while still burdened with the howling Thomas.

John Dunbeath said, "Here." He was beside her, lifting Thomas out of her arms and up against his broad shoulder. "Here, come along now, we'll go and find Ellen. She'll maybe have some candy for you to eat." Bearing Thomas with him, he made for the door. "Or a chocolate biscuit. Do you like chocolate biscuits?"

When they had gone, "My dear," said Roddy again.

"I . . . I can't help it . . ." Victoria gasped.

He could bear it no longer. Streaming face, running nose, sobs and all, he pulled her into his arms and held her against him, cradling the back of her head with his gentle hand. After a little, he reached up and took the red and white handkerchief from the breast pocket of his aged tweed jacket, and gave it to her, and Victoria was able to blow her nose and wipe her eyes.

After that, things got a little better, and the nightmare scene started to be over.

She went in search of Oliver. There was nothing else to be done. She found him down by the edge of the loch, standing at the end of the jetty, smoking a cigarette. If he heard her coming across the grass, he gave no sign of it, for he never turned round.

She reached the jetty. She said his name. He hesitated for a moment, and then threw his half-smoked cigarette into the sun-dappled water, and turned to face her.

Victoria remembered him saying, *If you so much as pick up a telephone, I'll batter you black and blue.* But she hadn't really believed the threat, because in all the time that she had known him, she had never seen the true violence of Oliver's uncontrolled rage. Now, she knew, she had seen it. She wondered if his wife, Jeanette, had seen it. If that, perhaps, was one of the reasons why his marriage had lasted only for a few months.

"Oliver."

His eyes rested on her face. She knew she looked hideous, still swollen from weeping, but even that didn't matter any longer. Nothing mattered except that the dreadful quarrel, for Thomas's sake, had to be patched up.

She said, "I really am sorry."

He still said nothing. After a little, he gave a long sigh, and then shrugged.

She went on, painfully. "It's difficult for you to understand. I know that. And I don't suppose I understood, either, because I'd never had a child of my own. But after I'd been with Thomas for a bit, I began to realize what it was like. I mean, having a little boy, and loving him." She wasn't doing it right at all. She was making it sound sentimental, and that wasn't what she was trying to be at all. "You get bound up with a child. Involved. As though it were part of you. You begin to feel that if anybody hurt it, or even threatened it, you could kill them."

"Do you imagine," said Oliver, "That Mrs. Archer was going to kill me?"

"No. But I did know that she was probably out of her mind with anxiety."

"She always hated me. They both did."

"Perhaps you didn't give them much reason to do anything else?"

"I married their daughter."

"And fathered their grandchild."

"He's my son."

"That's the whole point. Thomas is your son. You've told me over and over that the Archers have no legal claim on him. So how can it hurt you to be a little generous to them? He's all they have left of their daughter. Oh, Oliver, you must try to understand. You're perceptive and clever, you write plays that wring people's hearts. Why can't you come to terms with a situation that should be so close to your own heart?"

"Perhaps I haven't got a heart."

"You've got a heart." She began, tentatively, to

smile. "I've heard it beating. Thump thump thump, all through the night."

It worked. His grim expression softened a little, as though the situation had, in its way, a wry humor. It wasn't much, but emboldened by this, Victoria went down the jetty to his side, she put her arms around his waist, beneath his jacket, and pressed her cheek against the front of his rough, thick sweater.

She said, "They don't matter anyway, the Archers. What they do can't make any difference."

His hands rubbed up and down her back, as though he were absently fondling a dog. "Any difference to what?"

"My loving you," It was said. Pride, self-esteem no longer mattered. Loving Oliver was their only talisman, all she had to hold onto. It was the key of the lock that held the two of them, and Thomas, together.

He said, "You must be mad."

He did not apologize for any of the searing remarks and accusations he had thrown at her down the length of the lunch table. She wondered if he would apologize to Roddy and John, and knew that he would not. Simply because he was Oliver Dobbs. But that didn't matter. Victoria had bridged the breach between them. The wound of the hideous scene was still open, and agonizing, but perhaps, in time, it would heal. She realized that it was always possible to pick yourself up and start again, however many times you fall.

She said, "Would you mind very much if I was."

He did not reply. Presently he laid his hands on her shoulders and put her away from him. "I must go," he told her. "It's time I was going, or I'll miss my plane."

They went back to the Stable House and collected his suitcase, a couple of books. When they came out again, they saw Jock's old Daimler parked in front of the house, and Roddy and John standing beside it, waiting.

It seemed that everybody had decided to behave as though nothing had happened. "I thought it would be better to take the big car," Roddy explained. "There's not much room for luggage in the MG."

His tone was quite matter-of-fact, and Victoria felt grateful to him.

"That's great," Oliver opened the back door and heaved his case in, and the books on top of it. "Well," he grinned, quite unrepentant, even perhaps a little amused by the lack of expression on John Dunbeath's face, "I'll say good-bye, John."

"I'll see you again," John told him. He did not hold out a hand. "I'm not leaving till Wednesday."

"That's great. Bye, Victoria," he stooped to kiss her cheek.

"Tomorrow," she said. "What time does your plane get in?"

"About seven-thirty."

"I'll be there to meet you."

"See you then."

They got into the car. Roddy started the engine. The Daimler moved away, ponderous and dignified, tires crunching on the gravel. Down through the rhododendrons, over the cattle grid, through the gate.

They had gone.

He was terribly afraid that now it was all over, now he was alone with her, she would start to cry again. It was not that he was afraid of tears, or would even be embarrassed by them. In fact, he would have almost welcomed them. But he knew, too, that this was not the right time to take her in his arms, to comfort her as Roddy had done.

She was standing with her back to him. She was done with waving good-bye. To John, her erect and slender back seemed immensely courageous. He saw the firm set of her shoulders under the thick sweater, the long silky tail of fair hair, and was reminded of a colt his father had reared, long ago, on the ranch back in Colorado. Once frightened by a clumsy hand, only the most patient and perceptive of handling had finally brought it back to anything approaching trust. But little by little, letting the colt take his own time. John himself had achieved this.

He knew that he had to be very careful. He waited. After a bit, perhaps realizing that he was not going to simply melt away and tactfully disappear, Victoria pushed her hair out of her face, and turned to face him. She was not crying. She was smiling. The sort of smile that lights up a face, but does not reach the eyes.

She said, briskly, "Well, that's that."

He said, "They've got a good day for a drive. It'll be very beautiful, going over Struie."

"Yes."

"Don't you think we ought to go for a drive, too?" Victoria's smile froze and became agonized, and he knew that this was what she had been dreading; he was sorry for her and so he was going to be kind to her. He went on, quickly, "I have to go to Creagan, anyway. I have to go to the chemist. I've run out of shaving soap. And I thought the newsagent might have a *Financial Times*. I haven't seen the market prices for three days." This was not true, but it was a face-saver, and as good an excuse as any.

Victoria said, "What about Thomas?"

"We'll leave Thomas here. He's happy with Ellen."

"I haven't taken Thomas to the beach yet. I've always meant to take him."

"You can take him another time. If you don't tell him where you're going, he won't want to come."

She considered this. She said at last, "Well . . . all right. But I must go and tell Ellen that we're going out."

That was good enough. "You'll find them out at the back, on the drying-green. I'll get the car and meet you here in a moment or two."

When he returned, at the wheel of the hired Ford, she was back on the steps by the front door, waiting for him. He knew that in Creagan it would be windswept and cold, and she was wearing no sort of coat, but there was a spare sweater of his own lying on the back seat of the car, and he did not want to put off any time. He drew up beside her, leaned across to open the passenger door, and let Victoria get in beside him. Then, with no more discussion, they were on their way.

He took it slowly. There was no hurry. The more leisurely their passage, the more relaxed he hoped she would become. He said, casually, "How was Thomas?"

"You were right. He and Ellen are perfectly happy. Ellen's taken a chair out into the sun, and she's doing her knitting, and Thomas and Piglet are playing with her clothes pegs." She added, a little wistfully, "They looked very peaceful."

He said, "Thomas isn't your child, is he?"

Victoria, beside him, was very still. She stared ahead at the convolutions of the narrow road. Her hands lay clasped in her lap. She said, "No."

"I don't know why, but I always imagined that he was. I suppose Roddy thought he was, too. At least, he never gave me any reason to suspect that he wasn't. And he looks like you. That's the extraordinary thing. A bit fatter, perhaps, but he really looks like you."

"He isn't my child. But he's Oliver's. Thomas's mother was called Jeanette Archer. Oliver married her, but then the marriage broke up and she was killed in an aircrash soon after."

"How do you come into it?"

"I've been in it for years . . ." Her voice began to shake. "I'm terribly sorry, but I think I'm going to start crying again."

"It doesn't matter."

"Don't you mind?" She sounded surprised.

"Why should I mind?" He leaned forward and opened the cubbyhole on the dashboard, and revealed an enormous box of Kleenex. "See? I'm even prepared."

"Americans always have paper handkerchiefs." She took one out and blew her nose. "Crying's horrible, isn't it? Once you start, it's like a terrible addiction. However many times you stop, you always start again. I don't usually ever cry."

But this brave assertion dissolved, even as she made it, into tears. John waited peacefully, taking no notice, saying nothing. After a little, when the sobs had reduced themselves to chokes and then to sniffs and she had blown her nose, determinedly, once more, he observed, "If a person wants to cry, I never see any reason why they shouldn't. I always cried when I was a kid and being sent back to Fessenden. And my father never tried to stop me nor tell me that it wasn't manly. In fact, he sometimes looked as though he were about to burst into tears himself."

Victoria smiled wanly, but made no comment on this, and John decided to leave it, and nothing more was said until they reached Creagan. The little town lay bathed in cold afternoon sunshine, its streets swept and empty of the modest throngs who would fill it later on in the year as the summer season swelled.

He drew up in front of the chemist. "Do you want to do any shopping?" he asked Victoria.

"No. I'm all right, thank you."

He left her and went into the shop and bought the shaving soap and some razor blades. Next to the chemist was a newsagent, so he went in there and asked for the *Financial Times*, but they didn't have one, so he bought a bag of peppermints instead, and bore these back to the car.

"Here." He tossed them into Victoria's lap. "If you don't like them, we'll give them to Thomas."

"Perhaps Ellen would like them. Old people always like peppermints."

"These are toffees. Ellen can't eat toffees on account of her false teeth. Now, what shall we do?"

"We could go back to Benchoile."

"Is that what you want to do? Don't you want to go for a walk or something? Don't you want to go to the beach?"

"Do you know the way?"

"Sure I know the the way, I used to come here when I was knee-high to a bee."

"Haven't you anything else you'd rather do?"

"Not a mortal thing."

The beach at Creagan was divided from the town by the golf links, and there was no access by road to the sands, so John parked the car by the clubhouse. When he switched off the engine, they could hear the whine of the wind. The long pale grasses that flanked the fairways lay flat beneath its blast, and the brightly colored waterproof jackets of a couple of hardy golfers were filled with it, so that they resembled balloons. John pulled up the zipper of his old leather jacket, and reached back for the sweater that lay on the back

It was blue and very thick with a tall polo neck. She pulled it over her head and the tight, ribbed collar dragged her hair. She flipped it free and shook it loose. The cuffs of the sweater covered her hands , the hem reached below her narrow hips.

They got out of the car, and the wind pounced on the open doors and it was a struggle to get them shut. A path, a right-of-way, led down towards the sea across the fairways. Wild thyme grew underfoot, and there were hazards of whin and gorse. Beyond the links lay dunes of coarse grass, "bents" they were called in this part of the world, and there was a little caravan site, and small, ramshackle edifices, which in summer would open their shutters and sell chocolate and fizzy drinks and ice creams. The dunes ended abruptly in a sloping cliff of sand. The tide was out. Now there was nothing but white beach and the distant sea. Far away, the rollers creamed in, crested with spray. There was not another soul about, not a dog, not a scampering child. Only the wheeling gulls hung overhead screaming their disdain at the world in general.

After the soft, dry, sand of the dunes, the beach seemed very flat and firm underfoot. They ran, trying to get warm. As they approached the sea, shallow pools, fed from some mysterious source, reflected the brightness of the sky, and there were immense quantities of shells. Victoria's attention was caught by these. She picked up one and then another, marveling at their size and unbroken state.

"They're so beautiful. I've never seen shells before that weren't all broken to bits. Why aren't these broken?"

"I suppose because this is a shallow, sandy shore." He joined in her ploy, grateful for any diversion that would take her mind off her woes. He found the skeleton of a starfish, the delicate fossilized claw of a miniature crab.

"What's this?" she asked him.

He inspected it. "A sand gaper. And the blue one is a common mussel."

"And this? It looks exactly like a very small baby's toenail."

"That's called a banded wedge."

"How do you know their names?"

"I used to come and collect shells when I was a boy, and Roddy gave me a book so that I'd learn to identify them."

They walked on in silence, and came at last to the sea. They stood, facing the wind, and watched the breakers pouring in. The waves rose and curled and broke and hissed in over the sand, and the water was clear and clean and the color of aquamarine.

The shell lay, just out of reach of the ebbing tide. John stooped and picked it up, and placed it, wet and shining, in the palm of Victoria's hand. It was the color of coral, with a sunburst or raised ribs, semispherical in shape, so that if it had still been attached to its twin they would have formed a whole roughly the size of a tennis ball.

"Now there's a prize," he said.

She was openmouthed. "Whatever is it?"

"That's a queen scallop, and what a size of one."

"I thought you only found shells like that in the West Indies."

"Well, now you know you can find them in Scotland."

She held it away from her, taking enormous pleasure in its shape, the very feel of the shell. She said, "I shall keep it for always. Just for an ornament."

"And a keepsake, perhaps."

Victoria looked at him, and he saw the beginnings of her first smile. "Yes. Perhaps as a keepsake too."

They turned their backs on the sea, and started on the long return journey. The sands stretched forever, and the dunes seemed very far away. By the time they had reached the steep cliff of sand down which they had tumbled so easily, Victoria was beginning to flag, and John had to take her hand, and pull her, floundering and slipping, to the top. Halfway up, she began to laugh, and when they finally reached the summit, they were both breathless. In wordless agreement, they collapsed, exhausted into a sheltered hollow, where the sand gave way to a thick, coarse grass, and the tussocks of bents protected them from the worst of the wind.

Here, there even seemed to be a little heat in the sun. John lay back on his elbows, and let its warmth generate through the thick, dark suede of his jacket. Victoria sat forward, her chin on her knees, still gloating over her shell. Her hair had parted at the back of her neck, and his enormous sweater made her look even thinner and frailer than she actually was.

After a bit, she said, "Perhaps I shouldn't keep it. Perhaps I should give it to Thomas."

"Thomas wouldn't appreciate it."

"He would, when he's older."

"You're very fond of Thomas, aren't you? Even though he isn't your child."

Victoria said, "Yes."

"Do you want to talk about it?"

"It's difficult to know where to begin. And you probably wouldn't understand anyway."

"You could try me."

"Well . . ." She took a deep breath. "The Archers are Thomas's grandparents."

"I gathered that."

"And they live in Hampshire. And Oliver was driving back from Bristol, and he passed near Wood-bridge—that's where the Archers live . . ."

Slowly, hesitantly, the story unfolded. All the time she was speaking, Victoria kept her back turned to John, and he was forced to listen to the entire saga while staring at the back of her neck. He found this intensely frustrating.

". . . that night you brought me back from the Fairburn's party, and Thomas was crying—that was the evening they turned up."

He remembered that night, the evening before he had flown to Bahrain. The dark windy skies and the little house in the Mews; Victoria with her chin buried in the fur collar of her coat, and her eyes filled with apprehension and anxiety.

". . . and all come away for a little holiday. So we came to Benchoile on account of Oliver knowing Roddy. I told you about that."

"I take it you don't have a job to keep you in London?"

"Oh, yes I do. But I work in a dress shop in Beauchamp place, and Sally, the girl I work for, wanted me to take a holiday anyway. So she said I could have a

month off, and she's got a temporary girl in to help
out till I get back again."

"And are you going back?"

"I don't know."

"Why don't you know?"

"I may just stay with Oliver."

This silenced John. He could not comprehend how
any girl could want to stay with that raving egotist.
Despite all his original and laudable intentions of
keeping a fair and open mind, he found himself becoming slowly more and more incensed.

She was talking again. ". . . I knew how worried
Mrs. Archer must be, so I said to Oliver that I thought
I should write to her, and Oliver was furious because
he didn't want them to know where we were. But I did
write, although I explained to her about Oliver being
so difficult, and I asked her not to get in touch, but I
suppose Mr. Archer got hold of my letter."

Now that the telling was safely over, Victoria appeared to decide that the time had come to look John
in the eye. She turned to face him, her attitude confid-
ing, her weight resting on one hand, her long legs
curled up beneath her.

"And it was he who rang up Oliver at lunchtime. So
now you see why Oliver was so angry."

"Yes, I suppose I do see. But I still think it was a
fairly gruesome scene."

"But you do understand?"

It was obviously important to her that he did. But
for John understanding made things no better. In fact,
if anything, a good deal worse, for his most pessimistic
suspicions had proved themselves well-founded. It was
all in place now, the pieces of the jigsaw slotted together and the pattern clear. A person was selfish. Another person was greedy. Pride came into it, and resentment and even a sort of spite. Nobody came out of
it well, and only the innocent suffered. The innocent.

A noxious word, but how else to describe Victoria and Thomas?

He thought of Oliver. From the first encounter, there had been antipathy between the two men. Like dogs, they had circled each other, hackles bristling. John had told himself that this antipathy was reasonless, instinctive, and with the inbred good manners of a man staying in another man's house, had fallen over backwards in his efforts not to let it show. But the antipathy was obviously mutual and before long John found himself resenting Oliver's casual treatment of Victoria, his offhand attitude to Roddy, his lack of interest in his child. After a couple of days in Oliver's company he had to admit that he actively disliked him. Now, after the appalling scene over the lunch table, he knew that he detested him.

He said, "If you stay with Oliver, will you marry him?"

"I don't know."

"Do you mean you don't know if you'll marry him, or if he'll marry you?"

"I don't know." A flush crept up into her pale cheeks. "I don't know if he'll marry me. He's funny. He . . ."

All at once, John was filled with a boiling, unaccustomed rage. Brutally, he interrupted her. "Victoria, don't be a fool." She stared at him, her eyes enormous. "I mean that. Don't be a fool. You have a whole, wonderful life in front of you, and you talk about getting married to a guy, and you don't even know if he loves you enough to marry you. Marriage isn't a love affair. It isn't even a honeymoon. Its a job. A long hard job, at which both partners have to work, harder than they've worked at anything in their lives before. If it's a good marriage, it changes, it evolves, but it goes on getting better. I've seen it with my own mother and father. But a bad marriage can dissolve in a welter of resentment and acrimony. I've seen that, too, in my own miserable and disastrous attempt at making another person happy. And it's never one person's fault. It's the sum total of a thousand little irritations, disagreements, idiotic details that in a sound alliance would simply be disregarded, or forgotten in the healing act of making love. Divorce isn't a cure, its a surgical operation, even if there are no children to consider. And you and Oliver already have a child. You have Thomas."

She said, "I can't go back."

"Sure you can."

"It's all very well for you to talk. Your marriage may have broken up, but you still have your parents, your job. You have Benchoile, too, whatever you decide to do with it. If I don't have Oliver and Thomas, then I don't have anything. Not anything really precious. Not anyone to belong to, not anyone to need me."

"You have yourself."

"Perhaps I'm not enough."

"In that case, you dismally underestimate yourself."

Victoria turned swiftly away from him, and John was presented once more with the back of her head. He realized that he had been shouting at her, and this astonished him, because it was the first time in many months that he had felt sufficiently involved or aroused to shout at anyone. He said, gruffly, "I'm sorry," and when she did not move or speak, he went on, more gently, "It's just that I hate to see someone like you make such a goddamn mess of her life."

She said, sounding sullen as a child, "You forget. It's still my life."

"It's Thomas's too," he reminded her. "And Oliver's." Still she did not move. He put his hand on her arm and pulled her around to face him. With an immense effort she met his eyes. He said, "You have to love Oliver very much. Much more than he loves you. To make it work, I mean."

"I know."

"In that case you're going into it with your eyes open."

"I know," she said again. Gently, she eased herself free of his grasp. "But you see, there was never anyone else. There was never anyone but Oliver."

CHAPTER 14
Tuesday

The wind, he thought, was the same wind that blew in Scotland, but in London it took on a different shape. It sneaked from around corners, it tore the first buds from the trees in the park, and littered the streets with torn scraps of paper. It was not a friend. People pressed against it, their faces agonized, their coats wrapped tight against them. The wind was an enemy, invading the city.

The rain came as the taxi, which had brought him out from Fulham, turned at last into the complexities of Heathrow Airport. It came through tunnels and circled rotaries, a tiny entity in an endless stream of traffic. Lights flashed, reflected in the wet roadways; overhead a jet droned, waiting to land. There was the heavy smell of petrol.

This taxi, in a long queue of taxis, drew in at last under the canopy of the terminal building. Oliver got out, pulled his suitcase after him, and stood at the pavement's edge feeling in his pocket for the fare. The driver, waiting, let his eyes move over his passenger, his passenger's luggage.

"Here." Oliver handed the notes over.

"Sure I've brought you to the right place, mate? This is domestic flights here. Terminal one."

"Yes, that's right."

"Just saw the label on your case. You ought to be over in international flights, terminal three."

"No. This is the one I want." He grinned. "Keep the change."

"Well, it's you who's traveling. You ought to know."

He picked up his case and went in through the glass doors, across the polished expanse of the great building, up the escalator, following the signs that led to domestic departures.

The departure hall was crowded as usual, every seat taken with travelers waiting for their various flights to be called. There was the smell of coffee, and cigarette smoke and humanity. Oliver moved slowly down the room, looking about him, like a man with a rendezvous. He saw the woman with her five exhausting children; a pair of nuns. He saw the man in the tweed overcoat and bowler hat, immersed in his newspaper. His briefcase stood on the floor between his legs. Oliver stopped before him.

"Excuse me."

Startled, the man looked up from his paper. He had a long, pale face, a neat collar, a dark tie. He wore spectacles. A lawyer, thought Oliver. A businessman. He said, "I *am* sorry, but I saw the label on your briefcase. Are you flying to Inverness?"

"Yes," said the man, sounding as though he did not think it was any of Oliver's business."

"On the five-thirty plane?"

"Yes."

"I wonder if you'd be very kind and deliver a letter for me." He reached into his pocket and took out the envelope. "The thing is, I'd arranged to catch this flight, but I'm not going to be able to make it after all, and there's someone meeting me at Inverness."

The man in spectacles continued to look unenthusiastic. He probably thought the envelope contained some sort of an explosive device, and that he and the rest of his fellow passengers were going to be blown to kingdom come whilst in transit over the Pennines.

"This has just all cropped up in the last couple of

hours, and I can't telephone her—the girl who's meeting me, I mean—because she's driving to Inverness from Sutherland, and she'll have left by now."

The man in spectacles looked at the envelope and then back at Oliver. Oliver put on his sincere and open expression. The man laid down his newspaper.

"If I do take your letter, how shall I know the young lady?"

"Well, she's young, and she's got long fair hair, and she'll probably be wearing trousers. She's called Victoria Bradshaw." He added, as though it were a little lure, "She's very pretty."

But the other was not to be so easily seduced. "What shall I do if she isn't there?"

"She will be there. I promise you. She'll be there."

The man took the envelope at last, gingerly. "Wouldn't it be better to hand this over to the air hostess?"

"I suppose we could, but you know what they're like, always so busy giving people cups of tea. And anyway, I haven't got time to wait till she turns up, because I've got to get over to the international terminal and catch another plane."

"Very well," said the man at last. Having made the decision, he allowed a small smile to cross his chilly features. "You can leave it with me."

"Thank you," said Oliver. "Thank you very much. I'm really sorry to have bothered you. And I hope you have a good flight."

"The same to you," said the man in spectacles, and went back to his paper.

Oliver picked up his suitcase and turned away. He would go down the stairs and out of this building, and he would walk through the rain, over to terminal three, and check in to the New York flight, and after that he was on his own once more. He was on his way.

He was free. It was over. An interlude, a brief encounter finished. The actors had departed, and the stage lay empty. Like an untouched canvas, it waited for Oliver to inhabit it with his own people, his own private and absorbing world.

You're back then.

That's right.

She's gone, then.

Yes, she's gone.

You can tell. A house has got a funny feeling when the last child goes. You think they're there forever but they go. And there's nothing much left, really. Except the telly. There's always the telly.

"Oh, excuse me."

He had reached the top of the stairs. He turned and found himself face to face with the man in the bowler hat. It took an instant's mental reorganization before Oliver even recognized him. He carried his briefcase in one hand, and Oliver's letter in the other.

"I'm sorry, but the young lady I have to give this to, I can't remember what you said she was called. You've written it on the envelope, but your writing's not all that clear. Is it Miss Beronica Bradshaw?"

"No," said Oliver. "It's . . ." he hesitated, having to remember. "It's Victoria."

He supposed there came a time for starting to feel old. Not just mature, or experienced, or any of the other euphemisms. Just old. He was sixty. Jock had died at sixty-nine. If he, Roddy, were to die at sixty-nine, that meant that he had only nine years left to enjoy. Or did it mean that he had nine years to fill in before he was finally released? And if so, then how was he to fill them? He would not have Benchoile to cushion him against the cold winds of the outside world, and he knew—had known for some years—that to all intents and purposes he had outwritten himself. There was no longer a readable book inside his head, and scarcely the most banal of articles. His friends, his social life, which had once so satisfyingly filled his time, were fading. His contemporaries had started to die; the delightful women who had once charmed him were becoming grandmothers, unable to cope—as inflation swallowed everything and old servants went into retirement—with house parties and dinner parties and all the endless, pleasant diversions of former days.

Pouring his second drink of the evening, trying to cheer himself up, Roddy Dunbeath told himself that in many ways he was fortunate. He would become old and he would probably be lonely, but at least he would not be penniless. All right, so Benchoile was going to be sold, but Roddy Dunbeath was in a financial position that would allow him to buy, outright, some modest house in which to spend the rest of his days. Where this house was to be, he had not yet decided, but Ellen was another problem which loomed like a shadow at the back of his mind. There could be no question of abandoning Ellen. If none of her many relations could be persuaded to have the cantankerous old thing to live with them, then Roddy would have to take her on himself. The very prospect of living in a small house with no one but Ellen Tarbat for company gave him the shivers. He prayed, fervently, that it would never have to happen.

It was eight o'clock in the evening, and he was alone in his house, and it was this very solitude that had brought on his gloomy mood. Oliver was in London, by now—Roddy glanced at his watch—by now probably on his way back to Scotland. Victoria had departed in that immense Volvo to meet him at the airport. Thomas was in the bedroom downstairs, asleep, having been bathed and put to bed by Ellen. John was over in the big house, doing God knew what. The whole business of Benchoile seemed to have got the boy down, for he had been going around all day with a face like a wet weekend and with scarcely a word for anybody. To put the final lid on things, the weather had degenerated dismally with sleet showers and a force eight gale, and the summits of the hills were once more blanketed in snow.

Where, Roddy asked himself, was the spring? On such an evening, in such a mood, it was possible to believe that it would never come again. There would be some freak in the cosmos, the stars would start clashing, earthquakes erupt and the planet Earth be trapped forever in the grip of eternal winter.

Enough. That was as far as a man's depression could be allowed to go. Supine in his chair, his slippered feet sharing the hearthrug with his old dog, Roddy decided that the time had come to take some positive step to raise his spirits. He looked once more at his watch. He would go over to the big house and take a drink with John. They would then eat dinner together, and later, when Oliver and Victoria returned from Inverness, would all sit around the fire and listen to Oliver's news.

This pleasant prospect stimulated him sufficiently to make the effort of pulling himself up out of his chair. The newspaper that he had been reading sometime before slipped from his knees. Outside, the wind howled, and an icy draught came up the stairs and stirred the rugs on the polished floor. The Stable House was usually cozy, but no door or window built by man's hands could keep that northwest wind from penetrating. The room felt chilly. The fire was dying. He took logs from the basket, tossed them onto the dying embers, building up a good blaze that would still be alight when he returned later on in the evening.

He turned off the lamp and said, "Come along, Barney," and the old dog heaved himself up, obviously feeling, as Roddy was, his age. "You're not the only one," he told him, and he turned off the center light, and together, slowly, they started down the stairs.

Without occupants, the darkened room was still and quiet. The fire flickered. A log cracked and kindled into flame. There came a crack of splitting wood, and a shower of sparks erupted like fireworks, out onto the hearthrug. Unattended, they smoldered. Then a draught snaked in up the stairs, a spark flared for a second, and caught the corner of the abandoned newspaper. Tiny flames began to lick and then grew larger. They played up the leg of Roddy's chairside table, where he kept his books and his cigars and a pile of old magazines. They reached the tindery withies of the old basket where he kept his logs. Soon, the hem of the curtain had started to smolder.

John Dunbeath sat at the desk in the library, where he had spent most of the afternoon going through his uncle's papers, sorting out farm accounts from personal accounts, arranging neat piles for the attention of Robert McKenzie, for Jock's stockbroker in Edinburgh, for his accountant.

The old man had kept a neat and efficient tally of his affairs, and this task had not been complicated, but tedious and inevitably sad. For there were as well old diaries, dance cards, and faded photographs of people whom John had never known. Regimental groups taken in the Red Fort at Delhi; a snapshot of a party of guns in jungly surroundings gathered for what looked like a tiger shoot; a wedding. Some of the photographs were Benchoile. He recognized his father as a small boy, and Roddy, a slender stripling, wearing white flannels and looking as though he were about to burst into song, the juvenile lead in some prewar musical comedy.

The door opened and the present-day Roddy ambled in. John was pleased to see him and to have the excuse to stop working. He pushed his chair back from the desk and held up the photograph.

"Look what I've just found."

Roddy came to inspect it over John's shoulder.

"Good God. Inside every fat man there's a thin man struggling to get out. Where did you find that?"

"Oh, put away with some other old papers. What time is it?" He looked at his watch. "A quarter past eight already? I didn't realize it was as late as that."

"Quarter past eight on a vile cold winter's evening." He shivered. "I was nearly blown away just coming across the yard."

"Let's have a drink."

"Splendid idea," said Roddy as though he had not thought of it himself. He headed over to the table where the bottles and glasses had already been set out by Ellen, and John wondered how many private Scotches his uncle had already consumed, and then told himself that it didn't matter anyway, and it was none of his business. He only knew that he felt tired, and the prospect of a restoring drink was all at once very welcome.

He got up and went to build up the fire, and to draw a chair close to the blaze, for Roddy. Roddy brought the drinks over, and handed John his, and then sank into the chair with what sounded like a sigh of relief. John remained standing, and the warmth of the flames crept up his back, and he realized that he was stiff and cold from sitting in the bay of the window.

"Slainthe," said Roddy, and they both drank. "When are the others getting back, do you know?"

"No idea," John's dark face was impassive. "Around ten, I guess. Depends on whether the plane's on time or not. This gale might delay them."

"Are you really going back to London tomorrow?"

"Yes, I should. I'll probably be back again, next week or the week after, but we've got this big thing going just now, and I should be around."

"It was good that you were able to come."

"I've liked it. I'm just sorry that it had to end this way. I'd have liked Benchoile to go on."

"Dear boy, nothing can go on forever, and we've had a good run for our money."

They started talking about the old days, and as they both relaxed in the warmth, and each other's companionship, the time slipped pleasantly by. They were on to their second drink (or John's second drink and Roddy's fourth) when there came a scuffling sound from outside the door, the door opened, and Ellen advanced into the room. Neither of the men were surprised by this sudden appearance, for Ellen had long since given up knocking on doors. She was looking tired and particularly old. The wind and the bitter cold were bad for her bones, and she had been on her feet most of the day. Her expression showed this. Her mouth was buttoned up. She seemed determined to be put upon.

"I don't know when you two are wanting your dinner, but you can have it anytime you like."

"Thank you, Ellen," said Roddy, with a mild sarcasm that was wasted upon her.

"And when the others are getting back from Inverness I do not know, but they'll just have to make do with a bowl of broth."

"That'll be all they want," John assured her, and added, with some idea of placating her, "We'll be in the dining room in a moment. We're just having a drink."

"So I can see for myself." She hovered for a moment, trying to think of some other fault to find. "Did you check on the little boy before you came across, Roddy?"

"Um?" Roddy frowned. "No, I didn't. Was I meant to?"

"It seems it might have been a sensible thing to do instead of just leaving the mite there, abandoned for the evening."

Roddy became exasperated. "Ellen, I've only just

got over here. Anyway, we leave him happily every evening."

"Oh, well, never you mind. I'll go and look for myself."

She began to shuffle off, but seemed, in truth, so tired, so old, with her sticklike black legs and her trodden shoes that John couldn't bear it. He laid down his drink. "Here, Ellen, don't you worry. I'll go."

"It's no trouble."

"It's no trouble for me either. It'll take me one minute. And when I get back, we'll come and eat dinner, and then you can take yourself off to bed."

"Who said anything about bed?"

"I did. You're looking tired, and it's the best place for you."

"Well, I don't know . . ." Shaking her head, she made for the kitchen, and John started down the long flagged passages that led to the stableyard. Tonight they were as cold as dungeons, eerily lighted by naked bulbs which swung in the draughts. He seemed to be surrounded by looming shadows.

He opened the back door to the outside. The wind snatched at it and nearly blew it out of his hand, and for a second, that seemed like forever, he stood there in the doorway.

For ahead of him, across the cobbles of the yard, every upstairs window of Roddy's house was filled with dancing orange light. Smoke and flames gushed from the roof, and above the wind's fury, he could hear the terrifying sounds of the fire, a roar like a furnace, the splinter and crack of wood, sharp as rifle fire. Even as he stood there, a window exploded into a shatter of glass as its frame disintegrated in the heat. Instantly, flames leaped from the empty void, and John felt the heat of them sear his face.

Thomas.

He was across the yard and had opened the door before he considered the consequences. The stairs were already alight, and the wind caught the flames and the whole edifice turned into a sort of blast furnace from which he reeled. The smoke was suffocating. He turned from it, and holding his arm up to his face, made his way down the narrow passage and threw open the door of the first bedroom.

"Thomas!" He had no idea where Thomas was sleeping. *"Thomas!"*

This room was empty. The second door. *"Thomas!"*

Now, he was directly under Roddy's sitting room, and the smoke was blinding; his eyes began to stream and sting, he started to cough.

"Thomas!" His voice was a croak. He plunged on through the smoke and found the other door, the other bedroom.

Here, mercifully, the air was a little clearer.

"Thomas!"

A wail answered him. There was no time to be relieved, to give thanks that the child had not already died from asphyxiation, for it was clear that the charred ceiling of the room was about to give way at any moment. As John scooped Thomas up in his arms, there came a great load of plaster and charred lathe, spilling down from above and making a sound like falling rocks. He looked up, and saw the ragged crater of the hole, the inferno beyond. Thomas let out a scream, and John pressed the child's face against his shoulder and stumbled from the room.

He was scarcely through the door before the remainder of the ceiling collapsed, and the floor, the carpet, Thomas's bed, everything was obliterated beneath an avalanche of burning debris.

The London plane, fifteen minutes late on account of head winds, could be heard long before it was seen. The dark evening was stormy, the cloud ceiling very low, and when the aircraft did appear, it was with great suddenness, breaking through the murk at the end of the runway as it came in to land on the black, puddled tarmac.

Soon after this, the usual small activities began to take place. Trucks and tankers converged on the stationary plane. Steps were wheeled up to its side by two men in black oilskins. Doors opened. An air hostess appeared at the head of the steps. Slowly the passengers began to alight, to walk across the windswept apron towards the terminal building. They struggled with cases and baskets and awkwardly shaped parcels. The wind caught their clothes, they ducked their heads against the rain. One woman's hat blew off.

Victoria, with her hands in the pockets of her coat, stood just inside the plate glass doors and waited. One by one the other people, who had waited with her, claimed their various friends and relations. "There you are, pet. And did you have a good flight?" Affectionate kisses. There were two nuns met by a priest in a black biretta. "I've got a car waiting," he told them matter-of-factly. A woman with far too many children and no husband to help her, a few businessmen with briefcases.

The straggle of passengers thinned. There was still no sign of Oliver. She imagined him still sitting in the aircraft, taking his time, waiting until the first ugly rush was over. Then he would unfold his long legs, reach for his coat, make his own leisurely way down the aisle. He would probably stop to chat with the air hostess. Victoria found herself smiling wryly, because she knew him so well.

"Excuse me." The voice spoke from just behind her. Startled, she turned. She saw one of the businessmen, with his bowler hat and his stiff collar and his briefcase. "Are you by any chance Miss Victoria Bradshaw?" He held an envelope in his hand.

"Yes, I am.

"I thought you must be. This letter's for you. Your friend asked me to give it to you."

She did not take the letter. "My friend?"

"A young man with a beard. I'm afraid I never caught his name. He asked me to give you this."

"But isn't he on the plane?"

"No, he couldn't come. But I'm sure this will explain everything."

Victoria took her hand from her pocket and took the envelope. She saw Oliver's tightly formed black writing. Miss Victoria Bradshaw.

"But where is he?"

"He just said he couldn't make the flight, and he told me what you looked like and asked me to give you the letter."

"I see. Well, thank you. I . . . I'm sorry you were bothered with it."

"No bother. It was no bother at all," he assured her. "Well, I must be off. My wife's waiting in the car, and she'll wonder what's happened to me." He began to back away, eager to be off. He tipped his bowler hat. "I'll say good-bye."

"Good-bye."

She was alone. Everybody had gone. Only a few official looking people moved briskly about. A man in overalls wheeled a trolley of luggage. Shocked, confused, Victoria stood there, with Oliver's letter in her hand. She could not think what she was meant to do with it.

On the other side of the arrivals hall, she saw a small refreshment booth. She went across the polished floor and sat on one of the tall stools and asked for a cup of black coffee. A homely woman poured it for her from an urn.

"Do you take sugar?"

"No. No sugar, thank you."

She slit the envelope and took out the letter.

"It's a terrible night, isn't it?"

"Yes it is." She opened her bag and found her purse and paid for the coffee.

"Have you far to go?"

"Yes. I have to drive to Sutherland."

"Oh, my, what a way. Rather you than me."

She unfolded the letter. He had typed it, on his battered old typewriter. She was filled with cold apprehension. With her hand closed around the mug of hot coffee, she began to read.

> Fulham
> Tuesday
> February 24.

Victoria,

If I were any other sort of a man I should start this letter by telling you that it is a difficult one to write. But I'm not going to say that, because writing is the one thing I have never found difficult, even when it has to be a letter like this one.

I am not coming back to Scotland. I have spent most of the day with my agent, and he is very anxious that I should go to New York where a director called Sol Bernstein is already waiting to sign on the dotted line and to launch A Man In the Dark—with, I hope a tremendous fanfare of trumpets—on Broadway.

So I am going, catching a plane out of Heathrow this evening.

But he can't do this to me.

Oh, yes he can. He has.

I don't know when I shall return. This year, next year, sometime, never. Certainly not in the foreseeable future. There is too much at stake for plans to be made. Too much to think about. Too much buzzing around in my head.

I haven't made this decision without thought of you. In fact, I thought about you most of last night. The night is a good time to get things sorted out. It's dark and quiet and the truth comes more clearly. It's easier to see.

And the truth is that I could never stay with you, because I could never stay with any woman. A long time ago, when I left you for the first time, I told you that I'd never loved anybody, and it's still the same way. I suppose what I feel for you is something rather special, but still the only thing that really turns me on is what goes on inside my head and somehow putting all that down on paper.

This decision had nothing to do with what happened when we were at Benchoile. It has nothing to do with the letter that you wrote the Archers, it really has nothing to do with you. The few days we spent together were unforgettable, and you gave me the closest thing to delight that I have ever known. But they were days stolen out of time and now I have to get back to reality.

There are things that you will have to do. You'll have to get Thomas back to the Archers for one, and hand him over once more to their loving care. I still resent their hold over him. I still curl up at the sort of conventional life they will undoubtedly map out for him, but it is obvious that this is just one of those things that I am going to have to accept.

The Volvo is another problem. You probably

won't feel like driving it south by yourself. If this is the case, then ask Roddy if he will take it off your hands and perhaps find a buyer for it in Creagan. Tell him I shall be writing to him.

There is also the vexing problem of cash, but I have spoken to my agent and I will put his name and address at the bottom of this letter, so that if you get in touch with him when you get back to London, he will reimburse you and cover any expenses that you may have to incur.

So that's it. I did not mean to finish on such a mundane and mercenary note. I did not mean anything to finish quite this way. But happy endings are things that don't seem to be part of my life. I've never expected them, and in a funny way, I don't suppose I've ever wanted them.

She was crying. Now the words swam and shimmered before her eyes, and she could scarcely read them. Tears fell on the paper and blurred the handwritten signature.

Take care of yourself. I wish I could end by telling you that I loved you. Perhaps I do a little. But it could never begin to be enough, either for you or for me.

Oliver

Victoria folded the letter and put it back into the envelope. She fumbled in her bag and found a handkerchief. It wasn't any good crying. With a two-hour drive ahead of her through the stormy night, she had to stop crying. Otherwise she would drive into a ditch, or a river, or another car, and have to be dragged,

mangled, from the wreckage of the Volvo, and then
what would happen to Thomas?

After a little the kindly woman behind the bar, unable to ignore the obvious distress of her lonely cus-
tomer, said, "Are you all right, dear?"

"Yes," lied Victoria.

"Was it bad news?"

"No, not really." She blew her nose again. She tried
to smile, "I have to go." She got off the stool.

"Have another cup of coffee. Have a bite to eat."

"No, I'm all right. I'm really all right."

The Volvo stood lonely in the deserted car park. She
found the key and got in behind the wheel. She fastened the seat belt. High above, a hidden plane
droned, perhaps coming in to land. She thought of
being in an airplane, going somewhere, anywhere. She
thought of landing on some sunbaked airstrip surrounded by palm trees, in a place where nobody knew
her, where she could lick her wounds and start again.
Like a criminal, searching for a new life, a new identity.

Which was, of course, exactly what Oliver had done,
settling his few affairs with a single letter, shedding
his responsibilities like an old coat. By now he would
be in the transatlantic plane, high over the ocean, Victoria and Thomas already fading into the past, into
forgetfulness. Unimportant. Important was what lay
ahead. She imagined him, drinking a highball, filled
with anticipation for the excitement ahead. A new
production. Probably a new play. New York.

Oliver Dobbs.

*The only thing that really turns me on is what goes
on inside my head.*

This was the key to Oliver, his own personal, private key. And Victoria had never come near to understanding the private obsessions of his innermost mind.
Perhaps if she had been his intellectual equal, a bril-

liant bluestocking with a university degree, it might have been different. Perhaps if she had known him longer, or closer; if she had been a stronger personality, able to stand up to his moods. Perhaps if she had not always been so dependent upon him, had been able to give him something in return.

But I gave him myself.

That wasn't enough.

I loved him.

But he never loved you.

I wanted to make a life for him. I wanted to make a life for Thomas.

She was back to Thomas. At the thought of Thomas, the old, ridiculous, protective tenderness took possession of her. For the time being Thomas still needed Victoria. For his sake, she would be efficient, calm, practical. Thomas must be delivered back to his grandparents with as little upheaval as possible. She saw herself calmly packing, buying train tickets. Hiring a taxi, taking him to Woodbridge, finding the Archers' house, ringing the bell. She saw the door opening. . . .

But beyond that her imagination shied. Because once Thomas was gone from her life, then it really was the end. It would all be over. Not simply the reality, but the dream as well.

She started the car, switched on the headlights and the windscreen wipers and moved forward, away from the little airport and out onto the main road.

Two hours later she had reached Creagan, but it was not until she had turned into the single track road that led to Benchoile that she began to realize that something was wrong. The weather conditions, unpredictable as always, had begun to improve. The wind had dropped slightly, the clouds thinned, and as these were blown to rags across the night sky, the stars were revealed, and a pale new moon rose out of the east.

But it was not starlight that warmed the darkness ahead of her, and stained the sky like the glow from a whole city full of street lamps. It was not starlight that flickered and billowed and sent great storms of smoke up into the wind. She rolled down the window and smelled the reek of bonfires. Bonfires? More likely burning heather. Someone had started to burn heather, and it had got out of control and started a hill fire. But did one burn heather in February? And even if one did, surely the fire would have been extinguished by now?

Suddenly, she was afraid. She put her foot down on the accelerator, and the Volvo surged forward, swinging around the bends of the narrow road. The brightness of the fire seemed to grow no less. She had passed the Guthrie's house, she was coming at last to the final bend of the road. Then the house lay ahead of her, the gate and the pine trees, and she knew then that it was neither heather nor bonfires that burned, but Benchoile itself.

With a roar of its powerful engine, the Volvo racketed over the cattle grid and up the slope to the sweep in front of the house. The light of the flames made all as bright as day. She saw the cars lined up at random, the fire engine, the huge snaking hosepipes. There seemed to be people everywhere, all grimed and red-eyed. A man ran across the beam of her headlights, shouting instructions to a colleague, and she saw, with a shock, that it was Davey Guthrie.

The big house was untouched, although lights blazed from every window. But the Stable House . . . She brought the Volvo to a screeching halt, struggled with her seat belt, the door handle, remembered the hand brake. Panic, like the worst sort of sickness, threatened to choke her.

Thomas.

The arch to the stableyard was there, but Roddy's house was almost gone. Only the stone gable end had withstood the onslaught of the flames; it loomed, stark as a ruin, the void where the window had been bright as an eye, with the glow of the conflagration that still raged beyond.

Thomas, in his room, on the ground floor, in his bed. She had to know, but there was not time to ask, no time to wait for answers. She began to walk towards the fire, to run. The smoke was acrid in her nostrils, and the heat was blown towards her on great gusts of wind.

"*Thomas!*"

"Look out there . . ." a man shouted.

She had nearly reached the archway.

"Victoria!"

She heard the footsteps coming up behind her. Arms came around her, caught her, held her. She struggled to be free.

"Victoria."

It was John Dunbeath. Because she could not hit him with her hands, she kicked backwards at his shins with the heels of her boots. He swung her round to face him.

"Don't you understand?" she shouted into the blur that was John Dunbeath. "It's Thomas."

"Listen, stop . . ." She kicked him again, and he took her by the shoulders and shook her. "Thomas is all *right*. He's all *right*. He's *safe*."

She was still at last. She could hear her own breathing, labored, like a person on the point of death. When she felt strong enough, she looked up into his face. In the glow of the fire, she saw his dark eyes, red-rimmed and bloodshot, and there was dirt all over his face and down the front of his shirt.

She said, faintly, "He's not in there?"

"No. We got him out. He's fine. He's all right."

Relief made her weak as a kitten. She closed her eyes, afraid that she was either going to be sick or faint. She tried to tell John that her legs had started to feel like cooked spaghetti, but somehow could find neither the words nor the energy to speak them. By then it didn't matter anyway. Because by then John had already picked her up in his arms and was carrying her across the gravel and in through the front door of the big house of Benchoile.

By midnight it was more or less over. The fire was out, the ruin of the Stable House a still-smoking confusion of charred stone and fallen timber. The cars John had managed to rescue, backing them out of the garage onto the grass by the loch while Roddy telephoned the fire brigade. With them disposed of, and the cans of petrol that stood about, fuel for the motor mowers and the chain saws, he had felt a little easier in his mind for the safety of the big house. But even so, the garage roof had been swallowed and destroyed in the conflagration, and all that remained within it had gone as well.

And yet, the main house stood, miraculously unharmed. Within it, in various rooms, the survivors of the household were now bedded down. Thomas had wept, heartbreakingly, not from fear, but because he had lost Piglet. There was no way to tell him that Piglet was no more. Ellen had found him some other toy, a teddy bear that had once belonged to John's father, but at the very sight of this harmless, threadbare creature, Thomas had screamed more loudly than ever, and had finally gone to sleep with his arms wrapped around a wooden engine, the paint scarred and scratched and one of the wheels long since missing.

Ellen had come through it like the tough old thing she was. Only at the very end had she given way and started to tremble, and John had sat her down and given her a brandy, and Jess Guthrie had helped the old woman to bed. For Jess and Davey had been on the scene almost before Roddy had made his telephone call, and it was Davey who organized the team of fire fighters, and helped the men from Creagan—torn so abruptly from their own firesides—to set up the pumps and go about extinguishing the flames.

As for Victoria . . . As though he were controlling, reining-in a bolting horse, John's thoughts came to an abrupt halt. But one indisputable fact stood out. She had returned from Inverness alone, and nobody had had the time nor the inclination to ask her what had happened to Oliver. As far as John was concerned, her sudden reappearance in the midst of chaos, her mindless dash towards the holocaust which was all that remained of Roddy's house, had simply been the unthinkable climax of what had so nearly been a ghastly tragedy, and then he had had no thought in his head but to grab her back from the edge of the fire and carry her to safety.

He had taken her, for want of anywhere better, to his own bedroom, placed her on his own bed. She had opened her eyes and said once more, "Thomas is really safe, isn't he?" and he had time to do no more than reassure her before Jess Guthrie came bustling in to take over with soothing words and hot drinks. Now, presumably, Victoria was sleeping. With luck, she would sleep till the morning. In the morning there would be all the time in the world to talk.

So, it was midnight, and it was over. He stood at the edge of the loch, with his back to the water, staring up at the house. He realized that he was exhausted, drained of emotion and energy, and yet beneath this aching lassitude lay a calmness and a peace that he had not known for years.

Why he felt thus was a mystery. He only knew that Thomas was alive, and Victoria was safe, and Benchoile still stood, and Oliver Dobbs had not come back from London. He sighed with an enormous content as though, single-handed, he had successfully achieved some impossible task.

Around him, the stormy evening was slipping into a

peaceful night. The wind had dropped, the clouds
thinned to a few sailing shreds, like billows of mist.
Above, a sliver of moon hung in the sky, and the dark
waters of the loch were touched with the silver of its
reflection. A pair of ducks flew over. Mallards, he
guessed. For an instant he glimpsed them, silhouetted
against the sky, and then they were swallowed into the
darkness and their cry faded to an immense silence.

But there came other sounds. The wind in the topmost branches of the pines, the whisper of water nudg-
ing against the wooden piles of the old jetty. He
looked at the house and saw the comfort of lights in
windows. He saw the dark swell of the hills that rose
behind it.

His hills. Benchoile hills.

He stood there for a long time, his hands in his
pockets, until a fit of the shivers made him realize that
he was growing cold. He turned back for a final look
at the loch, and then, slowly, made his way up the
slope of the lawn and so indoors.

Roddy had not gone to bed. Roddy waited still in
the library, slumped in Jock's old armchair by the
dying fire. John's heart bled for his uncle. Of all of
them, Roddy was the one to suffer most. Not simply
because he had lost his house, his clothes, his books
and papers, all the personal and cherished possessions
of a lifetime, but because he blamed himself for what
had happened.

"I should have *thought*." he had said, over and over
again, his usual loquacity overwhelmed by the potential tragedy, by the ghastly realization of what could
have happened to Thomas. "I simply never thought."

But he had always piled logs onto his open fireplace, carelessly trodden out the random sparks on his
old hearthrug, never bothered about a fireguard. "One
of the last things Jock ever said to me was that I
should have a fireguard. But I never did. Put it off.

Lazy, procrastinating bastard that I am. Simply put it off."

And then, again, "Supposing Ellen hadn't had the wit to think about the child. Supposing, John, you hadn't gone along then to check . . ." His voice trembled.

"Don't think about it," John had interrupted quickly, because it didn't bear contemplating. "She did have the sense, and I did go. Come to that, it should have occurred to me to go without Ellen's prompting. I'm just as much to blame as you are."

"No, I'm totally to blame. I should have thought . . ."

Now, John stood in the chilling room, looking down at his father's brother and filled with a sympathy and affection that were, for the time being, of little use to Roddy. He was inconsolable.

A log crumbled into the dying fire. The clock showed a quarter past twelve. John said, "Why don't you go to bed? Jess has made beds up for all of us. There's no point in staying down here."

Roddy rubbed a hand over his eyes. "No," he said at last. "I suppose there isn't. But I don't think I could sleep."

"In that case . . ." He did not finish the sentence. He stirred the ashes of the fire, and put on more wood. In a moment the flames began to lick up around the dry bark. Roddy stared at them morosely.

"It's over," John told him firmly. "Don't think about it anymore. It's over. And if it helps to lessen your guilt, just remember that you've lost everything you possess."

"That's of small account. Possessions have never mattered."

"Why don't you have a drink?"

"No. I don't want a drink."

John managed not to look surprised. "Do you mind if I do?"

"Help yourself."

He poured himself a small brandy and filled the glass up with soda. He sat, facing his uncle. He raised his glass. "Slainthe."

A spark of wry amusement glimmered in Roddy's eye. "What an old Scotsman you're becoming."

"I've always been one. Or half one, at any rate."

Roddy heaved himself up in the chair. He said, "Oliver didn't come back from London."

"Apparently not."

"Why not, I wonder?"

"I have no idea."

"Do you suppose he's coming?"

"Again, I have no idea. I simply dumped Victoria on my bed, and after that Jess took over. No doubt we'll hear about it tomorrow."

"He's a strange man," mused Roddy. "Clever, of course. Perhaps a little bit too clever." Across the fireside, their eyes met. "Too clever for that little girl."

"Yes, I guess you're right.

"Still, she has the child."

"I have news for you. Thomas is not her child."

Roddy raised his eyebrows. "Really? Now you do surprise me." He shook his head. "The world is full of surprises."

"I have more surprises up my sleeve."

"You do?"

"Do you want to hear about them?"

"What, now?"

"You've already told me you don't want to go to bed. If we're going to sit here for the rest of the night, we might as well talk."

"All right," said Roddy, and composed himself to listen. "Talk."

CHAPTER 15
Wednesday

John Dunbeath, bearing a tray laid for breakfast, cautiously opened the kitchen door with the seat of his pants, and made his way across the hall and up the stairs. Outside a breeze, baby sister of last night's gale, stirred the pine trees and disturbed the surface of the loch, but already a cold and brazen sun, rising in a sky of frosty blue, was beginning to penetrate the house. Roddy's old Labrador had already found a bright lozenge of sunshine by the fireplace, and lay there, supine, basking in its frail warmth.

John crossed the landing and, carefully balancing the tray on one hand, knocked at the door of his own room. From within, Victoria's voice called, "Who is it?" and he said, "The floor waiter," and opened the door "I've brought you your breakfast."

She was still in bed, but sitting up and looking quite alert, as though she had been awake for some time. The curtains had been drawn back, and the first oblique rays of sunshine touched a corner of the chest of drawers and lay like gold on the carpet. He said, "It's going to be a beautiful day," and set the tray, with something of a flourish, on her knees.

She said. "But I don't need breakfast in bed."

"You've got it. How did you sleep?"

"As though I'd been drugged. I was just going to come down. The thing is, I must have forgotten to wind my watch, and it's stopped, and I've no idea of the time."

"Nearly half past nine."

"You should have woken me before."

"I decided to let you sleep."

She wore a nightdress lent to her by Ellen. It was peach pink crepe de chine, much hemstitched and embroidered and had, in fact, once belonged to Lucy Dunbeath. Over this, in lieu of a dressing-gown, was wrapped a white Shetland shawl. Her hair, tangled from sleep, lay forward across one shoulder, and there were dark shadows, like bruises, beneath her eyes. She seemed to John, in that moment, intensely frail. As though, if he were to take her into his arms, she would break into pieces, as fragile as china. She looked about her. "This is your room, isn't it? When I woke up I couldn't think where I was. Is it your room?"

"It is. It was the only bed that happened to be made up at the time."

"Where did you sleep?"

"In Uncle Jock's dressing room."

"And Roddy?"

"In Jock's bedroom. He's still there. We sat up talking till four o'clock in the morning, and he's catching up on his beauty sleep."

"And . . . Thomas?" She sounded as though she could scarcely bring herself to say his name.

John pulled up a chair and settled himself, facing her, with his long legs stretched out in front of him, and his arms folded.

"Thomas is downstairs in the kitchen, being given breakfast by Ellen and Jess. So now, why don't you start eating *your* breakfast before it gets cold?"

Victoria unenthusiastically eyed the boiled egg and the toast and the coffepot. She said, "I don't actually feel very hungry."

"Just eat it, anyway."

She began, half-heartedly, to take the top off the egg. Then she laid down the spoon again. "John, I don't even know how it happened. I mean, how the fire started."

"None of us do, for sure. We were having a drink in the library before dinner. But Roddy says he made up his fire before he came over. I suppose, as usual, the logs sparked all over the hearthrug, and there wasn't anybody there to put them out. Added to which, there was the hell of a wind blowing. Once it started, the whole room went up like a tinder box."

"But when did you first realize the house was on fire?"

"Ellen came to tell us supper was ready, and then she started fussing about Thomas being on his own. So I went along to check on him, and found the place blazing away like a bonfire."

She said, faintly, "I can't bear it. What *did* you do?"

He proceeded to tell her, playing down the circumstances as much as possible. He felt that Victoria had enough trouble on her mind as it was, without adding to it by graphic descriptions of the nightmare of Thomas's smoke-filled bedroom, the collapsing ceiling, the flaming crater, and the inferno overhead. He knew that the memory of that moment would return to haunt him, like some ghastly dream, for the rest of his life.

"Was he frightened?"

"Of course he was frightened. It was enough to frighten any man. But we got out all right, through one of the bedroom windows, and then we came back here, and Ellen took Thomas over, and Roddy rang the fire brigade in Creagan, and I went back to get the cars out of the garage before the petrol exploded and we were all blown to kingdom come."

"Did you manage to salvage anything from Roddy's house?"

"Not a thing. It all went. Everything in the world that he owned."

"Poor Roddy."

"Losing his possessions doesn't seem to bother him much. What bugs him is that he feels the fire was his fault. He says he should have been more careful, he should have had a fireguard, he should never have left Thomas alone in the house."

"I can't bear it for him."

"He's all right now, but that's why we sat up talking till four in the morning. And Thomas is all right too, except that he's lost Piglet. He spent last night with an old wooden engine in his arms. And of course, he's lost all his clothes as well. He's still wearing his pajamas, but this morning sometime Jess is going to take him into Creagan and buy him a new outfit."

Victoria said, "I thought he was still there. I mean, when I got back from the airport, and saw the fire. At first I thought it was a bonfire, and then I thought it was someone burning heather, and then I saw it was Roddy's house. And all I could think of was that Thomas was in the middle of it somewhere . . ."

Her voice had begun to shake. "But he wasn't," John said quietly. "He was safe."

Victoria took a deep breath. "I'd been thinking of him," she said and her voice was quite steady again. "All the way back from Inverness. The road seemed to go on forever, and I was thinking of Thomas all the way."

"Oliver didn't come back from London." He made it, not a question, but a statement of fact.

"No. He . . . he wasn't on the plane."

"Did he call you?"

"No. He sent a letter." With some determination, as if the time had come to put fancies aside, Victoria took up her spoon again and ate a mouthful or two of the boiled egg.

"How did he do that?"

"He gave a letter to one of the passengers. I suppose he told him what I looked like, or something. Anyway, the man delivered it to me. I was still waiting. I still thought Oliver was going to get off the plane."

"What did the letter say?"

She gave up the impossible task of eating breakfast and pushed the tray away from her. She leaned back on her pillows and closed her eyes. "He isn't coming back." She sounded exhausted. "He's going to New York. He's in New York now. He flew out yesterday evening. Some producer's going to put on his play, *A Man In The Dark*, and he's gone out to see about it."

Dreading the answer, it took a certain courage to ask the question. "Is he coming back?"

"I suppose he will one day. This year, next year, sometime, never." She opened her eyes. "That's what he said. Anyway, not in the foreseeable future." He waited and she finished, "He's left me, John," as though there could be any doubt still in his mind.

He did not say anything.

She went on, her voice inconsequent, trying to make what she was saying of small importance. "That makes it twice he's left me. Its almost becoming a habit." She tried to smile. "I know you said I was being a fool about Oliver, but this time I really, truly thought it would be different. I thought he would want the things he'd never wanted before. Like maybe buying a house and making a home for Thomas . . . and getting married, too. I thought he wanted the three of us to be together. To be a family."

John watched her face. Perhaps the abrupt disappearance of Oliver Dobbs, the paralyzing shock of the fire, had acted as a sort of catharsis. He only knew that the barriers between them, her frigid reserve, were tumbling at last. She was being, at the end of the day, honest with herself, and so had nothing left to shut away from him. He was filled with a marvelous sort of triumph, and recognized this as a carryover from his private elation of the previous night.

She said, "Yesterday, on the beach at Creagan, I

wouldn't listen to you. But you were right, weren't you? You were right about Oliver."

"I wish I could say 'I wish I weren't'. But truthfully I can't."

"You're not going to say 'I told you so.'"

"I'd never say that in a thousand years."

"You see, the real trouble was that Oliver doesn't need anybody. That's what's wrong with him. He admitted as much in his letter. He told me that the only thing that turns him on is his writing." She managed a wry smile. "And that was a smack in the face. I'd been telling myself it was me."

"So what will you do now?"

Victoria shrugged. "I don't know. I don't know where to start. But Oliver says I have to take Thomas back to the Archers, and I've been trying to think how I'm going to do it. I don't even know where they live, and I certainly don't know what I'm going to say to them when I get there. And I don't want to lose Thomas, either. I don't want to have to say goodbye to him. It's going to be like being torn apart. And there's the business of the car. Oliver said that if I left the Volvo here, perhaps Roddy could sell it. He said that I could drive it south if I wanted to, but I really don't want to, not with Thomas. I suppose I could get a plane or a train from Inverness, but that means. . . ."

John found that he could not stand it for another instant. Loudly he interrupted her, "Victoria, I don't want to hear another word."

Halted in mid-sentence, astonished at the roughness of his voice, Victoria stared open-mouthed. "But I have to talk about it. I have to do things . . ."

"No, you don't. You don't have to do anything. I shall see to it all. I shall arrange to get Thomas back to his grandparents . . ."

". . . but you have enough to think about . . ."

". . . I shall even placate them . . ."

". . . with the fire, and Roddy, and Benchoile . . ."

". . . though, from the sound of things they're going to require some placating. I shall take care of Thomas, and I shall take care of you, but as for Oliver's car, it can rot on a rubbish heap for all I care. And Oliver Dobbs, for all his genius and his sexual prowess and whatever it is that turns him on—can rot as well. And I never want to hear that self-centered son of a bitch's name again. Is that totally understood?"

Victoria considered this. Her face was serious. "You never really liked him did you?"

"It wasn't meant to show."

"It did, a little. Every now and again."

John grinned. "He was lucky not to get his nose punched in." He looked at his watch, stretched like a cat, and then pulled himself to his feet.

"Where are you going?" she asked him.

"Downstairs to the telephone. I have a million calls to make. So why don't you eat that breakfast now. There's nothing more to worry about."

"Yes, there is. I just thought of it."

"What's that?"

"My shell. My queen cockle. It was on the window ledge in my bedroom. In Roddy's house."

"We'll find another."

"I liked that one."

He went to open the door. He said, "The sea is full of gifts."

In the kitchen he found Jess Guthrie, peeling potatoes at the sink.

"Jess, where's Davey?"

"He's away up the hill this morning."

"Will you be seeing him?"

"Yes, he'll be down for his dinner at twelve."

"Ask him to come down and have a word with me, would you? This afternoon sometime. Say about half past two."

"I'll give him the message," she promised.

If my true love, she were gone
I would surely find another,
Where wild mountain thyme,
Grows around the blooming heather,
Will ye go, lassie, go?

He went into the library, shut the door firmly behind him, built up the fire, sat at his uncle's desk, and settled down to a positive orgy of telephoning.

He rang the office in London. He spoke to his vice president, a couple of colleagues, and his secretary, Miss Ridgeway.

He rang directory inquiries and was told the Archer's address and telephone number in Woodbridge. He made the call and spoke, at some length, to them.

With this safely behind him, he called the station in Inverness, and booked three seats on the Clansman for the following day.

He rang the lawyers, McKenzie, Leith and Dudgeon. He spoke to Robert McKenzie, and then, later, to the insurance company about the fire damage.

By now it was nearly midday. John did a few swift time-lag calculations, put a call through to his father in Colorado, dragged that good man from his early morning sleep and talked to him for an hour or more.

Finally, at the very end, he rang up Tania Mansell, dialing her London telephone number from memory. But the line was engaged, and after waiting for a little, he rang off. He did not try the number again.

CHAPTER 16
Thursday

It did not take very long to pack for the simple reason that they had nothing to pack. Everything that Victoria and Thomas had brought to Benchoile with them had been lost in the fire. And so they left bearing only a paper carrier containing Thomas's pajamas and the old wooden engine, which Ellen said that he could keep.

Good-byes were brief and brisk, for the true Highlander is neither demonstrative nor sentimental. As well, there was little opportunity for prolonged farewells. No sooner had breakfast been eaten in the kitchen at Benchoile than it was time to be off. Before Thomas had finished munching his toast, John Dunbeath was behaving like a family man with a punctuality complex, rounding them up and insisting that it was time to leave.

For this Victoria was deeply grateful. She even suspected that he was overplaying his role a little. His car was parked and waiting in front of the door, already loaded with his own suitcase, and John himself appeared to have deliberately taken on a new image, for he had abandoned the casual and comfortable clothes in which they were used to seeing him, and appeared at breakfast in the formality of a dark suit and a tie. The different clothes changed him. Not just the way he looked, but his entire manner. He was no longer the amiable, easygoing houseguest of the last few days, but a man used to responsibility and authority. A man to be reckoned with. He was in charge, not aggressively, but comfortingly, so that Victoria was left with the good feeling that nothing would go wrong. They would not have a puncture, they would not lose their tickets, there would be porters and reserved seats, and they would not miss the train.

"It's time to go."

Ellen put the last finger of toast into Thomas's mouth, wiped it clean and lifted him from his high chair. He wore tartan dungarees and a blue sweater, chosen for him by Jess Guthrie in the small shop in Creagan that was owned by her sister-in-law, so Jess had got discount. His new shoes were brown lace-ups, and there was a small blue anorak with red stripes to go on top. Ellen had brushed his red-gold hair flat to his head. She was wanting to kiss him good-bye, but decided not to with everybody watching. Her eyes had a way, these days, of filling with tears at the most inconvenient moments. Running, Ellen called it. "My eyes are starting to run," she would say, blaming the wind or the hay fever. She never cried. At times of great emotion, like anniversaries or weddings or funerals, she would shake a body's hand, but nothing more. So now, "There he is," she said, setting Thomas firmly down onto his feet. "Put your coat on," She picked up the new jacket, and stooped over him to help him with the zipper.

They were all on their feet. Victoria gulping the last mouthful of coffee. Roddy standing, scratching the back of his head, but not looking as disconsolate as she had feared he might. He seemed to have recovered with amazing rapidity from the shock of the fire and losing everything he owned. Indeed he was really being quite organized; had spent most of yesterday with the man from the insurance company, and had already started to make a little nest for himself in the big house, sleeping in his brother's old bedroom and tossing logs as carelessly as ever onto the fire in the library. The library fire was surrounded by a hearth of stone flags and a huge club fender, but still, said Roddy, he would get a proper fireguard. One of those chain curtains. He had seen one advertised. Just as soon as he could find the advertisement, he would order one for Benchoile.

"We must go *now*," said John, so they all left the kitchen and the remains of breakfast and trooped out, across the hall and through the front door. Outside, it was cold again and frosty, but it was going to be fine. It was good-bye. To the garden, the loch, the hills beyond, sparkling in the crystal clear morning air. It was good-bye to the friendly, peaceful house, good-bye to the sad charred remains of what had once been Roddy's domain. It was good-bye, Victoria knew, to a dream. Or perhaps a nightmare. Only time would give the answer to that one.

"Oh, Roddy," He opened his arms and she went to him, and they hugged. "Come back again," he said. "Come back again and see us all." He kissed her on both cheeks and let her go. Thomas, with the cheerful prospect of a car ride in front of him, had already climbed, independent of anyone, onto the back seat, had taken his wooden engine out of the paper bag, and had started to play with it.

"Good-bye, Ellen."

"It's been nice to know you," said Ellen briskly and stuck out her gnarled, red hand to be shaken.

"You've been so endlessly kind. You and Jess. I can't thank you enough."

"Away with you," said Ellen, brisk and much embarrassed. "Into the car, and don't keep John waiting."

Only John was allowed to kiss her. She had to stand tiptoe in her flat old shoes to receive his kiss, and then she had to fumble up the sleeve of her dress for her handkerchief. "Oh, my, what an edge to that wind," she remarked to no one person in particular. "It fairly makes your eyes run."

"Roddy."

"Good-bye, John." They shook hands, smiling into each other's faces, two men who had come together through a bad time.

"I'll be back sometime, but I'll call you and let you know when."

"Anytime," said Roddy.

That was all. They got into the car, fastened the safety belts, John started up the engine and they were away. There was scarcely time for Victoria to turn in her seat and wave a last farewell—scarcely time for a final glimpse of the two of them, Roddy and Ellen, standing there on the gravel sweep in front of the house. Roddy was waving, and Ellen was waving too, her white handkerchief a tiny flag. And then they were hidden, gone, lost behind the curving bank of the rhododendrons.

"I hate saying good-bye," said Victoria.

John's eyes were on the road ahead. "Me too," he said. He was driving very fast.

Behind them Thomas rolled his three-wheeled engine up and down the seat. "Meh meh, meh," he intoned to himself.

He played with the engine for most of the day, taking time off to sleep, to look out the windows, to be taken down the corridor at decent, regular untervals, to be given lunch, to be given tea. As the train thundered south, the weather, disobligingly, degenerated. They were no sooner across the border than thick clouds rolled up, obliterating the sky, and soon the rain started to fall. The hills were left behind them, the countryside became flat and incredibly dull, and watching acres of flat, wet plough wheel past the window, Victoria's own spirits sank accordingly.

She discovered that it was all very well being brisk and sensible about your future when you happened to be eight hundred miles from it, but now, with every moment and every turn of the wheel, it was drawing closer. She felt lamentably unprepared.

It was not just the distant prospect of the remainder of her own life, which would presumably, fall into some pattern of its own. As for Oliver . . . she was not thinking about Oliver just now. Later, she told herself, she would find the necessary moral courage. When she was back in her own flat, with her own familiar possessions around her. Possessions helped, whatever anybody said. And friends. She thought of Sally. She would be able to talk to Sally about Oliver. Sally's robust attitudes, her impatience with the vagaries of the opposite sex in general, would swiftly cut the whole disastrous episode down to size.

No, worse was the immediate and dreaded ordeal of having to hand Thomas back to the Archers; of having to say good-bye to him forever. Victoria could not imagine what she was going to say to his grandparents. Unfortunately, without much difficulty, she could imagine what they might be going to say to Victoria in her role of Oliver's accomplice.

There were other hideous possibilities as well. Suppose Thomas did not want to return to them? Suppose he took one look at the Archers, and burst into tears and had hysterics and clung to Victoria?

He had adjusted so easily to her in two weeks, had been so happy and become so affectionate. She found that she was torn in two opposite directions where Thomas was concerned; one half of her wanting him to need her as much as she needed him, the other shying like a frightened horse at the idea of any sort of a scene.

She looked at Thomas. He was sitting on the opposite side of the first-class carriage, his legs sticking straight out in front of him, his head, tousled by now, leaning against John Dunbeath's arm. John was entertaining him by drawing pictures with a felt pen on the pink pages of the *Financial Times*. He had drawn a horse, a cow, a house, and now he was drawing a pig.

"He's got a big nose that sticks out in front. That's for snuffling with and finding stuff to eat. And he has a tail with a curl in it." He drew the tail. Thomas's face broke into a smile. He settled down more cosily. "More," he ordered, and plugged his mouth with his thumb.

Victoria closed her eyes and leaned her head against the rain-streaked window of the train. It was sometimes easier not to cry if you didn't keep your eyes open.

It was dark long before they reached Euston, and Thomas had gone to sleep again. When the train stopped, Victoria picked him up in her arms. His head lolled on her shoulder. John carried his suitcase, and the little party stepped out onto the dark platform, into the usual confusion of barging passengers, trolleys, porters, luggage and mail vans. Victoria, weighed down by Thomas's considerable weight, felt overwhelmed. She supposed they must now trudge the length of the platform, wait in a queue for a taxi . . .

But she supposed wrong, and realized that in this supposition she had totally underestimated John Dunbeath. For from the confusion emerged a figure, grey-suited, with a grey uniform cap.

"Good evening, Mr. Dunbeath."

"George, you're a wonder. How did you know where we'd be?"

"Had a word with the ticket collector, he said you'd probably be down this end." With no more fuss, he relieved John of his suitcase. John duly relieved Victoria of Thomas. They followed the neat, uniformed figure down the length of the platform.

"Who is he?" asked Victoria, having to run every now and then to keep up with John's long legs.

"He's the office driver. I told my secretary to send him to meet us."

"Has he brought a car?"

"I hope he's brought my car."

He had. Outside the station, they were left waiting for a moment or two while George disappeared into the rainy darkness. In no time he was back, at the wheel of John's Alfa-Romeo. He got out and they got in, Victoria with Thomas still sleeping on her shoulder.

"Thanks a lot George, that was very good of you. Now, how are you going to get back?"

"I'll pop into the tube, Mr. Dunbeath. Very handy."

"Well, thanks again, anyway."

"A pleasure Mr. Dunbeath."

"How nice," said Victoria.

"Nice of him?"

"Yes, nice of him, but nice to be met. Not to have to wait for a taxi, or wait for a bus, or fight your way down the underground. Just nice to have a friendly face on a station platform."

"It makes all the difference between traveling hopefully and arriving," said John.

She knew what he meant.

The car sped west down the rain-drenched motorway. Three-quarters of an hour later, they had turned off it, and down the side road that led to Woodbridge. Now, there were little fields and hedgerows, and water meadows fringed with willows. Lights, shone, here and there, from the windows of small, red-brick houses. They came over a bridge, and a train screamed past beneath them.

John said, "That's lucky."

"What is?"

"Going over a bridge the same time that the train's going under it."

"What else is lucky?" She needed luck.

"Letters crossing. If you write someone a letter, and he writes to you and the letters cross, that's enormously lucky."

"I don't think it's ever happened to me."

"And black cats and picking up pins and new moons."

"There was a new moon the night of the fire."

"Disregard new moons, then."

At last, the lights of the village twinkled ahead of them. They passed the sign, WOODBRIDGE. The road swung around into a curve, and the long, wide main street sloped away before them. The car idled down to a gentle crawl. There were shops and a pub with a lighted sign. A church, set back behind a stone wall.

"We don't know where they live."

"Yes, we do. It's on the right hand side, and it's red brick, and it has a yellow door, and it's the only one in the street that is three stories high. There it is."

He drew up at the pavement's edge. Victoria saw the flight of steps that led up to the door from the pavement, the pretty fanlight, the tall lighted windows. She said, "How do you know this is the house?"

He switched off the engine. "Because I rang Mrs. Archer, and she told me."

"Did she sound furious?"

"No." He opened his door. "She sounded very nice."

Thomas, disturbed by the sudden cessation of movement, chose this moment to wake up. He yawned, bleary with sleep, rubbed his eyes, gazed about him with the confused expression of a person on whom some terrible trick has been played. He still held the wooden engine.

"You're home," Victoria told him gently. She smoothed down his hair with her hand, with some vague idea of tidying him up.

Thomas blinked. The word "home" apparently

meant little to him. He gazed out at the darkness. Then John opened the door and lifted Thomas and his engine up and off Victoria's knee. She reached around into the back of the car, retrieved Thomas's paper carrier luggage, and followed them.

They stood in front of the yellow front door, and John rang the bell. Almost instantly, as though the person inside had been waiting for them, there was a footstep and the door was flung open. From the bright, warm hallway, light poured out upon the three of them, so that they were caught in its beam, like actors spotlighted upon a stage.

"Good evening," said John, "I'm John Dunbeath."

"Yes, of course." He looked nice. Sixtyish, grey-haired, not tall, nor particularly impressive, but nice. He did not try to snatch Thomas from John's arms. He simply looked at Thomas and said, "Hello, old boy," and then stepped back, and went on, "I think you should all come in."

They did so, and he closed the door behind them. John stooped and set Thomas on his feet.

"I'll just call my wife. I don't think she can have heard the bell . . ."

But she had heard it. From a door at the far end of the narrow hall, she appeared. She had curly white hair and the sort of complexion that would go on being young, even when she was in her eighties. She wore a blue skirt with a cardigan to match and a rose-pink shirt with a bow at the neck. In her hand she carried her spectacles. Victoria imagined her, sitting in some chair, trying to read, or to do a crossword, anything to fill in the time while she waited for them to bring Thomas back to her.

There was a long silence. She and Thomas eyed each other down the length of the hall. Then she began to smile. She leaned forward, her hands on her knees. "And who is this," she asked him, "that Thomas has come home to?"

Victoria was frigid with anxiety, but she need not have had any worries. For Thomas, after an astonished silence, suddenly realized what was happening. Slowly, his rosy face became suffused by an expression of total, incredulous delight. He took a single enormous breath, and let it all come out in the first proper sentence that anyone had ever heard him utter.

"It my *Ganny*!"

He flung himself towards her, and was instantly swept up, lost in her embrace.

It was all very emotional. Mrs. Archer laughed, and cried, and then laughed again, and hugged her grandson. Mr. Archer took out his handkerchief and blew his nose. From upstairs, alerted by the noise, came running helter-skelter a young girl, round and plump and pretty as a milkmaid, and when Mrs. Archer could be persuaded to relinquish Thomas, he was engulfed in yet another pair of loving arms. Finally, he was set down and allowed to go to his grandfather, who had stopped blowing his nose, and who, in his turn, picked him up, and jigged him up and down, in a manly sort of way, which Thomas seemed to find wholly satisfactory.

While all this was happening, Victoria and John could do nothing but stand and watch. Victoria wanted to go, to get away while everyone was still happy and before any possible recriminations could set in, but it was hard to know how to achieve this without appearing rude.

It was Thomas who finally put an end to the great reunion scene. He wriggled himself down from his grandfather's arms, and with deadly determination made for the stairs that led to his nursery, where he remembered leaving a number of delightful toys. His grandparents sensibly let him go, and the little au pair girl went with him. As they disappeared around the bend in the staircase, Victoria took hold of John's sleeve and gave it a tug, but if Mrs. Archer noticed this, she showed no sign of it.

"I am sorry, keeping you standing there like that. But it's all just so . . ." She wiped away the last of her happy tears, and blew her nose on a lacy handkerchief. "You must come in and have a drink."

"We really ought to go . . ." Victoria began, but Mrs. Archer would have none of it.

"Of course you must stay, for just a moment. Come along in by the fire. Edward, I am sure Mr. Dunbeath would like a drink . . ."

There was nothing for it but to follow her, through a door that led into a pleasant, chintz-upholstered sitting room. A fire flickered pleasantly from an old-fashioned grate, there was a grand piano arrayed with family photographs, there were flowers, beautifully arranged, and the sort of cushions that looked as though nobody ever sat on them.

But it was warm and welcoming and under the influence of Mrs. Archer's obvious good intentions, her obvious gratitude, Victoria began to relax a little. The men had gone, presumably, to fetch the drinks, so she and Mrs. Archer were to be left alone together for a moment or two. Cautiously Victoria let herself down onto the sofa, and Mrs. Archer did not look disappointed about the cushions being squashed.

"Have a cigarette? You don't smoke. You must be tired. You've been traveling all day. And with a little boy, too. And I know how active Thomas can be."

Victoria realized that Mrs. Archer was just about as nervous as she was, and her manner was so different from the antagonistic reception that Victoria had anticipated that she felt totally confused.

She said, "He was good. He's always good. He's been good all the time we were away."

"It was you who wrote that kind letter, wasn't it? You're Victoria?"

"Yes."

"It was sweet of you. Very thoughtful."

"Oliver was furious."

"I wanted to apololgize about that. I would never have tried to ring you or get in touch, but my husband read the letter, and he was so incensed by the whole business, that I could do nothing to stop him telephoning Benchoile and having it out with Oliver. Nothing. It isn't very often," she added, her sweet face concerned, "that I don't get my own way, but there was nothing I could do to stop Edward making that call."

"It didn't matter."

"I hope not. You see, Edward never liked Oliver, even when he was married to Jeanette. But he is very fond of Thomas. And when Oliver just walked into our house, out of the blue, and stole Thomas, you can imagine the scenes. It had Helga in hysterics, poor girl, as though it could possibly have been her fault. And Edward saying he was going to put the police onto Oliver, and all the time I had no idea where the little boy was. It was a nightmare."

"I do understand."

"Yes. I believe you do." Mrs. Archer cleared her throat. "Your . . . your friend, Mr. Dunbeath. He rang me up yesterday to say you were bringing Thomas back. He told me, too, that Oliver has gone to America."

"Yes."

"Something about a play?"

Victoria said, "Yes," again.

"Do you suppose he'll come back to this country?"

"Yes, I suppose he will. Sometime or other. But I don't think he'll ever bother with Thomas again. I don't mean that he wasn't fond of him, and very good to him, but being a father isn't exactly Oliver's scene."

Their eyes met. Victoria smiled. Mrs. Archer said, very gently, "Nor being a husband, my dear."

"No, I suppose not. I really wouldn't know."

"He's a destroyer," said Mrs. Archer.

Perhaps no other person could have told her. She knew it was true. She knew something else as well. "He hasn't destroyed me," she told Mrs. Archer.

The men returned, Mr. Archer bearing a tray with glasses and bottles, and John following with a soda syphon. The conversation turned to day-to-day matters. The weather in Scotland, the weather in Hampshire, the state of the stock market, the variable fluctuation of both dollar and pound. John, without waiting for her to ask for one, quietly handed Victoria a whisky and water. This small service filled her with gratitude. She seemed to spend her time being grateful to him for one reason or other. It occurred to her then that his perception was remarkable, all the more so because he seemed to achieve it with so little fuss. He was, perhaps, the kindest person she had ever known. She had never even heard him say an unkind thing about any person, except to call Oliver Dobbs a son of a bitch, and he hadn't done that until Oliver had taken himself off to America, and there was no point in prevaricating any longer.

Now, she watched him, deep in conversation with the Archers. She saw his heavy, serious face, which could light up so unexpectedly in a smile. The dark, close-cut hair, the intensely dark eyes. He had been traveling all day with a small child, and yet he gave no sign of the sort of exhaustion that Victoria felt. He appeared as fresh and alert as the moment they had set out from Benchoile, and it was this resilience that she so envied and admired, because she knew that it was lacking in herself.

She thought, nothing defeats him. His disastrous marriage had left behind no apparent trace of bitterness. Things will always go right for him, because he likes people, but mostly because people like him.

Even over the telephone, it seemed, this genuine benevolence came through, for how else had he con-

trived, in the short space of the trunk call he had put
through to Mrs. Archer yesterday morning, to make
everything all right for Victoria, to somehow condone
the circumstances of Thomas's abduction, and to pave
the way for Mrs. Archer's reunion with Thomas.

One thing, she thought, I haven't had time to start
taking him for granted. Before she knew what was happening, they would be saying good-bye. He would
drive her to London, and leave her at the door of Pendleton Mews. There wouldn't even be the excuse of
carrying luggage to invite him in and up the stairs,
because she had no luggage to carry. They would just
say good-bye. Perhaps he would kiss her. He would
say, "Take care now."

That would be the end. John Dunbeath would walk
away from her, and be instantly absorbed back into
that busy, important life about which Victoria knew
nothing. She remembered the anonymous girlfriend
who had not been able to come to the Fairburns' party
with him. Probably the first thing John would do
when he returned to the peaceful familiarity of his
own flat would be to dial her number and tell her he
was safely back in London. "How about dinner tomorrow night?" he would say, "And I'll give you all
my news then." And her voice would float back at
him over the line, "Darling, how heavenly." Victoria
imagined her a little like Imogen Fairburn, beautiful,
sophisticated, and knowing everybody.

"We really mustn't keep you." John's drink was finished. He stood up. "You'll be wanting to go and talk
to Thomas before he goes to bed."

The Archers, too, rose to their feet. Victoria jerked
back to reality, began to struggle up out of the deep
sofa, but John took her empty glass from her, gave her
his hand, and helped her.

"I feel," said Mrs. Archer, "that we should offer you
something to eat."

"No, we really must get back to London. It's been a long day."

They all went out into the hall. Mrs. Archer said to Victoria, "Do you want to say good-bye to Thomas before you go?" But she said, "No." And then, because this sounded a little abrupt, she explained. "I mean, it wouldn't do any good, upsetting him again. Not that I think he would be upset, he's obviously so glad to be home, but . . . well, I'd rather just go, I think."

"I believe," said Mrs. Archer, "that you've become quite fond of Thomas."

"Yes." They were all looking at her. She wondered if she was going to start blushing. "Yes, I suppose . . ."

"Come along," said John, putting an end to all this by opening the front door. Victoria said good-bye, and was surprised when Mrs. Archer leaned forward to kiss her.

"You've looked after him so beautifully. I can't thank you enough. He looks rosy and well, and I'm sure the little experience has done him no harm at all."

"I hope not."

"Perhaps one weekend, when the weather is better, you'd like to come down one Sunday and see him. We could have lunch. You could take him for a walk." She looked at John, including him in this invitation. "You too, Mr. Dunbeath."

"That's very kind," said John.

"You're very quiet."

"I'm trying not to cry again."

"You know I don't mind if you do cry."

"In that case, I probably won't. Isn't it extraordinary if you know you can cry, and nobody is going to become upset or embarrassed about it, then you stop wanting to."

"Did you want to cry about anything in particular?"

"Thomas, I suppose. Thomas in particular."

"Thomas is fine. Thomas is nothing to cry about, except that you're going to miss him. Thomas has got a great home, and he's surrounded by people who love him. And what did you think of that welcome he gave his grandmother?"

"I nearly cried *then*."

"I have to admit to a lump in my throat myself. But you can see him anytime you want. Mrs. Archer liked you. It isn't good-bye to Thomas. You've got a standing invitation to go and see him."

"They were nice, weren't they?"

"Did you think they wouldn't be?"

"I don't know what I thought," She remembered something. "I didn't say anything to Mrs. Archer about the fire."

"I told Mr. Archer while we were in the dining room getting the glasses out of a cupboard. At least, I told him what had happened. I didn't enlarge too much on the possibility of Thomas being frizzled to a cinder."

"Oh, *don't*."

"I have to say things like that every now and then to lay my own private specter of what might have happened."

"But it didn't happen."

"No. It didn't happen."

They fell silent. The car nosed its way back along the narrow country road. A soft persistent rain blurred everything like mist. The windscreen wipers swung to and fro.

Victoria broke the silence at last. "I suppose," she said, I could cry for Benchoile."

"What a girl you are for thinking of things to cry about."

"It's just that I so hated leaving it."

John made no comment on this. The car traveled on, swiftly, down the winding road, but they passed the sign of an approaching lay-by, and he began to slow down. Moments later they came to the lay-by it-self, and here John drew off the road, pulled on the handbrake and turned off the engine.

The windscreen wipers ceased their demented dance. There was only the whisper of the rain, the ticking of the dashboard clock.

Victoria looked at him. "What are we stopping for?"

He switched on the interior light and turned towards her. "It's all right," he reassured her. "I am not about to ravish you. It's just that I want to talk to you. Ask you some questions. And I want to see your face when you answer them. You see, before we go a step further, I have to be totally and absolutely certain about Oliver Dobbs."

"I thought you never wanted his name mentioned again."

"I didn't. This is the last time."

"Mrs. Archer was talking about him. She was very wise. I didn't realize that she would be such a wise person. She said that Oliver was a destroyer."

"What did you say to that?"

"I said that he hadn't destroyed me."

"Is that the truth?"

She hesitated for an instant before replying. Then "Yes," she said. She looked at John and smiled, and it felt as though his heart was turning over. "It is the truth. Perhaps I've always known it was the truth, but I wouldn't admit it, even to myself. I suppose everybody has to have one great traumatic love affair in his life, and Oliver was mine."

"What about when he comes back from America?"

"Somehow, I don't think he'll ever come back. . . ." She thought about this, and then went on, in tones of the greatest conviction, "And even if he did, I wouldn't want to see him."

"Because he hurt you, or because you've stopped loving him?"

"I think I stopped loving him when we were at Benchoile. I can't tell you the exact moment. It just happened gradually. Now . . ." she made a vague gesture with her hands. "I don't think I even like him any more."

"That makes two of us," said John. "And with Oliver Dobbs disposed of, we can now go on to talk of other things. Just before I stopped the car, you said that you supposed that if you needed something to cry about, you could cry about Benchoile. And I think that this is as good a time as any to tell you that you don't have to. You'll be able to go back there, any time, and see them all, because I'm not going to sell it. At least not just yet."

"But . . . you said . . ."

"I've changed my mind."

"Oh . . ." She looked as though she were going to burst into tears, but she didn't do this. She said "Oh, *John,*" and then she began to laugh, and finally she flung her arms around his neck and kissed him.

He was immensely gratified, but as well taken totally unawares by her spontaneous delight. He had known that she would be pleased, but scarcely expected this throttling embrace.

"Hey, you'll strangle me!" But she took no heed.

"You're not going to sell it! Oh, you marvelous man! You're going to keep Benchoile."

He put his arms around her and pulled her close. She felt small-boned and fragile, and her fair hair was soft against his cheek, and she rattled on, excited as a child. "You said it wasn't viable, it wasn't practical." She drew away from him but he still kept his arms about her. "Without your Uncle Jock to run the place, you said that Benchoile would fall to pieces."

"Like I said, I changed my mind. I'm going to hang on to it, anyway for a year, till we see how things work out."

"What made you change your mind?"

"I don't know." He shook his head, a man still confused by the reasons for his sudden volte-face. "Perhaps it was the fire. Perhaps a man doesn't realize how much something means to him until he's in danger of losing it. That night, I had visions of the whole place going up. You weren't there, but it was only by the grace of God that the big house wasn't burnt to the ground with everything else. Late that night, I went out into the garden, and just stood there, and looked at it. And it was still standing, with the hills behind it, and I don't think I've ever been so grateful for anything in all my life."

"But who's going to run it?"

"Roddy and Davey Guthrie between them, and we're going to get another man in to help."

"*Roddy?*"

"Yes, Roddy. It was you who pointed out that Roddy is more informed and more interested in the land than any of us. He knows more about Benchoile than I could learn in a hundred years. The only reason that he's never become more actively involved before is because he's idle, and because there was always Jock there to do the thinking for him. I have a feeling that without Jock, and with a real job to do, Roddy has a good chance of laying off the booze and astonishing us all."

"Where will he live?"

"In the big house with Ellen. You see, all my problems have been solved by one inspired decision. They'll squabble like crazy, as they always have. But the big house is large enough to contain the two of them, without one murdering the other." He thought about this. "At least," he added, "I devoutly hope so."

"You really think it will work?"

"I told you, I'm going to give it a year. But, yes, I think it will work. And what is more, my father thinks so too."

"How do you know what your father thinks? He's in Colorado."

"I called him yesterday morning, we had a long talk about it all."

Victoria could only marvel. "What a morning you had on the telephone!"

"I'm used to it. In my office I'm on the phone most of the day."

"Even so," said Victoria, "I'd never think of calling someone up in Coloroado."

"You should try it sometime."

So, at least, for a little longer, Benchoile would go on. And perhaps John was right, and Roddy would take on a new lease on life. He was, after all, only sixty. Perhaps he would turn into a tremendously keen outdoorsman, felling trees and climbing hills, losing weight and generally becoming tanned and fit. The image was not particularly convincing, but there was no denying that it had distinct possibilities. And, living in the big house, perhaps he would be persuaded to enliven his social life a little. Throw small dinner parties, and have people to stay. Ellen would take the dust covers off the furniture in the drawing room, and rehang the curtains. Someone would light a fire in the fireplace, and people in evening dress would dispose themselves about the room while Roddy played the piano to them, and sang his old songs.

She said, "I know it will work. It has to work."

"So. With Benchoile and Oliver Dobbs safely out of the way, we can now get on to much more important things."

"Like what?"

"Like you and me." Victoria's expression became wary, and before she could start protesting, he went firmly on. "I thought it might be an idea for us to start over, from the beginning. It seems to me that from moment we first met, we set out on the wrong foot, and it's only now, after all this time, and so much happening, that we're finally fallen into step. And the first thing to be rectified is that I've never gotten around to taking you out for dinner. So I thought that when we get back to London, we might go out some place. If you want we can go straight there, and eat. Or you'd maybe want to wash up first and change your clothes, so I could take you to your flat, and then come around and pick you up later. Or we can both go straight to my flat and have a drink, and then go out to dinner from there. The permutations, as you will realize, are endless. The only constant is that I want to be with you. I don't want to say good-bye. Does that make sense?"

"John, I don't want you to be sorry for me. And you don't have to go on being kind."

"In fact," he told her, "I'm not being kind. I'm being utterly selfish, because it's what I want more than anything else in the world. I always knew I'd fall in love again one day. I didn't think that it would happen just this way. I didn't even think that it would happen so soon. But what I don't want is for you to get tangled up in a new relationship until you've had time to take a deep breath and look around and generally get used to the idea."

I don't want to say good-bye.

She thought, if this were a movie, it's where they'd start playing the really soupy theme music. Or there'd be an explosion of stars, or shots of sun shining down through branches laden with apple blossoms. None of these things were happening. There was just the car, and the darkness beyond, and the man, with whom already she seemed to have come so far.

She said, thoughtfully, "You know, I don't think I ever met any person as nice as you."

"Well, that'll do for a start," he told her. They watched each other, and she began to smile, and he took her face between his hands, and bent his dark head and kissed her smiling mouth. When he had finished kissing her, he put her gently from him, turned back to the driving wheel, switched on the ignition, started up the powerful engine. The car moved forward. Soon they came to the junction that marked the end of the quiet country road and the beginning of the motorway. The car came through a tunnel and then swept up the curved ramp. They waited to filter into the three-lane of cars which poured east.

Victoria said, "When we were with the Archers, I suddenly realized that I didn't want to say good-bye to you. But I never imagined that you wouldn't want to say good-bye to me."

A gap appeared in the traffic. Smoothly John slipped the Alfa-Romeo into gear; the engine changed tune, and the car swept forward.

He said, "Perhaps not wanting to say good-bye is just another word for loving."

The wide, fast road curved ahead of them, leading to London.

Dell Bestsellers

- [ ] TO LOVE AGAIN by Danielle Steel $2.50 (18631-5)
- [ ] SECOND GENERATION by Howard Fast $2.75 (17892-4)
- [ ] EVERGREEN by Belva Plain $2.75 (13294-0)
- [ ] AMERICAN CAESAR by William Manchester . . . $3.50 (10413-0)
- [ ] THERE SHOULD HAVE BEEN CASTLES
      by Herman Raucher $2.75 (18500-9)
- [ ] THE FAR ARENA by Richard Ben Sapir $2.75 (12671-1)
- [ ] THE SAVIOR by Marvin Werlin and Mark Werlin . $2.75 (17748-0)
- [ ] SUMMER'S END by Danielle Steel $2.50 (18418-5)
- [ ] SHARKY'S MACHINE by William Diehl $2.50 (18292-1)
- [ ] DOWNRIVER by Peter Collier $2.75 (11830-1)
- [ ] CRY FOR THE STRANGERS by John Saul $2.50 (11869-7)
- [ ] BITTER EDEN by Sharon Salvato $2.75 (10771-7)
- [ ] WILD TIMES by Brian Garfield $2.50 (19457-1)
- [ ] 1407 BROADWAY by Joel Gross . . . . : $2.50 (12819-6)
- [ ] A SPARROW FALLS by Wilbur Smith $2.75 (17707-3)
- [ ] FOR LOVE AND HONOR by Antonia Van-Loon . . $2.50 (12574-X)
- [ ] COLD IS THE SEA by Edward L. Beach $2.50 (11045-9)
- [ ] TROCADERO by Leslie Waller $2.50 (18613-7)
- [ ] THE BURNING LAND by Emma Drummond $2.50 (10274-X)
- [ ] HOUSE OF GOD by Samuel Shem, M.D. $2.50 (13371-8)
- [ ] SMALL TOWN by Sloan Wilson $2.50 (17474-0)

At your local bookstore or use this handy coupon for ordering:

DELL BOOKS
P.O. BOX 1000, PINEBROOK, N.J. 07058

Please send me the books I have checked above. I am enclosing $_____
(please add 75¢ per copy to cover postage and handling). Send check or money
order—no cash or C.O.D.'s. Please allow up to 8 weeks for shipment.

Mr/Mrs/Miss _____

Address _____

City _____ State/Zip _____

THE PASSING BELLS

by

PHILLIP ROCK

A story you'll wish would go on forever.

Here is the vivid story of the Grevilles, a titled British family, and their servants—men and women who knew their place, upstairs and down, until England went to war and the whole fabric of British society began to unravel and change.

"Well-written, exciting. Echoes of Hemingway, Graves and *Upstairs, Downstairs.*"—*Library Journal*

"Every twenty-five years or so, we are blessed with a war novel, outstanding in that it depicts not only the history of a time but also its soul."—*West Coast Review of Books.*

"Vivid and enthralling."—*The Philadelphia Inquirer*

A Dell Book   **$2.75   (16837-6)**

At your local bookstore or use this handy coupon for ordering:

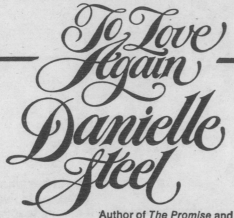